AN EXMOO ~E

Wedding Bells in Combe Tollbridge

ROSEANNA HALL

farrago

This edition published in 2025 by Farrago,
an imprint of Duckworth Books Ltd
1 Golden Court, Richmond, TW9 1EU, United Kingdom

www.farragobooks.com

A catalogue record for this book is available from the British Library

Printed and bound in Great Britain by Clays Ltd, Elcograf S.p.A.

The authorised representative in the EEA is Easy Access System
Europe, Mustamäe tee 50, 10621 Tallinn, Estonia.

Print ISBN: 978-1-7884-2547-6
eISBN: 978-1-7884-2548-3

Chapter One

The sun rose over Exmoor, and with it rose a light wind, spinning the last of the overnight mist into streamers of celestial gauze that melted into the blue of a fresh late summer morning as the breeze died slowly away.

Far below in the moor's deep, river-rushing combes and valleys the mist lingered, held by the stubborn fingers of creeper-hung trees to smother a thick carpet of lichen, ferns and moss. The air smelled rich and damp; the light was a shadowy, uncertain green. A driver must take extra care at this stage of the journey.

A motorbike appeared, its panniers laden, and began a cautious descent through the mist. The biker reduced speed, and quickly switched back on the headlights she'd only just switched off. She knew enough to respect the precipitous little road that led to the seaside haven of Combe Tollbridge. Hadn't her fishing friends told her, more than once, that the most dangerous moments in any voyage were when a vessel first leaves harbour – and when she's about to return?

'Till the engine be stopped and your anchor safe dropped, you watch so hard as ever.' That wily and picturesque fisherman, old Mike Binns, had tinkered with the wording of his new-minted traditional saw for an hour to get the balance right, but was pleased to think that in the end he'd got it.

Andromeda Marsh, more generally called Andy, thought so too; but Andy already knew the sentiment was true of any journey, by land or by sea. Five months earlier she had attended yet another funeral of a fellow biker who'd been killed within three miles of home. Now Andy Marsh was within three miles of Combe Tollbridge, and friends; and she'd been travelling for the greater part of the night – true, taking frequent breaks, with mugs of black coffee and sugar to suit – but she knew she shouldn't relax just yet.

She passed through Combe Ploverton. High on the moor the day might be advancing, but here the fog seemed to keep people at home. One or two could be seen going about their business: a postman delivered letters, a laundry van loaded and unloaded canvas bags outside The Slandered Pig, where the landlord's wife, Dora Tucker, hearing the rumble of the Triumph's engine gave Andy a cheerful wave before turning back to the list over which she and the van driver were amiably squabbling. Andy waved as cheerfully to Dora, and rumbled on her way. No traffic passed in either direction. It seemed the twin villages of Combe Ploverton and Combe Tollbridge were in a world of their own.

She throttled back as she finally entered Tollbridge, passing the corner of Hempen Row half expecting an early shopper or a returning night fisherman to appear out of the fog; but she saw nobody until she reached the old school building by the church. Here, blocking Stickle Street, hazard lights flashing, was a council truck. Burly figures yawned and muttered in hi-vis jackets, unloading with limited enthusiasm a cargo of plastic cones and a stop-go traffic lollipop.

The council gang heard the bike's approach, paused in their sluggish labours and looked about them. One man was quicker than the rest. Taking a second look he leaped for the stop-go sign and darted with it to the middle of the road. He turned the sign to Stop.

Andy stopped. She saw no immediate reason why she should but the gang, being local, must know the dangers ahead better than any visitor. More-and-so, in the local phrase, after driving through the night she knew she was tired. The fog might be thinning now, but it remained patchy: the most dangerous sort. Obediently, she lowered one booted foot to the worn tarmac of the road, idled the engine, and waited.

'This bike yours, midear?'

No hint of a traffic warning, just admiration; envy. Who could blame him? Andromeda Marsh smiled. 'You bet she is! Signed, sealed, and delivered – my very own ultimate lean, mean machine.' With a leather-gauntleted hand she stroked the petrol tank, and slapped it for emphasis. 'Every nut, bolt and piston!'

The stop-go man heard her voice – stared at a female biker – recovered himself, and sighed. 'You lucky devil.' He waved the lollipop at his colleagues. 'A Triumph Bonneville! Come and look at this, will you?'

Roadworks were forgotten. Andy, overwhelmed by hi-vis jackets and curiosity, found herself answering a host of questions and even managing to ask a few of her own.

As the hubbub died, the lollipop man grinned. 'This lot' – a jerk of his head – 'calls me Jason, but my middle name's Malcolm, same like my dad. My grandad's idea. A great one for a motorbike – had a Norton, himself – and my dad was born a year to the day Malcolm Uphill did his thing at the Isle of Man T.T. race. My grandad was there, and never forgot, so when Dad popped out next eleventh o' June, Malcolm was what Grandad had him registered. And my dad he carried on the tradition with me, though my mum insisted on Jason first, but I'm Malcolm in the middle and that's why.'

'Your grandfather saw Malcolm Uphill break the record? Wowser!' Andy might warily admit to having (once) achieved more than a hundred miles an hour on her Triumph – but (emphatically) only once, just to know how it felt. 'Cool or what!'

Jason grinned. 'Big fan, my grandad. After Uphill's accident, when Gramps wanted a roller shutter for his garage, no guesses who fitted it! They lived in Caerphilly, see, and every time we visited he'd have the Norton out on the road so we could watch him wheel it back in and hear him tell who'd done the installation – in person, he always said, and a real nice bloke.'

Andy, steeped in biker history, was even more impressed than Jason's workmates by this oblique brush with greatness. For some minutes the conversation continued, but the mist was clearing, and the postman's van could be heard rattling down the valley. Andy apologised for having delayed the start of the working day, said goodbye to her new friends, and set off again in the direction of the harbour.

She nodded to the few pedestrians she passed on her way from Stickle Street to Harbour Path, and was glad to see the sun burning the last of the mid-channel haze from the pewter waves of the Severn Sea, sluggish and glistening beyond the little harbour that still lay hushed in the shadow of Cliddon Hill, outpost of Exmoor.

Harbour Path finishes before Trendle Cottage, which lurks at the foot of steep edge-of-the-moor cliffs that drop almost sheer to the sea: cliffs too resolute for any long-ago engineer to have wasted time and money taking the little thoroughfare to a destination that nobody needed, then or now. There's no direct route through Combe Tollbridge. You drive in; you turn round; you go back the way you came.

Andy Marsh didn't turn round but turned right, just before reaching Trendle. The laden Triumph growled up the incline of narrow Meazel Cleeve towards The Old Printery and (she hoped) a bite to eat; she smiled in anticipation. Angela Lilley, who had rented the place from printer Sam Farley after he moved to more spacious premises, was a versatile and talented young woman employed by the local baker – but only part-time, in time spared from when she wasn't busy learning to spin and weave, barmaiding at the pub, or putting to rights the local museum Combe Tollbridge had discussed and casually assembled for years, but never organised. Angela, a born organiser, in her London life had been a librarian. The museum, Tollbridge now accepted, was really going to happen. One day. When young Angela could spare the time from her cooking, spinning, weaving...

Andy reached The Old Printery; the blinds were still drawn. Angela was usually up and about by this hour. 'An all-night shift at the bakery and she's sleeping it off,' deduced the unexpected visitor. 'But she didn't answer yesterday when I phoned. She might have gone away. An emergency? Or she might be round at her mother's.'

She nodded. 'Susan's not the best-organised person in the world, and right now she needs organising more than ever, so Ange has stepped in to save the day – yes, that's it, but Miriam will know for sure.'

Miriam Evans lived on Harbour Path, just around the corner from Meazel Cleeve. Close friend of Susan less-well-organised-than-her-daughter Jones, Miriam had taken on the competent Angela as apprentice and soon found her a promising spinner and weaver, even if it puzzled her that so good a cook should find mixing dyes for colour consistency so difficult. Angela likewise puzzled that anyone so skilled in crafting should find the securing of parcels with sticky tape the challenge that Miriam did. Angela had appropriated to herself any packing necessary and, deeming Miss Evans in all other respects too modest by half, persuaded her to adopt the trading name of Tiffler & Thrums. Business had boomed. Like her cousin Evan Evans the baker and his sister Tabitha Ridd at the Anchor, Miriam would gladly have employed Angela on a full-time basis; but Angela was enjoying herself too much trying out different jobs, and couldn't decide where (or when – or even if ever) she would settle down.

Andy climbed from her motorbike and removed her helmet. She stretched three times, touched her toes, and went to the door of The Old Printery. She clattered the knocker, rang the bell – and received the answer she'd half expected: none.

Meazel Cleeve, another of the various No Through roads in Combe Tollbridge, was never busy. Few passers-by, no sign of rain; so, okay to leave her bike, and her luggage, while she went in search of her friend.

She looked first, doubtfully, to Baker's Cottage at the top of the cleeve, home of Captain Rodney Longstone. Rodney, having some years ago taken early retirement from the Royal Navy, until the advent of Angela Lilley had been accepted by Tollbridge as a quiet man who didn't mingle. The divorce that had prompted his retreat from the submarine service was not only scandalous and embarrassing but also funny, if you had the right (or wrong) sense of humour. Tollbridge could enjoy a joke, but neither laughed to the captain's face nor sniggered behind his back, for he was thought to have been badly treated. Nevertheless, he chose to maintain a courteous distance from everyone until Prudence Budd, dying at one hundred and five, took with her to the grave the secret of the peppermint creams the captain bought daily from Farley's General Stores in the course of his round-the-village walk.

Angela had experimented, cracked the recipe, and thus be-come the first and closest of the friends Rodney Longstone at last began to allow himself to make.

'But surely not so close she'd be there at this hour of the day.' Andy frowned. Angela considered herself anti-man since her abrupt break with the treacherous Paul, but Andy suspected that her friend might be mellowing, and Rodney Longstone was the reason. Angela's father had died so young his daughter could barely remember him; her mother Susan had confided to Angela's London friend that an older man might be just what her daughter needed, in preference to the flighty, bed-hopping younger generation – if, indeed, she needed anyone at all.

'Nothing wrong with staying independent and fancy-free,' agreed Andromeda Marsh, who'd experienced man troubles of her own and could sympathise.

'Nothing whatever, if that's how you want it. I'm just not sure Angela really wants it that way.' Susan Jones, who as Milicent Dalrymple profitably ripped bodices in stylish but popular prose, sighed. 'For me, it's been rather different. I've coped with life since Andrew died because, as a single mother with few options, I've had to. But at least before I lost him we'd had the right sort of life together, and made enough happy memories to – to keep me going afterwards.'

She shook her head. 'Poor Angela *thought* she was having the same as me, didn't she? And you know what a shock it was when she realised she wasn't.' Andy, after a confused panic appeal from the shocked Angela, had delivered her friend as a pillion passenger far from the tumult of a London flat to the sanctuary of Susan's Corner Glim Cottage. Mother and daughter soon realised that living together no longer suited them, but separate homes quickly resolved the difficulty.

'In her place,' Susan had brooded, 'I'd be more than cautious about risking another experience like that, with any… *contemporary* relationship. But perhaps an older man would suit her: not a father figure exactly, but someone mature enough to understand.'

Andy, likewise understanding, had agreed; and soon learned that most of Tollbridge shared the sentiment. It was (she thought now) strange that the two persons most directly involved seemed the most oblivious to the expectations of their friends.

But even if she'd been willing to do it there was no point now in enquiring for Angela at Baker's Cottage. A second glance had showed that the captain's new Mini Cooper (much admired during one of Andy's previous visits) wasn't there, which meant the captain wasn't, either. Rodney would no more let anyone else drive his car than Andy Marsh allowed alien hands to take control of her Triumph. She saw the retractable collapsible tarpaulin cover suspended, neatly collapsed and retracted, up under the roof of the empty car port. The retired submariner, accustomed to working in confined spaces, had built this sturdy edifice as protection for his Mini against the prevailing salt-laden westerly winds that constantly drew moisture as they crossed the wide Atlantic and, after three thousand miles, found the Exmoor coast one of the first convenient places to dump most of it as rain.

'Miriam, then.' Andy patted her trusty bike farewell and headed, on foot, back down Meazel Cleeve towards the harbour.

Miriam Evans, a quick wiry figure with dark, greying hair, was deep in thought as she opened her door. It took several moments before she responded to the smile that greeted her, though the green pixie-cut streaked with pink that had been Andy's trademark hairdo throughout her career as a general handyman was difficult to miss.

'Andy?' At last Miriam seemed to focus. 'Well, here's a surprise! We had no word from Angela you were expected – she idn home today, o'course.' Andy's face fell. 'You'll be wanting a cup of tea,' said Miriam kindly, 'and a bite to eat; cake, maybe, if you've but just now arrived from London and no breakfast.'

Her tone was kindly and enquiring. Andy's nod and grateful look were answer enough for Miriam. 'Come you in, midear, and welcome – only, I've a special job that can't be too long delayed, so you'll have to excuse me working while we clitter-clatter together over the cups. I'll put the kettle on.'

Andy had watched Miriam weave on the large floor loom to which apprentice Angela could only aspire. Knowing her visitor's interest in all things mechanical Miriam had permitted Andy to attempt the treadles, and been impressed by the physical coordination she'd quickly shown. Andy said that riding a powerful motorbike kept you in good trim. Both she and Miriam had then looked at Angela, and shared a smile.

'And so does wool-working keep you fit,' said Miriam, as Angela studiously ignored her friends' amusement. 'My grandmother worked this-here loom well past eighty-five, and if I'm spared I hope to do likewise. The whole thing's original to Grammer saving the heddles, for they'm all metal, with which the salt air don't agree over too many years.'

'It's a splendid piece of kit.' Andy had been genuinely admiring, and was pleased now to meet again the elaborate wooden structure that completely dominated the tiny back room of Harbour Glim Cottage.

'Hey, that's what I call a bedspread!' Andy stood and marvelled at the fine white weaving that occupied the full width of the front roller beam. 'A counterpane? No, a king-sized sheet – from the look of it, though, more like for an emperor.'

Miriam pursed her lips. 'A sheet? Of a sort, I agree – a winding-sheet, if you young folk know the term these days. A cere-cloth. A shroud, midear.' She tried not to smile as Andy took a startled backward step.

Andy saw the smile, rallied, and stepped forward again. 'You mean to wrap a dead body in? For – for anyone I know?'

'No, no! Nothing o' that sort, I promise you. This is for old Thomas Joy, upalong to Ploverton – Sandy Joy, he's better known. Sinking fast in hospital, they tell me.'

Andy sighed, and shook her head. Miriam smiled again. 'Nobody you know, then; but I promised the man years back I'd make him the best winding-sheet ever seen in these parts, and I don't care to break a promise.' She settled once more to her weaving. 'He chose the fleece for himself, and cleaned it ezackly to my direction so I could spin it into the finest yarn I could contrive, to best dignify his coffin.

'And as to the coffin,' she added, as her guest gave her a curious look, 'why, Sandy his very own self made that!'

Chapter Two

Miriam hid her amusement: the young saw death as something that would never happen to them! 'A dab hand at caffendry, Thomas Joy. Meaning,' as Andy blinked, 'the man's a good carpenter, midear. Noted for it. Sandy can build a cupboard or turn a chair leg or hang a door so good as any in the southwest. Used the finest oak to make his own coffin, and once 'twas shaped to his satisfaction he stored it flat under the bed, with no more than carved oaken pegs to hold it together when the time should come. Wouldn have no loss of dignity to his handiwork with even one metal screw, he said, nor metal handles, so he carved them of oak, likewise.'

Andy rallied. 'Well, I can build a pretty nifty cupboard – and I don't mean flat-pack – and put up a mean set of shelves; and I can hang a door if it's not too heavy, but – my own coffin? That would be a bit... personal, I think. Creepy.'

'A craftsman of the old school, Thomas Joy. A job's a job, is what he would say. You'd have enjoyed to meet and talk with him, midear, and he'd have thought it a grand thing to meet another lady craftsman like yourself, for the man always thought well of me. For a time backalong he kept his own hens, and when the rooster began to fail and he couldn say why, he sent down word to ask if I'd take a look.' Miriam's small back-garden flock, in whose diet local seaweed played an important part, could never supply as many 'saltmarsh eggs' as her customers wanted.

'Did you find out what was wrong?'

'Indeed I did! That bird was crop-bound with potato peel, and serve him right for keeping t'other birds away while he gave hisself first chance at the tastiest food, only, none of the goodness was getting right down inside of him. He'd have starved to death if I hadn opened him up and cleared him out and stitched him back together – so neat, Sandy said, when the time came for the pot you would never have known what had happened.'

Andy chuckled. 'So if you keep chickens, you need to be able to sew!'

'I've had my birds more years than I can recall, and learned all manner of necessary skills. I was glad to help.' Miriam laughed. 'But I'm thankful he never asked me to do the same for Crusoe! His parrot,' she explained. 'There's roosters and to spare, you've but to ask around, but that parrot could never be replaced. Belonged to his son, poor lad. Only come to Sandy after Tommy was lost at sea.'

'That's sad. But if Sandy's in hospital now, where—?'

'With a neighbour; and his dog Turk, too. Sandy gave up his birds after they got the pip, being too clumsy for drawing them safe back to health – that is, to twirdle a feather down their throats and pull out the worms, which I would have done had he asked, only he didn. You need a delicate touch with fowl, and being a carpenter Sandy had more a hammer-and-nail way of treating the poor creatures.' Again she shook her head. 'But I do wonder now just when they'll be asking for another lend of my hens for Sandy's carpets!'

Andy stared. 'His carpets are made of feathers?'

Miriam, who had been constantly throwing the shuttle to and fro, working the treadles, rocking the beater, paused in her labours to laugh. 'Moth, midear! They found a plague o' liddle millers last time he was back from hospital – you ask Mike Binns and Gabriel, they'll tell you – the reason being, he'd bin held far too long in that place, and once he was set free he found the house thick wi' the creatures – carpets, blankets, clothes – and the pest man unable to come for a week, while going private would have cost a small fortune. So Mike and the rest come down here to borrow my hens, and took and shut 'em inside, and went with Sandy into the Pig, and waited.'

She laughed again. 'Tom Tucker, that's the landlord, told me they waited far over and above what was required and had a rare old time, the whole boiling' – Andy, knowing some of those involved, could easily believe this – 'and o'course it needed some powerful scrubbing and dusting after, on account of hens not being what you'd call indoor birds – but they'd seen off they millers, right enough. Almost never fails, if you've the patience – and the hens, o'course.'

'Of course. So that's how you got this gig – making his shroud, I mean?'

'That, and being the best weaver for miles, or so Angela keeps telling me.' Miriam's lips twitched. 'Light under a bushel, she calls it. So soon as the news came from upalong that poor Sandy was ailing and back in hospital, she was on at me – having already heard the tale – to warp up the loom with the twill I'd designed special for him and wouldn never let her talk me into making for anyone else, no matter how well it might look, until he'd had first use of it. Which,' she concluded sadly, 'by all accounts won't be long. Poor old Sandy.'

Then she brightened. 'But you were looking for Angela. Well, barring holdups they'll be more than halfway to Bristol by now, her and Susan. Angela slept last night at Corner Glim for an early start, Bristol being at least two hours distant, and she so particular about what her mother's to wear for the wedding. Not that Susan's too bothered, but you know Angela. She's planned out all the shops they're to visit this one day without having to stop overnight, with Susan begrudging time off her work on the new book.'

'So that's why there was no answer when I phoned last night to ask if she'd put me up for a bit while I got myself sorted. Mystery solved! But I'm surprised you haven't gone with them, being such friends.'

'A daughter's more than a friend, midear, and three's sometimes an awkward number. Susan knows I'd have bin willing – though I'd have made it Exeter, being closer – if I hadn this special job on, if she'd asked me, if Angela wadn here; but she is – and there's my promise to Thomas Joy besides, which Susan understood. Moreover' – Miriam paused again in her shuttle-throwing to contemplate her trousered legs – 'us both being, shall we say, of a certain age we'm not what you'd call fashion conscious, midear.'

'Neither is Angela! Not since she moved away from London, I mean, and was able to relax. To be herself, not what other people tried to make her.'

Miriam's bright-eyed glance took her in. 'You planning to move away likewise?'

It was all the encouragement needed for Andy to let off the steam that had bubbled inside her for so long. 'You bet! I'm sick of the place – the people – the lot!'

The shuttle flashed back and forth. 'Have a biscuit – some cake – and tell me about it.'

'Well... You know my Triumph?' Andy bit fiercely into chocolate cake. 'I guess that's how it all started – and then it got complicated...'

She sipped tea, and ate more cake. Blood sugar began to rise. 'There's a whole bunch of us out there with motorbikes – various types, of course, but all with lots of – of fizz. Buzz. Power. So, we like to get together the same way people with traction engines or fairground rides or vintage cars do, you know the sort of thing: rallies at the weekend, collections for charity… So, five or six months ago one of our guys was in a multi-vehicle pile-up.' She grimaced. 'Motorway closed both sides for hours, traffic diverted into another county, two air ambulances…'

'Sounds bad,' said Miriam.

'It was. He died. He wasn't the only one – it was a real shambles – but we knew him, so we gave him a grand biker send-off. All of us with black rosettes and ribbons, round-the-town escort for the hearse, guard of honour at the crem, wreaths shaped like helmets and gauntlets, even a motorbike… I did wonder about that one, because his bike was smashed up even worse than him, but his wife didn't mind so I guess it's just me; and we took a cash collection for the air ambulance.'

'I hope you raised a goodly sum.'

'We did! Not just from the club, but from people who'd met us before at rallies; even people who'd stood and watched the – the parade as we all went by. So that was something good to come out of it – but there's always a downside.' Andy took a second slice of cake. 'Yum, yum. This yours? Or one of Ange's finest?'

'I've no time for baking at present.' Miriam never paused in her weaving.

'Thought so.' Another mouthful disappeared. 'So, the bloke who died was treasurer of our club, and they asked me to take over. I thought at first it was because I've been running my own business a few years now – Handy Andy, no job too small – and I know my way around the paperwork and the legal stuff. These days you have to, so it was the obvious answer – but then I start-ed to wonder if it might be because I'm young, and female, and they thought I was less likely to make a fuss and more easy to shout down when I did – which I did, and I wasn't, when I found the books had more than a few mistakes in 'em and almost always *not* in favour of the charities.'

Miriam stopped throwing long enough to give the young woman a look of comprehension, but said nothing.

'I guess,' continued Andy judicially, 'it might just have been coincidence – or being unfamiliar with the system after there was a computer upgrade – but it got me worried, and I wouldn't sign off the accounts until I'd sent out a letter explaining why the delay. And the head honcho altered the wording! He tried to play it all down, which not only made me look a fool but was whitewashing, big time – and it still went out to everyone under my name – which drove me mad, and I said so. Loudly.'

'Well done,' said Miriam. 'And who could blame you?'

'You'd be surprised.' Andy sighed. 'Mud sticks – both ways. That bastard, excuse my French, is the treasurer's wife's cousin. Said he didn't want her upset by people casting nasturtiums on her husband's memory, and the man was dead and couldn't give his side of it and deserved the benefit of the doubt, and a whole heap of similar sh—' she broke off – 'uh, a lot of mealy-mouthed rubbish like that.'

She bit down hard on an innocent mouthful. 'Made me sick,' she muttered through crumbs, 'and pretty furious. So I sent out the original letter again, exactly as I wrote it, and said what had happened…'

Miriam kept quiet. The climax was drawing near.

Andy sighed. 'Like I said, mud sticks. Guilt by association, you know? With a helping hand or two – or three, I suspect, but I name no names because I couldn't *prove* anything – but I found my business starting to drop off. Nothing like so many callouts to jobs in people's homes, though the women's shelter still trusted me – but there were too many what I thought of as my regulars who made feeble excuses if I mentioned I'd seen other people's vans outside, rather too obviously fixing stuff I'd always used to do for them.'

'Nasty.'

'All whispers and rumour, nothing definite – not that I'd have sued anyone for libel, or is it slander? It costs money to go to law, and I was bringing home a fair bit less than I used to – but the absolutely final straw was when my number plate was cloned.'

'I've heard of such things.' Miriam watched more cake vanish into oblivion. 'Though not in these parts.'

'No real need, in such a quiet place. But in London, with cameras all over to watch traffic and parking and driving in a bus lane, or doing five miles over the limit from one zone to another, never mind crooks with getaway vehicles – not that I'm saying any of my old crowd were crooks – but suddenly I was getting a hell of a lot of tickets and fines I'd never had before, from places I knew I'd never been. I checked things out and at first plod wasn't that interested, but when I could prove black and white where I was with my bike at a certain time – so let's hear it for the women's shelter! – the police got their act together and said I'd almost certainly had someone clone my number, and the only safe answer was to get a new one. Which,' she ended grimly, 'cost even more money.'

'But worth it, midear, for the peace of mind?'

'Short term, yes, but who's to say the trouble wouldn't start up again once they saw my new plate and knew I'd got wise to their little game? Even if I stopped attending the rallies, they know where I live and places I work – used to work, that is. They'd only have to hang out near the women's shelter and wait: I sort 'em out pro bono, you see. That building isn't the most up to date, but maintenance is all they can afford – which is where they made their mistake with that last parking fine. It wouldn't have been so hard to check where I was at the time, but they got over-confident and it backfired on them – whoever they are, but I name no names, remember.'

'I remember.' Miriam's smile was appreciative. 'Very tactful.'

'Sensible!' Andy was almost cheerful. 'So here I am, not a stain on my character, with a clean record and a new number plate – and I'd like to think a new life, too. Worked okay for Ange, didn't it? Best thing she ever did, she says, leaving town.

She loves it here, cooking and weaving and helping out at the pub, new faces, new friends, new opportunities…' She laughed. 'I tried dropping a few hints to the yellow-liners about my chances of a part-time job, but they were too interested in the bike to notice.'

Miriam took this for the latest slang, but couldn't be sure. 'Yellow-liners? The workmen who wear them fancy bright jerkins?'

'These were fluorescent green rather than yellow, but no, not the jackets, I meant the lines they came to paint on the road.' Andy saw Miriam's puzzled look. 'The old lot were badly faded, weren't they? So, new double yellow lines down the gutter for No Parking, zigzags and "School Keep Clear" by the gates.' She checked her watch. 'They'll be finished by now, I should think, and gone on to the next job.'

Miriam had stopped work to stare in bewilderment at her guest. 'Yellow lines outside the school?'

'Well, yes.' Andy was equally bewildered. Combe Tollbridge might be a backwater, but even here the twenty-first century couldn't be kept out. 'That's how it's done,' she explained gently. 'Reduce traffic jams and road-blocking when parents drop their little dears off in the morning or collect 'em in the afternoon – health and safety stuff, you know?'

'No,' said Miriam. 'That's to say, I take your meaning, but I can't see the point. Talk about a waste of time and money. Didn't you know – didn't *they* know – Barney Christmas bought the old school for holiday flats or similar, when the council closed it down? Eight, nine years back it must have bin. The younger ones here go by bus or took by their parents up to Ploverton, and the secondary's even farther afield. There's no need for any yellow lines to be renewed outside the school. No need at all.'

Chapter Three

In Farley's General Stores and Post Office, the tongues of those shoppers assembled to gossip rather than shop wagged with their customary vigour.

'Mickey's divorce was long ago,' old Hilda Beacon was saying. 'And tidn as though there was any blame attached to him – or her.'

'Both sides the same, so he've ever said,' said her younger sister Daisy. There was a general nodding of heads; dissenters who held the marriage vows to be unbreakable did no more than frown. It couldn't be denied that Mickey Binns always maintained his divorce had been by mutual consent, when he and the fellow geologist he'd met at college grew slowly apart in their years travelling the world. He, finally, had wished to settle down; she'd still wanted to travel. The marriage couldn't last, but there were no hard feelings.

'And friendly,' Daisy went on. 'The vicar shouldn these days hold it against them for a proper wedding in church, when Susan's bin a respectable widow many more years than Mickey's bin divorced.'

A deep wordless sigh was heard from the counter where Tilda Jenkyns, who with her twin Debbie Tucker shared the duties of deputy postmistress, was currently in charge. Tilda was a widow of even longer standing than Susan Jones.

'I don't believe Mr Hollington to hold it against them in the least.' Debbie, like Mickey, was a long-term divorcee, though in her case the parting had been far from amicable. Once the papers were signed her ex had left town, to the regret of none. Not even his blood relations lamented his loss. 'It's no more'n they want for themselves, or rather, Susan does, and Mickey, he'm agreeable to the bride's choice, as is only to be expected.'

'And so she told Mother.' Tilda sighed again. 'Explained it all so kindly and gentle, it almost made up for the disappointment, though there's no denying it was a blow—'

'But saved her all that work.' Debbie was more practical than her sentimental sister. 'More-and-so, who's to say Mother or Louise or both together could have finished a lace veil in the time, with their fingers... well, not so young as once they were.'

Even in this twenty-first century, the oldest inhabitants of ancient fishing communities still practise many of the crafts known to their ancestors – both from habit, and with the hope of passing on the mysteries to those of younger generations who wish to learn them. Men as well as women knit the traditional 'jumper' that distinguishes, by individual variations on a local theme, one wearer from another: an all-important distinction for those whose business lies upon great waters, or even the offshore waters of the Severn Sea. One boat lost can too often mean more than one drowned body washed finally ashore. 'Nine days down and nine days up,' goes the theory, 'and crabs pinching for food with every tide.' A patterned jumper will help ensure the correct name will be carved on the tombstone of one who might otherwise be known only unto God.

Gabriel Hockaday, Tollbridge patriarch, with his brother-in-law Mike Binns (father of the divorced Mickey) is among these dedicated knitters. Gabriel's prowess with a jumper is renowned, while Mike (a bright cockney evacuee who never went back when the war ended) prefers the quicker satisfaction of a warm woollen beanie. Both men will make and repair nets, as can their fellows and many of their women-folk; but the apparent immortality of modern fibres means that most female net-makers have long since reverted to the related, and far more delicate, art of lacemaking as learned in their youth.

When news of the betrothal of Mickey Binns to Susan Jones broke upon a delighted village, a feud that began in their schooldays seemed likely to be ramped up to danger level as Tollbridge's two most skilled lace-makers, Louise Hockaday and (in her ninth decade, still the official postmistress) Olive Farley, each resolved that to her bobbins, and hers alone, should fall the honour of making a lace wedding veil for Susan Jones.

'Mother straightway sewed a fresh cover-cloth for her pillow,' said Tilda Jenkyns now. 'The same green as ever but for good fortune in the marriage it must be new, she said.'

'And Louise likewise,' said her twin, 'though Louise have always more inclined to blue. Which suited both, o'course – something old, something new, and everyone happy!'

'And both buying their doings from poor Amelia Martin,' chipped in old Mrs Beacon, 'which is a benefit to all. Amelia must surely be glad of the money, being rather less wishful to work these days, her poor eyes getting so much worse through this muscular deceleration they say she's got.'

Hilda's word-scrambling could be a challenge, but this time everyone recognised what she was trying to say, and murmured in sympathy. Only Hilda's sister Daisy ventured to correct her. 'Surely there've bin no talk of money? Didn Amelia say the new cover-cloths were her share in the wedding? More-and-so, I know she'll be glad of the room. Outspilling from every shelf and cupboard, she says, all them fabrics and ribbons and trims and fandangles she've bought over the years for her hats – and small use they'm like to be to her for how much longer, she says, poor soul. The fingers may be willing, but...'

Tilda shook her head. 'Poor Amelia,' she echoed. 'She takes it as it comes, o'course, for what else can she do? So sad – and so brave.' Again she sighed.

'Sad indeed,' said Mrs Beacon. 'Doctor Gally's told her, even these days tidn so easily sorted if the wrong kind, there being two, as Amelia's seems to be. But they've bin so kind and helpful upalong to the surgery, getting leaflets for her and a nurse to read and explain them, and telling her of all these visionary aids that can make her see so well as possible while the poor soul's still able.'

Her audience puzzled briefly over the visionary, but only briefly. There were further murmurs of sympathy.

'As to Doctor Stan,' Daisy interposed, 'he didn even smile, Amelia said, when she asked him on the quiet, just in case, if maybe Doctor Gally might have made a mistake—'

'As if he ever would!' broke in her sister with scorn. The Ploverton partnership of doctors Galahad Potter-Carey and Sterndale 'Stan' Bennett was highly regarded in and around the twin villages. Not only were the two medics knowledgeable, compassionate and down to earth in their approach, they were honest. If they didn't know, or weren't sure, they never hesitated to press for a second or even third opinion to get the best possible treatment for their patients.

'Just as well young Angela's took Susan off to Bristol for a wedding outfit,' said Debbie Tucker, as general mirth at the idea of Dr Potter-Carey's making a mistake died away. 'Not as she'd have bin inclined to ask Amelia for making more than the hats anyway, much as Susan likes to shop local, for which we're thankful – but there's sure to be photos, and they'll want something smart and up to date for publicity, I don't doubt, authors being the way they are these days all over the world.' Susan's successful bodice-ripping as Milicent Dalrymple was brought to an enthusiastic readership via the Hot Pink Press imprint of noted publishers Messrs Thoroughgood & Whiting of London, Sydney and New York.

'Maybe Amelia *is* a touch old-fashioned,' Debbie's twin conceded, when again old Hilda Beacon laughed.

'And if Susan don't so very much want it, you can be sure Angela will know what's due to her mother and choose it for her!'

Smiles and nods rippled round the little group. 'Give young Angela a ladder and doubtless she'd be up the church tower fixing the clock, too,' someone said.

'Yes, it's a puzzle Mr Hollington didn have it put right so soon as he knew something was wrong,' said someone else. 'When was it the clocks changed – end of March?'

'And ever since the chimes starting with dong, and the ding tacked on the front end o' the next quarter. Tidn ezackly dignified.' Debbie sniffed. 'Even more so for a church.'

'And waiting for October to see if the changing hour sets it right – which maybe it won't,' said Daisy, 'the mechanism being so old and costly to repair, the vicar says. Maybe that's Susan's true reason for choosing a registry wedding rather than church.'

'Surely not,' gasped Tilda; but Mrs Beacon was eager, as always, to have the last word over the sister who was her junior by ten whole months.

'If they'd wanted church they could've waited for November to wed, couldn they? Tidn as if there's like to be any particular rush for them to tie the knot!'

'Hardly love's young dream,' it was agreed. 'Still, better late than never, and good to see the matter settled after this long age.'

Mickey Binns, home-loving globetrotter, had admired the celebrated author from her first days in Tollbridge. His admiration became apparent to all save, it appeared, Susan herself. Popular opinion held that only reluctance to be thought a fortune hunter had stopped him popping the question some years before. Mickey hadn't been too obviously bothered by his long-ago divorce, but for all the college education that had seen him wander the world as a mining engineer before coming home to help his fisherman father, he was a quieter chap than the sprightly Mike – and it was possible that Mike's occasional teasing over his silent worship served to make his son all the more backward in coming forward.

When not engaged in matters connected with fishing, Michael Binns *père et fils* shared the duties of Tollbridge's private bus and taxi service with their Hockaday relatives. Mickey contrived to have the author as his passenger rather more often than numbers might expect, and Susan Jones raised no objection; but it came as a surprise to both when, on a day trip to Bristol for research purposes, Mickey found himself saying something that could be taken as a proposal of marriage, and Susan had chosen so to take it.

Tollbridge rejoiced at the news, and fell to making plans before the breathless surprise of the two contracting parties had subsided. Old friends Mike Binns (as Mickey's father) and Gabriel Hockaday (as senior to his brother-in-law) squabbled for the honour of walking the fatherless bride down the aisle; older friends Louise Hockaday and Olive Farley each prepared to weave her a veil of Honiton lace, and serious consequences were only averted by the compromise offered by the bride as soon as she heard of likely trouble.

'We'll have a quiet ceremony at the register office, followed by a church blessing here and then a party at the Anchor, everyone invited,' Susan said. This advice had been offered by Angela – 'Mother, no! I'm too old to be a bridesmaid!' – who had also offered to plan the various menus required.

'My side of the church,' Susan went on, 'would look so empty, compared with Mickey's, at a formal church wedding. Angela and I have so few relations able to come all this way – and most of our friends are Mickey's, too. It would feel… uncomfortable.

'But,' she added as Louise and Olive exchanged looks, 'of course we'll pull out all the stops for the party – and a few for the blessing, too.' She smiled. 'Angela says I must buy three new dresses! But she says I needn't have a different hat for each outfit. She – we – thought that a lace fascinator might do for all three occasions, and I was wondering...'

Olive and Louise, both secretly relieved they'd been spared the worry of a rushed job, had suggested butterflies for the fascinator, amid a cloud of flowery sprigs. Each in her youth had been taught a different pattern, which together would look elegant when skilfully assembled on a silken headband by Amelia Martin.

'And Amelia's eyes aren't yet so poorly she can't sew straight, if given sufficient time, for so small a job as this,' the two old ladies had reassured the bride. 'As to the rest, she'll not be needed for that!'

'The rest?' Susan stared. 'Oh, but I thought—'

Olive and Louise exchanged mischievous glances. 'You leave it all to us, midear,' said Louise with great firmness. Olive nodded sternly at her side. Susan duly left it. The schooldays feud had been subsumed into a joyful conspiracy of parchment pattern-pricking, flying bobbins and secrecy.

'As for the church clock,' said Mrs Beacon now, 'what *I've* heard is, Mr Hollington sets the difficulty upon the Reverend Field back in Queen Victoria's time, him having grand ideas for the betterment o' the building and any argument being disrespectful to the cloth, for all the cost – which, with Mr Field bringing down an architect from London, ended with the windows a sight too small for easy access to the tower inside.'

'Men!' muttered Debbie Tucker, and rolled her eyes.

'The Perrins never complain of it,' someone objected. The Perrin family, clockmakers and repairers, are proprietors of a local firm that has served the area through more horological generations than most people can number.

'The Perrins set their ladders up *outside*.' Mrs Beacon looked smug. 'The twirdling of a knob to move the clock hands forward idn so hard from outside, but when it's a case of climbing through one o' they liddle windows to get inside, they say a ladder's not enough and it can't be safely done at a reasonable price. Which is why the vicar waits for October, in hopes the mechanics will sort theirselves out when being moved eleven hours forward up a ladder, rather than pay for a scaffolding tower to get right inside.'

'Scaffolding would be so wrong for the wedding pictures.' Tilda Jenkyns sighed, and shook her head.

Daisy tried to sound a cheerful note. 'Anyone else hear the motorbike earlier? I wondered if it might be that friend of young Angela's with green hair, the clever girl as puts up shelves for folk and wires their electrics. My recollection is she'm small enough to squeeze through a window and set the clock to rights, if given proper instruction—'

'Oh, no.' Firmly, Debbie shook her head. 'Angela's always said, Andy will undertake most jobs for which she'm able, but she don't like heights and won't climb ladders, which go with scaffolding, remember. She might not even care to climb the tower steps inside, could the job be done that way – which o'course we don't know if it can. I reckon Mr Hollington has the right of it. Leave well alone. Wait and see.'

The meeting still had this motion under consideration when there came a rattle at the door and it opened to the clanging of the bell. In strode Louise Hockaday, her yellow thumbstick thumping with every emphatic step. It was clear to all that she was big with news, and eager to impart it.

As every eye turned in her direction, her own quick gaze took in and summed up the company present. The total didn't appear to please her. 'Where's your mother?' she demanded of Mrs Tucker. 'Olive did really ought to hear this, Debbie. She might know the reason, even?'

'Sometimes she might, but she idn so good this morning. The weather *will* get into her knees, poor soul, do what she may – as you well know, o'course.' Of course Mrs Hockaday knew her former playfellow's weakness. Each of Olive's knees had been replaced some years earlier after a prolonged and prideful delay, because the way Louise had crowed when Olive's left hip was replaced, decades before the knees, had left the invisible score-sheet far too heavily weighted on the Hockaday side for Olive Farley's liking. The twins had finally chivvied their mother into accepting the inevitable, which (reluctantly) she had; but even now she used a wheeled walker indoors, and two sticks – one red, one green, designed for the appropriate hands – to move, slowly and painfully, about only the flatter parts of Combe Tollbridge; which in reality meant the harbour area, and little else beyond.

The thumbstick, with the hollow handle into which a custom-built brandy flask fitted neatly, remained Louise's one concession to arthritis. Secretly hating the way her oldest friend was being reduced by age, at the same time that she arranged for Olive's sticks to be spray-painted in the Hockaday garage Louise had chosen a cheerful yellow for herself to make the sad oppression of the walking sticks more fun. In public she had argued that if she fell over and lay unconscious on the ground, she would be so much easier to find in the dark; and the brandy would come in handy while she waited.

'Poor soul,' echoed Louise automatically, eager to deliver her bombshell. 'The fog's bin a touch slow to lift today, but lift at last it has – and you'll never guess in a million years what's bin done upalong to the old school under cover of the fog, while there was nobody there to see!'

Chapter Four

High on Watchfield Point, the former coastguard headland that overlooks Combe Tollbridge and falls almost vertically into the sea, artist Jane Merton stood chatting with friends. She cast anxious glances from the sky to the rippling water, and back again. Yesterday she had caught the weather forecast: it promised well. She'd tapped the barometer to make sure, and tapped it throughout the day; she consulted the weather-wise, and fretted, and spent the night restless with creativity. She breakfasted in a silence her husband knew better than to break. Jasper's smile was rueful as he saw her leave Clammer Cottage, her sketchbook and camera in their woven bag as impatient as their owner for the mist to clear, hoping for the exact effect she wanted.

As Jane turned from Hempen Row into Stickle Street, vivid spectral images danced before her mind's eye, blinding her to everything else. She failed to notice the work-gang arrive outside the old school, hurrying on her way to the harbour bridge and the steep Coastguard Steps with mental fingers crossed that soon she would see the clifftop view just as her original vision had inspired her.

'Not long now, I reckon.' The reassurance came from Sam Farley. Tollbridge born and bred, landsman Sam could read the weather as well as any fisherman. He owned and ran, single-handed, the Coastguard Printery he'd set up in the former headland station that had been closed by the brute but realistic force of locally applied economics. 'That old mist idn like to linger out there, as the cap'n here I'm sure will agree.'

Former naval person Rodney Longstone reminded his friends that he'd spent most of his career in submarines 'where a periscope isn't very good at weather forecasting', adding that he nevertheless believed Sam to have the right of it. The last of the fog would soon disperse once the sun had risen (the captain checked his watch) high enough over Cliddon Hill to shine on the grey-brown waters of the Bristol Channel, in its broader identity known also as the Severn Sea.

Captain Longstone had by public opinion been volunteered to the setting up of a Tollbridge Coastal Watch, in lieu of the lifeboat service many would have liked to re-establish but which, as everyone accepted, in so small a community was no longer viable. Rodney and his little committee had agreed the necessary basics but, with naval thoroughness, the captain said he preferred to take his own measurements and investigate preliminary costings before any professionals should be brought in. He, Sam Farley and Jasper Merton spent an afternoon with a sextant, notebooks, two tape measures and a ball of string with metal pegs of the butcher's skewer type; the captain was now back for one final survey before leaving for his regular trip to Taunton, in the course of which (he promised) he would make even more detailed enquiries, just to be sure.

This promise had reassured the young printer. When the idea of a Coastal Watch was first mooted, Sam's unspoken concern (given that a spot near the old coastguard station was the obvious place to set up headquarters) had been that the watchers would all too frequently apply to him to let them use the printery's kitchen, the loo and the telephone down whose trusty landline he conducted his business. Combe Tollbridge is a noted not-spot for cyber communication. Even on the summit of the Watchfield cliff, at certain times of day there's no guarantee a mobile phone will be able to connect and stay connected with the outside world for very long.

Rodney Longstone had run a happy ship; at Christmas he still exchanged cards with officers and men who'd served with him. He understood them, and guessed what worried Sam without having to be told. He'd done his best to reassure.

'We do plan to work as an independent unit,' he said. 'We'll try our best to leave you in peace – though I can't promise you won't be asked to lend a hand with digging the foundations!' The shy smile that accompanied this amiable threat had become more evident in recent months, as friendship with Angela Lilley brought the quiet captain further out of his self-imposed shell.

Sam grinned back. 'You've but to say the word, Cap'n, and I'll show the lot o' you I can turn a spit or take a mattock to hard ground as good as any in Tollbridge – out of working hours.' He was happy now to make coffee for his friends, as they enjoyed their gossip while Jane awaited the weather's convenience.

Before the first blow from a pickaxe can fall it must be decided where exactly it should be delivered. Jane's husband Jasper, who since the pair's arrival in Tollbridge had gradually become accepted as second only to Susan Jones in understanding how to look things up on a computer, had researched the legal requirements for erecting a small, self-contained building at the correct distance from a building that was already there.

In this endeavour he was quietly assisted by local entrepreneur Barnaby Christmas, the greater part of whose mysterious wealth was thought to be property-based. Barney liked to keep his financial affairs private. Many years ago, an impoverished young man, he'd left Combe Tollbridge to seek his fortune in the wider world – had apparently found it – and considered it now the business of few to know how it might have been made. It amused the old man to tell a different outrageous (but always just credible) story any time anyone ventured to ask, though he rarely joked with Jasper Merton – who from the first had treated him with respect – because Jasper was currently in his employ.

Mr Christmas had saved his young employee, and Tollbridge in general, time and effort by pointing Mr Merton towards the various directives, regulations, and catch-questions that mattered most. Jasper downloaded and printed reams of detailed pages, with salient points highlighted in different colours; he made summaries of all important sections because he guessed only the captain would bother to read everything through; and under Barney's guidance there were now likely to be few, if any, unexpected shocks.

The fog was gone, the sky was blue, the air was crisp and clear. Coffee mugs were drained, and returned with thanks to Sam; he and Rodney Longstone duly set about their survey measuring, pegging out, poring over the original notes. Few corrections were needed, none of which was major. Rodney looked at his watch, and nodded: still time to spare before leaving for Taunton. Naval training is thorough. He and Sam could double-check their corrections to the notes, and then that should be an end to the matter. Both men forgot Jane, even as they half heard the young artist moving about nearby.

Jane gazed at the Bristol Channel and saw, just as she'd hoped, wide Exmoor shadows retreating from the light across the waves. Darkness and brightness, cloud-speckled depths and the chill glint of autumn waters shimmering in gently restless movement; gulls screaming a welcome to the sun as it rose to warm the world...

There was something else. 'Oh.' Jane lowered her camera, and blinked. 'No. A trick of the light, that's all.' She tried to believe it. 'Just a trick of the light.' She shook her head; looked again; rubbed her eyes. 'It's still there...' Her voice began to tremble. She breathed deeply; her heart thumped; she felt giddy. 'Oh, no – it must be some sort of brainstorm!'

Her plaintive cry made the other two pay attention. 'Something wrong, midear?' asked Sam, and then – 'Oh!'

'Oh indeed.' Rodney followed his gaze. 'Quick, Jane, your camera – we've no idea when it will fade, and this one is marvellous. You might be able to sell it to a newspaper if you don't wobble and blur it – hurry, now!'

As he'd intended, the voice of command shook Jane from her stupor. She sagged with relief that her companions seemed to be sharing her hallucination, and forced her hands to be steady as she followed Rodney's advice and raised her camera.

'A container ship, you reckon?' Sam squinted under the eyeshade of his hand.

'Oil tanker?' The captain squinted in similar fashion. 'Maybe liquid gas – either way, heading for Milford Haven, I think.'

Jane's gasp was audible. 'An oil tanker in the sky? Milford Haven's miles away!' Yet the clicks and whirrs of her camera never ceased.

'It's a fata morgana,' said Rodney. 'A mirage; as you called it yourself, a trick of the light. If the weather's unusually calm they can be caused by layers of air at different temperatures: it's called thermal inversion. Think of a hot summer day when it seems there's water on the road ahead, and when you get there everything's dry as a bone.'

'Now that,' Sam corrected him gravely, 'is a ghost ship – leastways, so Gabriel or Mike or any of them others would tell 'ee, should they see it. Doom and disaster, they'll predict, the minute they can find some old tale that appertains to the sight!' He chuckled. 'Long ago there could be three-masted schooners or pirate brigs in the sky as harbingers of evil, but there's bin nothing such in these parts in my lifetime save once, when someone made a film and had a ship in full sail smuggling up and down the coast, Minehead way – which was real enough, and no ghost.'

'What a wonderful memory to have.' The captain thought of Nelson's glorious, victorious wooden walls, and sighed. 'She must have made a grand spectacle – and so close to home.' He brightened. 'Imagine the fun of being a film extra on a ship in full sail – even being paid for it, perhaps!'

Sam applied a regretful damper. 'As to that, nobody come here asking for volunteers, so none in Tollbridge had the chance, which no doubt saved much argument. Fishermen are a different breed from them that sail for pleasure, or to win races.' He laughed. 'The film folk would have had old Gabriel telling 'em what they were doing wrong the moment he set foot on deck, and Mike to back him up, and the pair of 'em walking the plank for mutiny before the anchor was properly raised!'

Rodney had to concede the point. 'But it would have been a grand spectacle,' he said again. 'In the days of full sail, it's easy to understand how such a mirage would terrify the superstitious into predicting the worst. I hope you get some decent shots, Jane.' Jane waved a quick acknowledgement, but didn't interrupt her work. 'It could be a good marketing opportunity for you too, Sam. This is the first fata morgana I've seen, or even heard of, since I moved to Tollbridge, though I saw a couple during my service years; but submarines don't spend a lot of time on the surface! Anyway, they're unusual. The two of you might get together for a set of postcards – oh, I believe…'

'Yes,' said Sam, 'looks like it begins to fade. Keep snapping there, Jane! Could be a small fortune to be made, like the cap'n says!'

As the air continued to warm, the oil tanker in the sky shimmered and shivered against the blue, then disappeared silently into the emptiness of the heavenly vault.

Jane blinked herself back to reality. 'Did I imagine that?' She fiddled with her camera to reassure herself, and displayed the results of her efforts to her friends, who were suitably impressed as she scrolled through the images. 'I've seen nothing like it before. Thank goodness I had my camera, but... It looked so real, and so do my snaps – and the movie I took... Everyone will think they're just mock-ups I did in my studio, and the way things are these days with photoshopping, who's to know I didn't?'

'We can't be the only ones to have seen it,' Rodney pointed out. 'It will have been visible for some miles up and down the coast. It didn't last long: national news probably won't bother, though I'd guess our local stations might – but how many of 'em will have top-quality film from a camera, rather than a phone, to use is quite another matter.' He spoke with meaning, and Jane took the hint and said she'd go straight home and talk to Jasper.

'There's a theory,' went on the captain, 'that it was some sort of mirage that caused the *Titanic* disaster. It was an unprecedentedly calm, clear night, with the moon already set, and many vessels in the area reporting strange optical conditions. Captain Smith truly believed it was safe to steam at full speed through ice-cold waters, but he didn't realise that above the freezing sea the air was much warmer. It had drifted across from the Gulf Stream, settling in different layers of temperature; there was thick haze on a doubtful horizon, so that none of the lookouts could see clearly – and suddenly, out of that haze, the iceberg appeared. They spotted it just those few seconds too late.'

There was a respectful pause. Rodney broke it. 'But you, Jane, spotted our particular optical illusion in good time and, I hope, made the most of it. Get going before you miss your chance. Leave us to finish our survey – so that I can get going, too!'

'Aye-aye, sir.' Jane threw him a swift salute before stuffing the tools of her trade back in their bag, repeating thanks to Sam for the coffee, and hurrying in the direction of Coastguard Steps towards home and her husband. Jasper, founder and owner of Packlemerton's Publicity, was undoubtedly the best person to advise on how she could market her morning's work for fair and reasonable profit.

Jane jogged along Boatshed Row without meeting anyone, and after crossing the little bridge over the Chole was about to make for Clammer Cottage and commercial advice when she realised it wouldn't delay her so very much to detour past the post office. Would it? She and Sam and Rodney Longstone might be mistaken in supposing there was public interest in the sight of a Milford Haven-bound oil tanker floating in mid-air. Shouldn't she at least try out the idea on those members of the public currently in Farley's General Stores, who might have missed the phenomenon, before risking her husband's ridicule at having so misjudged the marketing possibilities?

'Idiot,' she told herself. 'Be honest. You just want to brag about it.'

She found her feet had already directed her down the narrow path connecting Bridge Lane to The Legger; she hesitated over popping first into Widdowson's Bakery, but remembered Angela wasn't there, being on her way, with her mother, to Bristol. As to the baker, the absence of his apprentice meant Evan Evans would be working on his own, and wouldn't care to be disturbed by anyone except a paying customer. If Jane bought cakes from Evan she could hardly justify buying at the post office, too. And the audience would be larger in the post office...

Farley's doorbell jangled, though so intense was the ongoing chatter that few heads turned as Jane came in, ready to whip out her camera at the slightest excuse.

The turning heads included that of Louise Hockaday, whose eyes gleamed on seeing her young neighbour. 'You tell 'em, midear! I can't be the only one to have seen – you tell 'em what *you* think it all means!'

Everyone waited. Jane blinked. She'd known that superstition still held local respect; she herself would without thinking toss a pinch of spilled salt over her shoulder, or touch wood for luck. Taught as a child by her godmother Miriam she would never set a half-cut loaf of bread cut-side-down on the board, for fear of invoking the storm spirits who would sink the fishing boats this unlucky shape resembled; yet Jane had always supposed her friends' respect to have been modified over the years by modern thought and education. They could laugh at themselves and among themselves, and they only believed in omens and ill-wishing when they were telling the tourist tale to visitors who came to the little village and needed to be encouraged to linger, and to spend money.

'Captain Longstone explained it very well, I thought,' she said at last. 'With the calm weather we've been having recently, it made sense. It's not as if it was a – a three-masted schooner, or a pirate brig, it just means there were different layers of air at different temperatures. Anyway, it's gone now, though I did get some photos and a film, if you're inter—'

'Pirates?' Louise pounced on the word, glaring round, daring anyone to argue. 'Didn I *say* they must have come here outside the law – warn there could be mischief afoot?' All heads but that of the puzzled Jane duly nodded. 'Remember, there's bin nothing said by Barney Christmas, so with nobody having any sensible reason' – once more her triumphant glare swept the little group – 'mischief is surely all it can mean. The property belongs to Barney, when all's said and done, and—'

Then Louise's brain caught up with what her ears had heard. She stared at Jane.

'Layers of air? What's temperature to do wi' the price of eggs? We'm all in confusion over them yellow lines painted this very day in the road next the old school, the men packed up and driving off so soon as they clapped eyes on me, and no time to ask 'em – and you must have seen the same, walking past as I did!' Jane was given no time to reply. 'That school have bin closed and empty these eight years or more, with Barney biding his time for the money to come right and start building the holiday apartments he talked of—'

'So far as I recall 'twas a hotel he wanted,' someone said, when it was clear that Jane was still trying to make sense of everything.

Louise shrugged. 'He bought it, he paid for it, he had his plans worked out and' – her thumbstick banged the floor – 'economic circumstances went against him, so he've always said when asked. But Barney still owns the old school – so far as is known,' she had to concede. 'But we've heard nought to the contrary – and didn he go on paying insurance for the chillern to use the playground with no benefit to hisself, till that motor-bike gang came one night and cut up the tarmac and he had to lock the gates?'

'As for motorbikes,' someone began, but Louise was still going strong.

'Your Jasper's thick as inkle-weavers with Barney Christmas, young Jane. Has he said aught to you?'

This question at least could be answered. 'Has Jasper said anything to me? Well, he wouldn't, if it's business. He's serious about client confidentiality. He never says anything to anyone about his clients until he's allowed.' Jane giggled. 'And then, if there's what looks like a leakage of information you can bet it was part of a deliberate plan, which he *might* tell me about then – or he might not. It just depends.' On what, and what they were all discussing, continued to puzzle.

She reached into her tote. 'I've been up on Watchfield Point with my camera,' she began, 'and got some rather good shots of—'

Old Hilda Beacon laughed. 'Getting in practice for the wedding, midear? You'd be the one to ask, such friends with Angela as you are!'

'Or Chris Hockaday,' put in Daisy, one eye on the prize-winning photographer's grandmother. 'I've read in my paper there's many folk these days have drones at their wedding to be a touch different from everyone else.'

Louise looked smug. 'Our Chris would do a grand job, no doubting – if asked.'

'Susan idn keen on fuss and fidget no more than Mickey,' said Debbie Tucker, whose married life had within two years of tying the knot become divorce-level grim.

'But such happy memories,' sighed the widowed Tilda Jenkyns. Tilda's wedding album, too precious to be opened, lay wrapped in tissue paper in a lonely bottom drawer.

'I wonder how fares the trip to Bristol,' someone said, with a glance at the clock. 'Reckon Angela's found anything for her mother to wear yet?'

'And how many shops she've dragged poor Susan to visit,' said someone else.

'There'll be no chocolate with marshmallow sprinkles today!' This was now the author's default mid-morning beverage: her favourite Turkish delight was banned until after the wedding. 'Angela won't let her mother forget her diet, shopping or no shopping.'

Jane smiled, but was quick to speak in her friend's defence. 'Angela just wants Susan to look her very best for Mickey's sake – and I suppose for the photos too, but I've no idea who's taking them – because Susan's mostly so laid back about things and never bothers much, and Angela thinks it's time for once she did. She likes Mickey a lot – Angela, that is – and Mike, and everyone – and she knows how much fun the village will have at the blessing, and the party. She worries that if she leaves Susan to sort it on her own she'll make one outfit do for all three occasions, and people will feel short-changed.' She suppressed another smile. 'Of course, since Angela came to live in Tollbridge she's been so busy with so many different jobs she hasn't had the time to treat *herself* to new clothes, either.' Saying nothing of Rodney Longstone, she wondered if anyone else had similar thoughts and was likewise keeping quiet for fear of tempting fate.

'A great sorrow for Amelia Martin to have her eyesight turn against her,' someone said. 'Time was she could've matched Susan half-a-dozen outfits, hands behind her back and standing on her head!'

'Ah,' said old Hilda, 'and as to heads, never mind making from new, Amelia could work miracles putting frill-de-dills to any hat bought by other folk from any o' the big shops.'

'Trimmed and retrimmed year upon year, season upon season,' agreed her sister, 'all according how much was spent on the original purchase. But now…'

'Such clever fingers, poor soul.' Tilda Jenkyns likewise paid tribute. 'Why, you'd never recognise your own winter hat the next spring, not once Amelia took it for tiddivation, never mind anyone else's—'

Louise Hockaday was horrified. 'But nobody, surely, would go to Mickey Binns's wedding in a made-over hat! Not when we've all bin waiting these long years for Susan to say yes – most of us,' she added for Jane's benefit, 'but you'll be buying something new along o' the rest of us, won't you, midear?'

Jane was starting to say she certainly would, when Hilda Beacon spoke over her.

'Well, o'course she will! Is there any that won't? Me and Daisy, now, tomorrow we'm on the bus across to Minehead, and choosing a pair of real smart liddle fornicators to go with our best summer frocks. All the rage for weddings, so the fashion papers say!'

Chapter Five

Susan's little car crawled down Stickle Street, passed the Bridge Lane fork and reached the entrance of narrow Three Square Passage. Stifling a yawn, Susan executed the turn less neatly than usual as she made for the sanctuary of home, hot chocolate with – she sighed – marshmallow sprinkles, and the chance to put her feet up.

It was the end of a wearisome day. Angela's offer to drive back from Bristol had been refused, in Susan's final attempt to assert herself. She'd given in to almost everything else suggested by her daughter – she hadn't realised that Angela held such strong views on even mid-haute couture – because the combination of a born organiser and a multitude of fashionista saleswomen had been too much for a distracted author to withstand. Susan lost count of the shops into which she was dragged. She never knew how many clothes she tried on; her mind glazed over, and it didn't take long for the very sight of a full-length mirror to make her shudder.

Angela channelled Nelson to remind her mother that Tollbridge expected its bride to do her duty. By the end of that day Susan had been talked into the purchase of three entirely different outfits, with shoes and bags to match.

Costume jewellery was mentioned once, but never again. Susan thought of this minor triumph every time a personal shopper insisted each new outfit would need a new hat; she snapped up a discreet but elegant Alice-band comb she would ask Amelia Martin to turn into a one-does-for-three fascinator, and stood firm.

It was only after she had manoeuvred her car to a thankful stop in the parking space squeezed from the original pocket-handkerchief garden of Corner Glim Cottage that Susan realised what she had left undone.

'Angela, I'm sorry! I meant to drive on to Meazel Cleeve but you were so quiet, I forgot you were in the car.' Perhaps this wasn't tactful. 'I mean—'

'No problem, Mother.' Angela's tone held just a hint of condescension. 'Don't fuss! Let me help you unload the bags and boxes, then I'll leave you alone. I'll take the clothes round to my place to make sure everything is hung up properly, and won't get creased.' Angela thought little of Susan's ability to treat her new wardrobe as the day's expenditure demanded. It wasn't that the best-selling Milicent Dalrymple couldn't afford to look stylish; but when working from home (which was most of the time) she so seldom needed to dress smartly that, in the throes of creativity (which must include wedding plans) there was a risk she would forget how very carefully smart clothes should be handled in order to maintain their smartness until they were required.

'I'll keep the dresses in my bathroom for a few days while you break in the shoes.' Susan stifled a groan. 'When the steam's done its thing, you can come round and we'll have the fashion parade for Miriam to see if you need any final tweaks like – oh, letting out a seam or taking it in' – Susan had curves, of which she wasn't ashamed, but tried to resist bulges – 'or altering a hem or anything.'

Angela, not as fond of hot chocolate as her mother, was soon on her posh-shop carrier-laden way back to The Old Printery. She walked more slowly along Harbour Path than her normal easy pace: she, too, was tired. After that early start, it had been a busy day. Like Susan she would be glad of a chance to put her feet up – though she might just stop off at Harbour Glim Cottage to let Miriam know the travellers were safely returned. She might beg a cup of tea before tackling the short, sharp steepness of Meazel Cleeve...

'But not a sniff of what's in these bags does she get until Mother says okay,' resolved Angela. 'I may be thirsty, but I won't be bribed.'

She was still smiling as she drew near Miriam's door, and was startled to hear brisk tapping on the window. A face grinned at her from the small front room, even as the door banged open and there stood Miriam.

'If it's not the very one we've bin expecting! How did 'ee fare over to Bristol, midear? From the look o' those bags it seems you managed, after all, talking Susan into some fire-new duds for the big day.' In private conversation with her closest friend Susan had been vocal on the bossiness of daughters and how she planned to resist it – but Miriam knew her apprentice. It was no surprise now to see the number of carriers Angela brought with her, or the expensive names that adorned them. 'Come along in and see who's here for you, and show us what luck you've had!'

'I'll come in, thanks, but you can't – Andy?' The emerald pixie cut, streaked with pink, appeared crowning the well-known grin that widened over Miriam's shoulder. 'Andy, what on earth are you doing here?'

'Waiting for you and learning to twirdle. Miriam's let me try winding on the umbrella swift, too. Harder than it looks, isn't it?'

Angela laughed. 'You're better coordinated than me: I bet you picked it up in no time.' She dusted her feet on Miriam's mat, and carefully set down the carrier bags. 'I've just left Mother making hot chocolate. Safer to come away before she knocked the mug over, and ruined the clothes, and we had to repeat the whole performance – which would be too much for either of us. You know how chocolate never really washes out.'

The others knew, Miriam adding that tea was far less marking than chocolate. If Angela wanted to join them in a cup, with perhaps a slice of cake, she'd be very welcome.

'Thanks, I'd love one – but I won't show you what we've bought.' And for the next half-hour Angela stuck to her guns, giving a lively account of the day's doings and listening with interest to Andy's story, as earlier narrated to Miriam. Then, apologising to her hostess, she said it really had been a tiring day and, while she was truly delighted on behalf of her mother and Mickey, there was a lot to be said in favour of elopement.

'I'll carry the bags; you can just walk,' suggested Andromeda Marsh, as they made their farewells and headed for The Old Printery. 'It's the least I can do after foisting myself on you for – well, I hope not too long, but I've no idea just yet.'

Angela flashed her an understanding smile. 'Been there, done that, and you know I sympathise – and thanks, they are a bit inconvenient after a day like today! If you could just take the biggest?' Bags duly changed hands. 'I want to keep what's in them a secret until the big reveal, remember.' A bathroom adorned with de-creasing clothes would be impossible to keep secret from a house guest, but Andy could be trusted.

Little else was said as the pair climbed Meazel Cleeve, but at Angela's gate Andy nodded towards Baker's Cottage and observed, in a deliberately casual tone, that Rodney Longstone's car, which hadn't been there when she and her motorbike arrived, was now safely back from wherever the captain had been all day.

'Taunton.' Angela was equally casual. Too casual? 'It's a regular trip, every fortnight. He says it's good for the car, quite apart from anything else, but he's still on the Reserve list and it kills two birds with one stone, he says.' She was too busy with her front door key to notice Andy's grin. Angela's mother (thought Angela's best friend) seemed to have the right idea. A self-contained young woman, made by circumstance perhaps older than her years, might well find a more suitable life's partner, companion, spouse, whatever in someone half a generation her senior.

'You and Susan could have begged a lift with the captain today and saved yourselves the trek to Bristol,' she suggested, returning the carriers to their guardian. 'Or aren't the Taunton shops any good?'

Angela smiled. 'To be honest I think it was a sentimental thing, though Mother would die rather than say so! It was while Mickey was driving her to Bristol that he got round to asking her – at least he sort of hinted, she said, and then she realised he was never going to come right out with it, so she sort of accepted, because *she* would never come right out and say yes in case it had been a joke she'd taken the wrong way – though Mickey's nothing like his father, thank goodness – but however it happened,' finished Susan's daughter crisply, 'it's high time it did, and I'm so pleased for both of them. The whole village is thrilled! So I want everything to go well in every way, and have it a proper occasion – three occasions, I should say – which has to include the dressing-up. You come and help me put this stuff on hangers to drop the creases, and while we're doing it you can tell me the rest of the story.'

'What rest?' Andy was another who could offer a too-casual response.

'Come off it! You told me what you said you'd told Miriam, and she didn't say you left anything out – but I've known you long enough to know you didn't tell her the half of it. I'll fetch the hangers while you start shaking things out, and then you can spill the beans.'

There was a wicked gleam in the eye that met Angela's. 'Okay, you're right – but I certainly showed the bastard, pardon my French, and he'll think twice before he tries another trick like that. He's not the only one who can be tricky – *and* it cost him! He and my landlord are in cahoots – cousin, brother-in-law, can't remember, don't care – but when I had a rent increase come out of the blue, and didn't argue over and above what you'd normally expect – and not a word about a rent tribunal – I guess he assumed I was so desperate to stay in town he could pretty much get away with murder. Only by then, with the smear campaign and everything, I'd already made up my mind that I'd had enough. All it needed was the final push to get me going, which it was.'

'What did you do?'

Andy gurgled with suppressed mirth. 'Waited till my last official day, emptied the flat – don't get your knickers in a twist, most of my gear's in storage and won't be coming here – and changed the locks. I left the new keys at the women's shelter, and wrote snail mail to my landlord telling him where to collect 'em.' She grinned. 'And I told him they wouldn't be handed over until he produced a receipt from the air ambulance that attended the crash that started all this, for his donation of the exact amount of the deposit he still owes me.'

Angela applauded the principle of Andy's good intention, but was surprised her friend hadn't spotted the obvious catch. 'It's brilliant, Andy, but – if the flat's legally his, all he has to do is get himself a locksmith—'

The wickedness in Andy's eye, gleaming brighter still, cut her short. 'I *knew*,' cried Angela, 'you hadn't told Miriam the half of it!'

Andy shrugged. 'Older generation, out-of-the-way village – hard to know how she'd react. You know her well; I've barely spoken to her before today, when she was the obvious place to look when—'

'Never mind that! What did you actually *do*?'

'I told you I wrote snail mail to my landlord, rather than text or what-have-you. It can take a week for a letter to creep through the postal system in our part of town.'

'I remember. So?'

'Before leaving my flat for the last time, I played the prawn trick.' Angela's mouth fell open. 'With the odd kipper for garnish. In every single room.'

'Every room?' Angela recovered at last. 'Which explains the snail mail – and a second class stamp, of course.'

'Of course.' Andy was buoyant. 'You know I'm a pretty good woodworker. I can fix skirting boards and floorboards and put in fake knotholes to add character, if that's what people want. That son-with-no-father will sure as Hecate have his work cut out trying to find where I hid those… biological specimens, shall we call 'em? I know, I know, a waste of good food – but in a very good cause. After a week of warm weather that flat won't find a tenant in a hundred years without my help.'

Angela couldn't deny her friend's undoubted skill in both carpentry and cunning. 'You do plan to help him, when he asks?' She didn't say *if*. 'But – how is he to get in touch if you don't mean to tell people where you've gone?'

'The shelter again: it's the obvious place. Then they hand over my second letter, saying he's to give my entire flat deposit to them within the week.' Andy sighed. 'I've helped them out for so long I feel guilty about leaving them in the lurch this way. It's the least I can do, in the circs. My final donation.'

'And he's had to pay it back twice, to two different charities. Brilliant! I suppose he gets a third letter with diagrams, once he hands over the money?'

'Full details and photos – of every single prawn, cross my heart. Every flake of kipper too, in case you wondered. I may be vindictive, but I don't want anyone calling me spiteful.'

By now the display of Susan's wedding finery was complete, Andy's narrative having been interspersed with little cries of admiration as the two friends worked together shaking, smoothing, and enviously stroking the three luxury outfits Susan had been persuaded would truly, honestly suit her and, yes, Mickey was sure to like them, and so would everyone else in Tollbridge and she really should stop making such a fuss.

'Now, coffee – and plans.' Angela led the way from her tiny bathroom to the slightly larger kitchen. 'You must have some. If not – talk about burning your boats! I don't blame you for chucking London, and it would be lovely if you wanted to settle in Tollbridge. All the old-timers agree the place needs livening up – not too much, we're too small and it isn't as if there's anywhere to expand except up – but some new blood in old houses would be just the thing. Barney Christmas has plans for Boatshed Row, you know.'

'I know, he buys 'em up as people die off, and he's waiting to get the last one, then he means to burn the whole place down as a sort of revenge – no, call it a public Up Yours to the days when his family was so poor they couldn't afford to heat the place, even when it was snowing a blizzard.' Any visitor to Tollbridge who spent more than half an hour in the pub was sure to hear the rags-to-riches story of the local tycoon, with suitable and imaginative embellishments. 'Honestly, Ange! So you think he might hand me the matches and pay me to get on with it? Vindictive, I won't argue with that – vengeance is mine, and so on – but the prawn trick is one thing. Arson's quite another, although – if the money was right—'

'Don't be silly.' One of Angela's looks stayed this flight of fantasy before it left the ground. 'By all accounts, Barney's mellowing. Jane says Jasper's talked some sense into him! Considering the age difference, the two of them get on really well, both being in business even if not the same way. Barney left home with nothing and came back rich, and to this day nobody knows how he did it, or how much he's worth. Packlemerton's Publicity is another one-man band, but – well, anyone with internet access knows Jasper from his website, and they can find out even more if they check him online at Companies House.'

'You don't see an age difference as a problem, then? To... friendship, I mean.' Andy judged Rodney Longstone to be, at most, twenty years older than Angela. Mr Knightley had been sixteen when Emma was born; Jane Eyre was a generation younger than Edward Fairfax Rochester...

'Why should I?' Again Angela was casual. 'Jasper and Barney don't. They've been making plans together like a couple of children with a Great Big Secret. All they'll say is that we'll be told in due course – the Ploverton doctors are somehow involved, too – and if it goes the way they hope, the village should benefit financially as well as them – but they give no details, though of course Barney never has given much away, on principle.'

'Mike Binns says he's a – a reg'lar old pinch-fart.' Andy made a brave attempt at the accent. 'I adore that man! I think he means miser.'

Angela laughed. 'Gabriel calls Barney a snibble-nose who'd skin a flint for a penny, which is the same thing. Barney enjoys playing up to them, just as long as it doesn't interfere with his business. What he *has* let slip is that it means refurbishing Boatshed Row, which is why I mentioned it, Handy Andy' – with emphasis – 'because refurbishment means plenty of the kind of handiwork you're so good at. If you're here on the spot you can get going – and get paid – just as soon as the mystery plans are made public.'

Andy was cheerful. 'As old Christmas always says, it's worth a try!' Barney's catchphrase was long established in the area, and frequently quoted.

'Time will tell. And if we're wrong about the doctors, and it's refurbishment as ordinary houses they've got in mind, I've wondered if Mickey and my mother might fancy living there. Mickey will move to Corner Glim Cottage after the wedding, only I can't help worrying they'll both find it hard to adapt, at their age. When she first bought the place Mother had it remodelled for single living, which is why she found it so hard when I dumped myself on her after the Paul business. Once I moved out from under her feet and left her on her own, everything was fine.'

'Susan's a working woman. She needs her space if Milicent Dalrymple, or whatever she finally decides to call herself in her new identity, means to carry on writing.'

'Well, of course she does! A writer's what Mother is, whatever she calls herself – and she says she'll recognise the new name when it comes along, so she's not worrying.'

Andy was intrigued: her imagination was not that of a creative. 'So, how exactly does it come? Where did she get Milicent Dalrymple?'

'It's logical enough, if you have that sort of mind.' Angela had a different sort of mind. 'It seems to work for Mother! Years ago she went on a school exchange to France, and fell in love with a special gingerbread they make in Poitou called Melusine, after some woman who was half a serpent because she'd left her father on a mountain, or something – not that Mother cared much for the legend, but she did enjoy the cakes and never forgot them. No modern equivalent comes anywhere near, I'm told.' The baker's apprentice laughed. 'I've given up trying: you can never bring back memories exactly as things were, can you? So when she wanted a romantic pseudonym she anglicised Melusine to Milicent; and I think the hero of some book she'd just read was the Duke of Dalrymple; and there you are.'

Andy nodded. 'Gingerbread dukes and best-selling authors – well, why not? As for being an author, why can't they live somewhere else and Susan keep her cottage and just use it as an office? Off to work every day like a commuter. It's not as if she'd have far to walk: nowhere's far from anywhere, around here.'

'Off to work from where, exactly? That's what worries me. They can hardly go and live with Mike in Hempen Row, can they!'

'That poor old man – his only son leaving him after all these years. He'll be so lonely.' Andy tried to sound as if she meant it, but couldn't quite manage it. 'I wonder how he'd like me as a lodger – just for company, you know?'

'You must be mad! You'd never cope. Seriously, who could? If Mike didn't tease you half to death, there's Gabriel Hockaday just a few houses down. He'd be for ever popping in to egg Mike on.' Angela shook her head. 'You know, once they've finished trying to take over the wedding that pair will have far too much time on their hands for anyone's peace of mind. Makes you think.'

'What I think,' said Andy, 'is that where those two old rascals are concerned, ignorance is definitely bliss. Why borrow trouble before you have to? You just leave well alone!'

Chapter Six

Combe Tollbridge had long known that when the taxi was booked by Susan Jones, Mickey Binns was her preferred driver. Susan often took a taxi when she didn't want to drive herself; she might use the minibus, but when travelling for reasons of authorial research it was understandable she should prefer to discuss her work with someone of similar age and education, like Mickey. It had become a close, though not too personal, relationship. If Tollbridge in general (and Mickey in particular) might prefer the relationship to be even closer – well, they'd waited this long age, hadn they; and a little longer wouldn hurt, would it? Just so long as they didn leave it *too* long!

Then Susan had been inspired to create Vesta the Investigator, and was duly driven to Bristol by Mickey to research the old music hall where the real-life Vesta Tilley could well have performed. Susan achieved as much of her research as circumstances allowed and then, contending with finally freed emotions and the constraints of Bristol's traffic, the newly betrothed in their first official partnership survived the motor-way, the cross-country aftermath, the perils of Porlock Hill and the narrow, steep and twisting roads beyond. Mickey had parted with reluctance from his lady at Corner Glim Cottage and driven in a daze up Stickle Street. He parked the taxi, and came only slowly out of the clouds. He couldn't really believe it, but – he knew he wasn't dreaming. Inside, he was one huge smile. He only hoped his father hadn't worried too much over his more than two hours' delay arriving home.

One glimpse of his son's face had been enough for Mike. The finest black beard (and Mickey's whiskers, slightly grizzled now, remained splendid) could not hide a son's proud expression from a sharp-eyed father who'd been watching the clock, thinking of the passenger – and wondering.

'Anything... special to tell me, boy?'

'Any reason there should be?' Mickey loosened his shoulders. 'Sorry, we didn't mean to be so late, but there was a sight too much traffic out there today for my liking.' He smiled to himself. 'All in all, though, we did well enough.'

'Did you, though!' Mike regarded him quizzically. 'More than well, maybe?'

Mickey thought he was being discreet. 'Susan got well started on her research: some pamphlets, photos, lots o' notes; she seemed pleased with how things went, yes.'

'Yes,' echoed Mike hopefully. 'She said that, did she? Yes?'

Mickey had hesitated, hugging the blissful secret to himself for just a few moments more. 'Susan's always took pains over her research, Dad. You know she likes to see things properly when she can, not just books or the computer.'

Mike pounced. 'Susan's seen things properly, have she? High time she did!'

Mickey wanted to tell him he had no idea what he meant. The words wouldn't come. He opened his mouth – and even more words wouldn't come.

'Now,' said Mike, 'I hope I'm not mistook – about Susan saying yes, I mean. She did say yes, didn she?' Suddenly he was anxious. 'And to the right question – not about her books? You said she said yes!' His voice quavered. 'See here, you wouldn be making fun of a poor old widow-man, would you, whose one hope at the end of a sad and weary life is to see his only son happily settled, so he can set out on his final voyage in peace—'

'You play-acting old fraud!' Now Mickey found the words he wanted. 'All right! Yes, I asked Susan to marry me, and yes is what she said, and you know full well you're like to outlive the pair of us – and Angela, too – with years to spare.' Then he thought about this. 'Which is to say, you will so long as you're not thrown overboard when someone's had enough of your nonsense. And if I'm the one does the throwing, don't expect me to change my mind and jump in after you. I'll be holding the *Priscilla* to her course dead ahead, and no more than you deserve.'

Mike had been so thrilled at this confirmation of long-held hopes that, although over the years he'd prepared his role with great care, he was now happy to sacrifice all idea of himself as a sorrowing parent, wounded to the heart by the callous desertion of his only child. 'She's really took you at last? You'm to be wed? That's wonderful!' He leaped at Mickey and clouted him across the shoulders. The younger man staggered sideways. 'Congratulations! When's the great day? Just wait till I tell Gabriel!'

'Now hold on,' begged Mickey. 'We thought we'd announce it in the Anchor tonight, once Susan's spoken with Angela. We can tell everyone—' But he could have spared his breath. Mike was already rushing for his boots, cramming on his beanie, darting from the cottage like a man half his age. He punched a gleeful fist in the air as he sped along Hempen Row, uttering wild cries of triumph that echoed around the cliffs and woods to rouse birds from their roosts and startle even the local goats, who run wild as they please about the neighbourhood and are rarely startled by anything, being every bit as bold as those in Lynton or Llandudno, if not yet their equal in notoriety.

The Anchor announcement had set the tone for a riotous and illegal night extended for hours past official closing time into a morning of headaches and hoarse voices. Gabriel and Mike shouted louder and longer than any, at one point almost coming to blows over which had the better claim to be the one to give the bride away. Susan, so long a widow, had no close family members of appropriate age, health or dignity beyond Angela, who'd already been cast by the two village elders as brides- maid – which suggestion startled both mother and daughter. Angela tried to calm the situation by proposing Miriam Evans, as her mother's first friend in Tollbridge, for the job of walking her mother down the aisle.

'A smart hat, a classy trouser suit,' said Angela, 'and say she's being Veshta Tilley.' Her eyes were slightly out of focus. 'I mean *Vesta* Tilley, Mother. Miriam.' Her smile was wider than anyone had seen it in Tollbridge. 'Very shuitable.' She nodded gravely.

Susan's new non-murder mystery series, to feature the great- est of all Victorian male impersonators, remained very much at the notes-and-thinking stage. Susan hadn't yet chosen her pseudonym, or worked out a plot; she was still coming to terms with her characters, and the technical niceties of corsets and wigs, greasepaint, top hat and tails. 'Clever,' she said, 'but would you do it, Miriam?'

'No,' said Miriam. 'Not in fancy dress not being me. I'll walk beside you, as me, if—'

Mike Binns burst into song. *I'll walk beside you, through the world today—*'

Gabriel joined in, gazing with exaggerated sentimentality from bride to groom as he warbled: *'While dreams and songs and flowers bless your way—*'

The duo suddenly became a trio. *I'll look into your eyes and hold your hand / I'll walk beside you through the golden land!*' After which Barney Christmas fell silent, scowling at Mike and Gabriel before smiling apologetically at Susan and Mickey.

It was generally agreed that Susan had every right to choose the wedding she wanted. She was, after all, the bride; but, as more cider went down, spirits rose higher and higher. Everyone had waited too long for this news. The Anchor seethed with plans both farfetched and (occasionally) practical, though as noise levels increased it was hard to know which was which. The bride and groom exchanged looks of resignation. They would allow Tollbridge to have its say and let off steam; once things had calmed down, the happy couple could explain what had already been settled.

The one thing they hadn't settled was what Gabriel and Mike might do on learning the ceremony would take place at the register office, quietly, with cousin Jerry Hockaday as best man and Susan's daughter Angela the only other official guest, the legal requirement being for two witnesses 'of sound mind,' said Susan, 'which rules out Mike and Gabriel, surely.'

'You reckon? They'll turn up anyway, demanding their rights, and they'll doubtless set all the rest to wait outside and ambush us with confetti afterwards.'

'Rice would be better than paper; rose petals better still. I'll drop a hint to Louise. She'll keep them in check if anyone can.'

'I doubt it.' Mickey tugged at his beard. 'Mark my words, we'll have them two old devils for official witnesses and your Angela wearing – oh, I dunno, purple satin with a flower garland on her innocent head before either of you can blink.'

Susan had indeed blinked at this startling vision, before starting to giggle.

Just as the principals had guessed, by refusing to take No for an answer the two old gentlemen (and, at Susan's insistence, Louise) were duly added to the register office party. The gleeful patriarchs had then made sure their special status was widely known and Tollbridge, with reluctance, accepted that the register office was out of bounds. The ban was easier to accept once everyone realised Jerry Hockaday was best man, and there could be no regular bus service on the day of the wedding. Tollbridge threw itself whole-heartedly into plans for the church blessing and the post-blessing jollifications in the Anchor...

And the two old gentlemen, giddy with success, had grown more and more out of control as the great day drew closer.

'Your Chris for the still photos,' Mike said to Gabriel, as the pair made their homeward way after limited overnight success among the lobster pots had been redeemed by a legally doubtful visit to the pub. 'Young Jane, o'course, to take the film – for, award-winning or no, not even a grandson o' Gabriel Hockaday can do two things at one time together.' Jane's fata morgana sequence, improved by technology but correctly accredited, had been shown on local television and admired, although so few locals had seen the real thing that the ghost ship, as she had feared, was regarded as little more than a clever piece of artistry.

Gabriel looked pleased at the compliment, but saw a difficulty. 'With Susan being so famous her publishers could plan for her to have folk from national telly, and likely wouldn't want her having neither of our people.'

'Mickey's a quiet chap. He won't want none but his cousin to shoot him, for comfort – and Susan's always bin very good about buying local where she can.'

Gabriel tried to think positive. 'National news would bring more visitors, o'course.'

This was inarguable. Combe Tollbridge does not greatly benefit from the regular tourist stream that runs through other parts of Exmoor and beyond: in Tollbridge it's more an irregular trickle, with the occasional flood of limited duration.

'A pity,' said Mike slowly, 'nothing happened with young Jasper's notion of a Christmas get-together. All went very quiet, didn't it, after setting everyone talking?'

Gabriel nodded. 'Talk's how it remains. Changed his mind, seemingly, now he'm on to something new with Barney Christmas and the upalong doctors, though he've not come right out and said aught one way or t'other.' He sighed. 'Ask around as I may, I'm unable to ascertain what any of 'em has in mind about anything!' The admission grieved him, though he knew his brother-in-law had had no more success than himself in finding out what was being so keenly discussed by the Tollbridge tycoon, his publicity 'flack' – a term Gabriel had once overheard, questioned, and brought out now with pride – and Doctors Galahad Potter-Carey and Sterndale Bennett, of Combe Ploverton.

'We'll just have to wait and see,' was his regretful conclusion. 'Things will happen as they will. Nought else to be done.'

In a cider-rich and thoughtful silence broken only by the thump of sea-boots, the two continued their slow ascent of Stickle Street.

'I've read,' said Mike at last, 'how a duck race can bring in the crowds.'

'Gulls, you mean? Not so many ducks in these parts.'

'I mean ducks! With the Chole running fast after rain, a host of rubber ducks would make a fine sight bobbing down the river from Ploverton bridge, say, to the harbour—'

Gabriel's eyes began to gleam. '—to be catched in nets against pollution of the seas, rubber being more costly but plastic these days a very bad thing: an idea, certainly.' He brightened. 'We could sell the nets after, and say they're local made.'

'Ye-es.' Mike began looking for likely snags. 'And so they would be, had your Louise and Olive – the village's best netters, saving ourselves – not bin so busy making lace frill-de-dills for the wedding.'

'True enough.' Gabriel stroked his Father Christmas beard. 'More-and-so, if starting a race down the river from Ploverton, I wonder if it should be pigs in place of ducks?'

'What! Give free advertising to Tom Tucker?' The landlord of Ploverton's Slandered Pig had long been a friendly rival to distant cousin Jan Ridd of Tollbridge's Anchor. 'Not so sure Jan or Tabitha would take too kindly to that.'

'They'd say first, pigs don't swim, they fly! And very unlikely birds they make, but either better than anchors, to float or fly.

Stands to reason.' Gabriel sighed. 'Maybe you'm in the right, and ducks would be more tactful as well as more in keeping – only, with pigs we could talk Tom and Dora into paying for 'em. Ducks, we'd have to find the money ourselves.'

'It all comes down to money. Whatever's raced – pigs, or ducks, or – or goats, even – they must needs be bought, thus defeating the whole purpose, if it didn work in bringing folk to visit. Oh, well. Just a thought.'

'Worth a try,' said Gabriel, thinking once more of Barney Christmas. Mike nodded, but said nothing. The two friends trudged on. 'About visitors,' said Gabriel at last. 'Have you the feeling same as me, Barney might be having second thoughts over the holiday rents he spoke of all them years since, and never built? T'other night, you may recall, when we were questioning the lines painted by the school, and Barney said he'd no idea and twadn nought to do with him—'

'—and he wouldn waste his hard-earned money phoning the council to ask, the old snibble-nose—'

'—then young Jasper jumped in quick and said, anyhow 'twas too dark, with no moon and no street lights and no sense going upalong to look—'

'—and Barney just shut up,' finished Mike. 'Yes.'

'Yes. Jasper silenced him, and Barney took heed. Not like the man, somehow.'

They pondered the matter for a while.

'O'course,' said Gabriel, 'we have to concede there's little in Tollbridge to keep folk here beyond a few hours, during the day – but Barney's not one to let that deter him, when a while back he was so keen. A smart hotel or a holiday rent as originally planned, that would mean they can choose to stay here for sleeping and meals and then travel to other parts for the day, coming back again to spend the night.'

'And spend the money in the pub – either o' the pubs,' said Mike. 'Star-gazers say they find the Pig of greater convenience, remember, being so much closer to the moor.' The vast, wild expanse of Exmoor is famous round the world for its wide, dark, unpolluted skies and astronomical opportunities. 'A sad waste that shooting star didn land here last week. There'd have bin folk enough visiting to look at the thing if we could but have found a piece or two of it.'

A few nights earlier in the south of England the eyes of the sleepless, and a multitude of security cameras, together with telescopes amateur and professional, had tracked for many miles across the sky a meteor of singular brightness. The shooting star ended in a fountain of sparks high above the Severn Sea, although nobody could tell the exact spot. Even computer calculations gave no definite answer, but it was generally agreed that any surviving fragments of the visitor from outer space must now lie somewhere in the watery depths that separated England's south-west peninsula from the southern coast of Wales.

'When it happened once before,' said Gabriel, 'it landed on someone's front drive and they parked a car there so nobody should dig it up and take it, as I recall.'

'And they gave it to a museum,' said Mike. 'I think.'

The two old gentlemen had reached the corner of Hempen Row, where stood the small and long-redundant tin tabernacle that was destined to become, in time, the Budd Memorial Museum. As one man they contemplated the derelict.

'Once Mickey's wed to Susan,' said Gabriel, 'you'll be near enough granfer to young Angela, and able as such to speak with authority. When we gived her the job of setting that museum to rights, did we expect her to be so very dawdly over it?'

Mike leaped to the defence of his nearly relation. 'We never expected her to achieve so much as she have done, in the time,' he shot back. 'A busy little worker, Angela, when only a few hours each week are paid for and she'll do more than that when she can, as you ought to know, Gabriel Hockaday. That girl's like her mother. Thorough. Looks things up to make sure, writes it all down, sets it in order—'

'Which is the cause-for-why Susan had Mickey drive her to Bristol for a looky-see o' the old music hall,' agreed Gabriel quickly. 'And didn that end well!'

Mike was again all smiles. 'So it did, so it did. But a wedding – that's a one-off. What we want here is something folk can tell their friends will still be here to see another time.'

Again the two pondered.

'As I recall,' said Gabriel at last, 'that shooting star wadn so very much worth the seeing, from the photos. A gurt lump of coal was what it most resembled, to my mind.'

'Coal.' Mike looked at Gabriel.

Gabriel looked back.

Their eyes began to gleam.

'One goat in the woods looks much like another,' said Mike.

'One tree in the woods,' said Gabriel. 'One sheep on the moor…'

'One stone in a wall!' The air between them almost crackled as the brothers-in-law exchanged grins.

'Or,' said Gabriel, 'on the ground.'

'Hammer and chisel,' cried Mike.

'Paint stripper,' countered Gabriel.

Cheerfully debating the point they charged side by side down Hempen Row, in search of these essentials.

Chapter Seven

The Clammer Cottage household's daily walk, with shopping, usually involved both Jane Merton and her spouse: today, however, Jasper excused himself on need-to-think grounds. Would Jane mind, this once, going out on her own? 'Don't buy anything too heavy. If you do, I'll catch up later and carry it, but right now there's other stuff to catch up with – so "later" means rather more than just a few minutes. Okay?'

'Okay.' Like all creative persons, Jane understood the need for personal space. She was happy to walk by herself: she sometimes preferred it.

Thus it came about that Jane, on her return, witnessed one of those little episodes that would, suitably embroidered, become Tollbridge legend. The principal actors were too deeply involved (and too vocal) to notice her as she headed discreetly towards her home at the end of Hempen Row.

At this point in the Chole's exuberant rush from Exmoor to the sea the river takes a sharp bend to carve already steep terrain into an even steeper spur of land on which, long ago, the cottages of Hempen Row were built. These cottages march down only one side of the narrow Row: nothing opposite has ever blocked the view, or ever will. The land falls away at too sharp an angle for historical safety, while twenty-first-century building expertise, in theory possible, in practical terms would present too great (and too expensive) a challenge.

Hempen Row was established in distant, happier days with no red tape and little outside interference. Tollbridge knew when to ignore bureaucracy; over the years each property had encroached far enough upon the original Row to leave adequate passage for a pony and cart, and rather more space for flowerbed and/or vegetable patch, as required. Squatters' rights to these gardens were claimed by skilful edging of the plots with large white stones, relocated from time to time by the cottagers with, on each occasion, the relocation proving to the cottagers' ultimate benefit.

Louise Hockaday was fond of flowers. In the sea-level shelter of the cliffs Olive Farley could (and did) grow different specimens from her own, but the higher aspect of the Hockaday garden gave Louise an advantage when hours of sunshine were added to the equation. There are parts of Combe Tollbridge that remain, in the gloom of winter, without direct sunlight for days at a time.

Louise cherished her garden. Should Gabriel incline to mischief, he could sometimes be deflected if his wife set him and Mike to digging, mulching, weeding or planting as the season demanded. At least once a year a bucket or two of whitewash would be mixed and applied to the boundary stones of both gardens, whether needed or not.

On one such legendary occasion the brothers-in-law, bored with obedience, had stopped work in protest only to prove the truth about idle hands and Satan. For reasons that even Louise could never learn, they began a heated debate about exotic dancers. In Mike's wartime infancy he had overheard his elders discourse on London's celebrated Windmill Theatre ('We never close') and the glory of motionless nudes ('We never clothe') with or without gauze drapery in appropriate places.

Gabriel held that you might as well watch statues wearing knitted scarves and spangles. One thing had led to another.

Before long Mike was balancing a half-empty bucket on his woollen beanie. As Gabriel jeered, his brother-in-law began to shimmy. Arms outstretched, he curvetted, dipped and swayed. Whitewash slopped in a rising tide from one side of the bucket to the other.

Mike lost his balance: so did the bucket. As it fell it sprayed whitewash far and wide; as it landed, it chipped a sizeable chunk from one of the stones.

When he'd finished laughing, Gabriel had picked up the chipped-off chunk and examined it. He held it out to the muttering Mike. 'Now, here's a piece o' good luck, soce! Could come in handy some time.'

The chipped-off white chunk was jet black inside. So was the stone on the ground.

Mike stopped grumbling. 'Coal?' He bent to peer at the broken stone, then straightened to consider Hempen Row's other gardens. 'Reckon they'm all the same like this?'

'Reckon they could be.' Gabriel winked. 'Set aside against a rainy day, at a guess – only, so many years since, we've all forgot.'

'Fell off the back of a lorry? Packhorse, I should rather say.'

'Shipwrecked trader from Wales, more like.' Gabriel gestured across the pewter seas to where the Welsh coast was a dull grey line, seen through a faint blue haze. 'Less profit to smuggling coal, when there's spirits and baccy and similar goods not desirous of paying tax to the authorities...'

There was a thoughtful silence. You never knew who might be listening.

The guilty pair had carefully overturned the damaged stone to hide its broken edge, sacrificing the Hockadays' new scrubbing brush in an attempt to remove from the underside the earth stains and lichen of centuries that were now all too visible on top. Only when the bristles had been worn to stumps did it occur to Gabriel that a coat or two of whitewash would have covered up the crime with a lot less effort.

On the better-late-than-never principle the pair cheerfully mixed more whitewash; the splashes around the garden proved harder to conceal than the broken border stone. Louise returned from shopping to ask how two grown men could take so long and make so much mess in the performance of just one simple task, no matter how much drink they might have took – which was in any case no excuse, and what had they to say for theirselves?

There was no coherent response. Boots shuffled, elbows nudged, and muted laughter was punctuated by hiccups.

Louise had prescribed strong, sweet tea in generous quantities, and marched indoors to the kitchen. Here she discovered the sad corpse of her scrubbing brush.

She had not been pleased.

Basely, Mike abandoned Gabriel to his fate but seized the chunk of coal, hurrying home to destroy the evidence in his grate. Then he worried that whitewash might not burn; it could give off fumes – explode, even! If he asked Mickey – well, a secret told today and the whole world knows tomorrow.

He made himself another mug of tea, and pondered. When twilight came he dug a hole in a corner of the garden. With luck, nobody would notice anything…

And down the years nobody, not even the exasperated Louise, ever had.

'So,' said Gabriel now, 'well begun is half done. Not that we knew it at the time.'

'It was a good start,' agreed Mike. 'So we'll have it out dreckly minute, move the rest along to even the gap, with some weeding to hide all disturbance of the ground – and then there's nought to show, beyond the fact we've bin tiddivating the place!'

'Louise likes things to be tidy,' said her husband.

The two set to work with various tools and incoherent plans.

The broken coal-stone was rolled out of the way to make room for the manoeuvring of its neighbours into new positions. With an enthusiastic spade, Gabriel flattened disturbed soil.

Mike scraped vaguely with a garden fork. Both old gentlemen, encouraged by cider, felt pleased at the result: nobody would notice anything out of the ordinary!

Mike took the shears to clip cunning and ragged patterns in the grass. Gabriel leaned on his spade, watching with a critical eye; he grew bored; his eye began to wander. He froze. Could that be a loose bit of whitewash against the solid black? Had Mike, after all, bin right about hammer and chisel rather than paint stripper? Best make sure!

He gazed about him: no hammer, no chisel. But the shears – his shears, not Mike's – were sharp: they would do!

Gabriel made a lunge, with intent to poke and prove (or disprove) the point.

Mike's natural instinct was to hold on. He'd begun to enjoy himself, and didn't see why he should stop. He gripped hard, and pulled back.

Gabriel didn't let go. The shears snapped open. The two old men, each tugging on a wooden handle, glared at each other as the hinge creaked and groaned.

Gaping metal jaws caught the sun with an evil glint as Mike and Gabriel swayed to and fro, boots digging into the ground. Gabriel was sure he could prove he'd had the right idea from the start: paint stripper would surely do the job. No need for hammer and chisel! Mike, who'd almost forgotten the original discussion in the fun of camouflage, had been concentrating on a skilful un-tidying of the border and wanted to finish this unusual task before he even thought about anything else.

Jane Merton, turning into Hempen Row, saw flashes of movement; heard voices raised and rising in argument. She winced. Those shears looked sharp – were sure to be sharp: Gabriel, like his brother-in-law, took good care of the equipment he used. One lapse in concentration could be fatal to either or both of the combatants. She would make her way as quietly as possible past the squabble, and hope that it wouldn't last long.

'And what,' cried a voice behind her, 'do you pair think you'm about?' Louise, homeward bound from lacemaking at the post office, had no such qualms about interruption. Brandishing her thumbstick she quick-marched down the Row, ready to deliver a piece of her mind to anyone in sight. 'My garden shears!'

Jane merged tactfully into the background, too interested now to think of going home. She guessed that Louise would prevail, but couldn't guess how the quarrel might end; she knew herself to be by fifty or sixty years the best person to rush to phone for help if anything went wrong. Never had the not-spot status of Combe Tollbridge for mobile signals seemed more unfortunate.

Louise scolded, Gabriel blamed Mike, and Mike justified himself loudly until the inevitable occurred – a dull *crack!* and a bang. Shouts turned to curses as two old men with beards fell heavily backwards, each clutching in triumph one wooden-handled blade from a broken pair of shears.

Jane waited nearby long enough to hear both men catch their breath and each start blaming the other for the accident. She saw them scramble to their feet, rubbing bumps and bruises while Louise scolded both impartially and they ignored her. None of the three saw Jane as she hurried back to Clammer Cottage and an appreciative audience.

But Jasper was still at work; Jane heard the keyboard rattle in their tiny spare room as she opened the front door. She made herself a mug of herbal tea, sweetening it with honey for shock. Now it was all over, she found herself shivering. Nobody's luck could last for ever. This time nobody's head had smashed against anything, and there had been no signs of concussion; nobody had broken any bones, or been stabbed. Loss of dignity, yes; bumps and bruises too – but the greatest physical threat seemed likely to come from Louise!

Jane forced a smile. After all these years Mrs Hockaday must be resigned to behaviour of this sort. Tonight, holding their regular court in the Anchor, the reprobates would be turning the episode into a highly coloured anecdote, loving every minute. At their age they must of course be allowed their fun – but Jane still felt shaken by what might have happened to those (by now, surely fragile) old bones, and those indomitable (so far, but for how much longer?) spirits who played so great a part in village life.

She sighed, sipped her sweetened tea, smiled again, and began doodling in her sketchbook. Losing track of time, she didn't look up when Jasper emerged at last from his study; she was too busy setting the final touches to an epic duel on a boulder-strewn plain between two bewhiskered warriors clad in leather armour, woolly hats and enormous boots. A female figure who might be Justice, or Equity, or Nemesis – Jane couldn't waste time looking it up – stood at a distance to oversee proceedings, brandishing a staff. She might be about to hurl a thunderbolt; she might be conducting an invisible orchestra – *yes!* Jane drew a helmet on Equity's head, and added horns. The Ride of the Valkyries!

She sat back, realised she hadn't drunk her tea, tapped the mug with a rueful pencil, and looked about her to share the joke with Jasper. Realisation had dawned that he was sitting quietly on the other side of the table, his laptop before him, smiling and awaiting her convenience.

'I didn't finish my tea,' she told him, laughing. 'Hello.'

'Hello, back. While you've been doodling I've had a few thoughts about skirret, among others.'

'Have Skirret and the others been thinking about you?' She came properly into mental focus. 'Who is Skirret – someone else working for Barney Christmas, right? You're going to tell me at long last what it's all about!'

'No – no – and no.' Jasper slid his laptop and wireless mouse across the table. 'Good try, though. Barney will reveal all when he's ready, which he almost is or I wouldn't have the time to think about other things – but skirret's not a person, it's a root vegetable. Take a look while I make another cup of tea. The Tudors grew tons of skirret until the potato came along to put its nose out of joint: blame Sir Walter Raleigh if you've never heard of it before. I certainly hadn't, and I doubt if I'm the only one.'

'You're not,' said Jane, mousing through the first few pages he'd left open.

Jasper warmed to his theme. 'Skirret might taste better, sort of parsnipy and sweet – but the humble spud's far easier to peel, and quite as nutritious. Dig up a root of skirret and you've basically got a tangle of anaemic carrots, smothered in soil. Think of the time you'd waste scrubbing them.'

'Not me,' said Jane. 'Kitchen maid or tweeny.' She studied the laptop image. 'Talk about outgrowing your strength! Anaemic carrots is right. On top it looks just like spindly cow parsley – are you sure it isn't? And what's so special about the stuff, anyway?'

Jasper brought steaming mugs to the table and sat down. 'It's unusual but, talk about a heritage vegetable!' He grinned. 'Pliny the Elder mentions it: says to boil it in honeyed wine for added flavour. So does Hildegard of Bingen.'

'But she was a mediaeval nun, wasn't she? Honey, I can believe; but wine?'

'Some sort of mention: I forget what. I remember she was twelfth century, but it wasn't really popular until two or three hundred years later. There's references to growing it as far north as Scotland – they call it crummock – and everyone saying how tasty it is; recipes, too. You can dig it up and eat it raw, snack or salad, as well as cook it – Angela would have a field day – and the flowers make good feeding for bees, and other pollinators.'

Jane, smiling thanks for her tea, abandoned the laptop and began ticking off points on her fingers. 'Easy to grow, tasty to eat, environmentally friendly; a heritage vegetable that would make a good talking point for people who need that sort of boost. Let me think.' She cocked her head to one side, and frowned. 'Oooh, it's a puzzle. I'm baffled.'

Jasper, with dancing eyes, primmed his lips and nodded. Jane sighed.

'I may of course be wrong, but – and this is the wildest of guesses, but – could it be you've at last found something to do with the old hemp garden?'

'What on earth can have given you that idea?'

'I can't imagine, idiot; but I'm really pleased. Best news I've had for yonks!' She raised her mug in a toast. 'Thanks for this; I needed it. But honestly, it's high time you stopped all this faffing about indoors and started on the fresh-air fun and exercise that was the original plan when we moved here. I'd love to be able to leave off nagging you about blood pressure and stress – so come on, give! What started you on your skirrety way?'

'It was when Angela talked the other night about fancying a challenge but accepting that more… adventurous menus wouldn't suit the Anchor at all. You don't come to a little place like Tollbridge wanting five-star cuisine: you want good plain food, well cooked and presented and in keeping with the general atmosphere.'

'You mean Gabriel and Mike would make fun of anyone who tried. Oh! Remind me to tell you afterwards about – no, afterwards. Skirret, now. Details, please.'

'I always said I wanted to grow vegetables.' Jane nodded. 'Naturally I wondered first about hemp, with us owning the old hemp garden and living in Hempen Row.' The founder of Packlemerton's Publicity sounded wistful. 'Think what a splendid hook, all those historical associations – but then I imagined some jobsworth getting the wrong idea and ordering a drugs bust, with sniffer dogs everywhere looking for cannabis.'

'Even more publicity when they realised their mistake! And Mike Binns would be thrilled. You know how fond he is of dogs.'

Jasper waved this away. 'It just didn't appeal, somehow – all the paperwork and legal complications; same with tobacco.' Jane stared. 'Yes, that's been tried as well. If we're talking of history, Charles II got in such a strop over the tobacco import taxes he no longer got from America, with people buying local instead, he had Parliament make it illegal to grow tobacco in this country.' He answered the obvious question before she could ask it. 'Hampshire, Gloucestershire, Somerset, Devon: any sound familiar?' He laughed. 'By the 1950s, when you could get a proper official licence, some guy Duncan was seriously trying to make it pay in this part of the world, but the experiment didn't last long. The climate probably had more to do with it than the law, though.'

'This is England,' said Jane. 'It rains.'

'And it's cold for more days than it's hot: which makes it weird anyone now can make money growing tea, but they do, only farther south in Cornwall. They grow Manuka bushes, too. I read somewhere that honey sourced from plants growing near the sea has a hint of salt, and here we're about as close to the sea as you can get and I know Miriam's saltmarsh chicken and eggs do the business, but – honey is something else that didn't really appeal. Done properly, beekeeping's hard work.'

'And bees sting – and get killed by these Asian hornets that sneak in from the continent and build ginormous nests that need professional exterminators – and there's some disease that wipes out beehives row by row, isn't there?'

'Varroa, you mean? And I believe there are others.'

'Bound to be. Better keep away from livestock. So what are the likely problems with skirret?'

'Not many, I think, though now we've talked it over I'll do more serious research – and for other heritage vegetables, too. Purple carrots, maybe: orange was only ever a fashion, and fashions change! But skirret, definitely. Once you've got the cut-off roots set right you can pretty much leave the plants to their own devices—'

'—leaving you to get on with whatever you've got to do for Barney Christmas.' Jane, back at the screen, resumed manipulation of the mouse. 'You know, I like the sound of this. I really do. And I really think we – you – should give *Sium sisarum* with appropriate friends and relations a proper try!'

Chapter Eight

The Anchor saw the usual evening crowd in the usual convivial mood. Barney Christmas, after another session with the Ploverton doctors, dropped hints that there might, before long, be some news of future plans. There *might* be.

Asked again about the yellow paint by the school he was more forthcoming. 'Just because there's routine maintenance done at that building o' mine don't mean the council, nor anyone else, can take it upon theirselves to do what's never bin asked for – and won't be paid for! We've had words.' He glared. 'They *say* they'll be coming to burn it off, but not when – meaning, no doubt, another risement in our taxes to make up for their mistake. I've told 'em I'll be on the watch for such tricks, and won't pay out one penny piece more.'

He sat back, his arms folded, his mouth a stubborn line. His eyes flickered towards Andy Marsh at the bar, chatting while Angela poured drinks.

Jasper, a little restless at the old man's side, had spent the afternoon researching and downloading a ream of paperwork relating to skirret. He was impatient for the morning.

Jane politely listened to, and (slightly) sympathised with, Mike and Gabriel's account of how Louise had thwarted their scheme to turn long-ago, long-forgotten coal into tourist gold.

Jane understood Mrs Hockaday's views on shooting stars, honesty, and the neatness of her garden, but thought it tactful not to say so. It seemed the matter of the rather less long-ago, and certainly not forgotten, scrubbing brush had come up in the course of conversation. From what was now not being said by Gabriel and Mike, Jane was sorry she'd missed that part of the entertainment.

Mickey Binns and Susan Jones discussed with family and friends their wedding plans, deflecting the most extreme.

'I'm with Andy.' Susan nodded across to Miss Marsh, who raised a glass and grinned. 'I don't like heights. I prefer to keep my feet firmly on the ground.'

'And me,' said Mickey, 'I'm not so young as once I was – though you, midear' – with a quick hug for Susan – 'remain every bit so lovely as when I first saw you, a fine figure of a woman.' The grizzled beard gently brushed her cheek. 'Only, I'm not sure how easy I'd find it to lift you up and over that-there church gate, whether tied with satin ribbon or a hempen rope – so be reasonable, friends.' He surveyed his audience. 'When did we last do such at a Tollbridge wedding?'

'When was the last wedding?' came the query.

'Far too long since,' was Sam Farley's quick reply. Sam had begun to notice that moving his printery from Meazel Cleeve, where there were neighbours, to the old coastguard station had indeed given him bigger windows, better light, and a larger working area; but Watchfield Point was proving a lonelier spot than he'd thought, especially after dark. The reappearance in Combe Tollbridge of Andromeda Marsh had made him more conscious of this than ever.

'So then, high time us were gived another chance!' someone said.

'But,' said Susan gently, 'the wedding ceremony *as such* isn't at the church, remember, just the blessing. What do other people think? Should the lych-gate custom still apply?'

'You can look it up and let us know, midear, being the one with book-learning and my son here' – Mike thumped Mickey across the shoulders – 'no longer of such an academic persuasion – and making out he's a bad back, besides.' Mike hated any reminder, direct or oblique, that he, too, must grow older, must become frail. Why, his sixtyish son was a mere youth – and he himself still in his prime!

'Or,' said someone, 'hinting you've the need to go on a diet, Susan.'

'I'd box his ears if I thought that,' cried Mike. 'I never raised my boy to speak discourteous to any female, sweetheart or otherwise. No!'

He toasted his daughter-in-law elect in the double-handled mug, and looked round at his cronies. After he and Gabriel had so resolutely insinuated themselves into the ceremony proper and got away with it, both old gentlemen, their special status acknowledged, had affected a lofty indifference to any view that might be expressed by the rest of the village regarding the forthcoming nuptials. If challenged, the pair would insist that as Susan and Mickey wanted it that way, then that was the way it must be. Tollbridge could let its collective hair down at the grand post-blessing party. There was no doubting everyone would then celebrate to their heart's content in the Anchor's skittle alley, overspilling later out of doors if the weather was kind.

'As for the blessing,' said Gabriel, 'being in church we'll celebrate just so far as the vicar will allow and no farther, which is for Mr Hollington to decide.' A cough, a wink. 'Him and his good lady being afterwards expected at the party, same as for Aunt Prue.'

The Reverend Theodore Hollington, slow at first to come forward, had been encouraged by his wife and parishioners to join the dancers who accompanied Prue Budd's impromptu table-top fandango in the Jubilee Hall, on the occasion of her birthday. It was the last memorable event to be held in the hall before it burned down. Tollbridge had been dismayed to learn how twenty-first-century requirements of health and safety must always trump the speed, efficiency and risk-taking of late Victorian builders who got things done. Even now, months after the conflagration, the paperwork continued its tedious crawl through the legal and financial hoops the village was sure its ancestors would have happily ignored; the descendants were just as willing to ignore them but the vicar, with the rest of the hall committee, stood firm. The Anchor's skittle team learned to yield to the greater community good on public occasions, moving 'upalong to the Pig' for match nights even though the Ploverton alley was cambered, and the Anchor's was not.

Andy Marsh, returning with her glass refreshed, sat down not quite as close to Sam as the printer might have liked. 'How I wish I'd been here then,' she said. 'One hundred and five years old and still kicking up a storm – respect for Prudence Budd, is what I say. I'd have been right there beside her on that table, no question. Way to go, Prue!' She sipped happily at her cider. Sam winked. Andy grinned back.

'I thought you didn't like heights,' put in Susan before anyone could dampen the merry mood by giving Andy the less cheerful finish to the story.

Or was it? A careless step, a fall, a broken bone, and a gradual but trouble-free care home decline had indeed been the old lady's way to go. Everyone agreed that everything had happened more or less as she might have planned it; many wondered privately if this was what she had in fact done. Respect for Prudence Budd, locally always great, was never greater than after the village had lost her for good.

'It's okay if you don't look down,' said Andy, 'or if you *can't*, like through a table-top. Between the rungs of a ladder you can always see the ground. On a scaffolding tower, on solid boards, you can't, so that's not too bad. I guess it's part of the job, and there's always the poles to grab if you feel you might be slipping.' She laughed. 'But, talk about illogical! I'd really hate to go up in a hot air balloon. Just imagine watching the ground drop away from you through the holes in the basket-weave – yet I'm fine with going abroad for my hols because aircraft have solid floors, and I don't look out of the window until all that's out there is clouds. Crazy, I know, but that's how it is.'

Susan smiled. 'You're still braver than I am, Andy.'

'We're all different.' Andy nodded to Mickey. 'I'd hate to go fishing. Fish wriggle, and flap about, and they have to be killed and gutted and – ugh, is what I think. Sorry.'

'We're all different.' Mickey returned her smile.

Sam Farley's smile was wider. 'And this from someone more'n happy to play the prawn trick on a rascally landlord! In every room, you told me. Prawns – and mackerel, I think you said. Swim behind the skirting board of their own accord, did they?'

Barney Christmas, as was so often his way, had been enjoying the give-and-take of conversation without joining in. He still said nothing, but now he pricked up his ears.

Andy didn't notice she had caught his attention. 'Prawns and kippers – but you're right, it's illogical. I did tell you I was crazy.'

'Not so very crazy.' Gabriel toasted her in cider. 'Worked, didn it?'

Andy nodded. 'Seems so. The shelter texted me thanks very much, and followed it up with a note to The Old Printery. I told them my Triumph will be needing regular motorway sessions to keep the engine at concert pitch, so if they can't find anyone local for their odd-jobbing they can still call on me, if it's not urgent. Old Ange will tell you I build a pretty mean kitchen cupboard, with concealed lighting or overhead spots, as required!'

Gabriel asked about dimmer switches; Mike spoke vaguely of 'puddles of oil shining on the ceiling' he'd once heard his son describe. Mickey enlarged upon strobe effects, and everyone threw themselves into dreaming up ever more exotic electrical demands that Andy might be asked to fulfil…

…until Jan Ridd appeared from the other bar. For a silent few moments he surveyed the scene before approaching the crowded table where Mike and Gabriel held court.

'They've just rung from the Pig,' he said. 'Sandy Joy's gone at last, rest his soul.'

Merriment faded. The company stilled. Andy knew this was no time for an incomer to speak, and kept quiet.

Gabriel Hockaday cleared his throat. 'Poor old devil. Rest his soul,' he echoed, pledging the late Joy in a deep swig from his mug. Mike, Mickey and the others followed his sorrowing example.

'So what age was he, then?' Sam Farley (early thirties) looked to the village elders. 'Knowed him my whole life and he wadn never young in my eyes, that I can recall.'

Mike and Gabriel, nearest in age to the deceased, pondered. 'I reckon,' said Gabriel slowly, 'ninety-seven, though he've bin over ninety for so many years I could be wrong.'

'Ninety-eight, I'd say,' came the automatic correction from his brother-in-law; but Mike's heart wasn't in the skirmish. He drank again, and shook his head. 'Wadn no helping him escape this time, more's the pity.'

He and Gabriel shared rueful grins, with a hint of mischief. Their eyes began to gleam. 'The one that got away' – Mike was smiling now – 'if not for ever.'

'Which nobody does,' said Gabriel, 'though old Sandy gived it a bloody good try!'

Those in the know likewise relaxed, and laughed. Laughter is infectious.

'Miriam told me a little about him,' ventured Andy, 'while I watched her weave his – his shroud?' Everyone nodded; everyone knew. 'Sandy was a carpenter, wasn't he, and kept chickens, and his coffin under the bed; and his only son was lost at sea.' She smiled at Mike Binns of the suspiciously auburn beard. 'Alexander Joy, for posh? Or was he another redhead… like you?'

Gabriel snorted. 'Thomas, rightly,' he said before Mike could utter, 'but Sandy on account of, as you say, him being a caffender, and knowing all the tricks. There was a flag stuck once at the top of Ploverton church, and no ladder long enough and the roof not safe. Young Tom, as then he was, he got his coarsest sandpaper and tied some to each leg and shinned up that pole and brought the flag down – after fixing the tanglement, too – and ever after, he was Sandy. Nothing red about his hair I can remember.' He glanced sideways at Mr Binns, but restrained himself from saying more.

'His son was Thomas, too.' Mike sighed. 'Young Tommy. A sad thing for a widow-man to lose his only son – and in such a way! That was a cruel loss.' There were times when the old rascal's sorrow was all too obviously play-acting. This was not such a time.

'Cruel indeed,' said Gabriel, after a long pause. 'By rights that boy should of bin safe at sea, being as how he was born in a bag, and always kept it by him.' He saw Andy's puzzled gaze, and nodded to Susan. 'You'll know the proper wording, midear?'

Susan nodded back. 'His caul: his amniotic sac, if we're being posh. If you're born in a caul – I forget the odds, something like one in every hundred thousand births – but anyway, they say you'll never drown if you take it to sea with you.'

'As Tommy always did – except the poor lad was exploded, not drowned. Sandy took it hard,' said Mike. 'Anyone would.' He turned his eyes away from his only son. 'Caught a mine left from the war in his net. Yelled at the rest to get back, but it swung to the side of the boat afore he'd finished cutting it loose and…' He waved his hands in a helpless gesture. 'Saved all their lives but his own, poor Tommy. Sandy Joy's only son.'

Gabriel could guess something of Mike's thoughts. 'Saved everyone's life and the dog, remember. Kicked him 'cross-deck down an open hatch, and not a bone broken.'

Mike, known for his love of dogs, brightened. 'But couldn face going to sea again, poor beast, and who can blame him? Turk, the pup was named, for his first Christmas when he got somehow into the larder with... unfortunate results.' He chuckled. 'Sandy used to keep hens, see, so turkey was a proper treat – or would've bin, if they'd ever had the chance to eat 'un! The family never forgot that Christmas, you may be sure.'

Gabriel nodded. 'Every dog they've had since has bin Turk. After the loss of young Tommy, the dog was sociable enough while a boat was tied up, only, the minute you made to start the engine, down went his tail and he'd shiver and shake so his legs wouldn hardly carry him ashore. Sandy said twadn fair to force him, even with his breeding.'

Mike laughed. 'There was a descent from my Bran, see, in Turk – Bran being the little black dog Gabe and I saved from shipwreck during the war. A regular spark in her eye, that dog, same like her son that was mine from a pup, sent me across the water after his mother had gone back home to Wales. So, Turk, he surely made up for lost time once he was living on dry land each day – and night.' Another laugh. 'Many a dog still in these parts have a dash o' that seafaring blood. You can always tell by their coats: black and shiny with the bit of a ruff round the neck, just like my Bran from so long ago.'

'Miriam told me his dog's with a neighbour now,' said Andy.

'Joseph Tuggs,' supplied Gabriel. 'Grocer upalong to Ploverton, now retired. Him and his daughter Lottie that keeps house for him, they've took him in, this Turk, as they did before, and Crusoe too – that's the parrot young Tommy trained up in all manner of tricks, parrots being long-lived creatures. Far more so than dogs.'

'Joe's grown powerful hard o' hearing this past couple o' years,' said Mike. 'Crusoe won't trouble him overmuch, I reckon, though Lottie will doubtless have bought herself more earplugs – and grudged every penny piece!' He glanced across at Barney Christmas, who ignored him. 'A parrot needs proper company, and Miss Charlotte made complaint enough last time poor Sandy was in hospital about the shrieking and the chatter, an old man and a dog being insufficiently lively for a bird of character.'

'And the feathers,' said Gabriel. 'Remember how she *would* carry on when Sandy's hens ran free about the garden, and the feathers blew over the wall?'

Everyone was smiling now, the initial shock having given way to the next stage of mourning: the memories.

'Miriam told me,' said Andy, 'how she opened up one of his crop-bound birds and sewed it back together again and it survived.'

'Born survivors, the Joys,' said Gabriel. He saw Mike's face and hurried on: 'Threaded more than once as a child, old Sandy, yet up to this last time he've always come back.' He shook his head. 'That's hospitals for you.'

'We'd never have got away with it a second time.' Mike, too, was regretful. 'But it's a comfort to remember we managed it that once.'

Andy, though puzzled by the childhood threading, decided to ask first about the hospital escapade that had glinted in Miriam's eye. 'You brought him home and the house was full of moths, wasn't it?'

Everyone laughed, Mike and Gabriel most heartily of all. Andy sat back and prepared to enjoy the anecdote she knew was coming.

'The great escape,' said Mike, with a grin.

'Hospitals,' said Gabriel again. 'Wasting away afore our very eyes, poor old Sandy, on account o' the food—'

'—and the teeth. You can't chew proper if you got no teeth.' Again Mike looked over at Barney. 'Saving money's fine in moderation, but can be took too far – though Sandy never went so far as to stop the funeral, as doubtless there are some that might have done.'

'My teeth,' said Barney, 'are altogether my own, whether paid for in honest cash or as originally granted by the Almighty. Each and every one.' He bared these adornments in a wide, ferocious grin. 'More-and-so, sharing idn in my nature. Never was, never will be.'

He grinned again for Andy's puzzled look. 'Sandy Joy, he lost his teeth young and carved hisself a new set from oak, only they didn last so long as expected and he took to sharing with Joe Tuggs's brother, being both about the same size, and neither with a wife to nag 'em into paying for a new set each when 'twas seldom they'd have the same need at the same time. A wise economy.' His look dared anyone to argue. 'Howsumdever, 'twas old Tuggs's turn at wearing 'em when the man died, very sudden, and Sandy – well, he didn feel able to approach Joe Tuggs in the matter, having already bin given an earful by Lottie when he tried asking tactful. A female of decided views, Charlotte Tuggs. So Thomas Joy went to the funeral and never breathed a word, though when others threw earth or flowers on the coffin he chose to drop a spanking new toothbrush...'

As appreciative chuckles died down, Mike resumed the tale. 'Which is why, when he caught a chill that week and it went to his chest and no shifting it, Sandy hadn the necessities for eating what they tried to feed him in that place.'

'Hospital food.' Gabriel shook his head. 'Didn care for it anyhow, teeth or no teeth. Nobody would.'

'Wouldn let 'em stick no needles in him, neither,' said Mike. 'Told us, them being so insistent on liquid food he could do a damsight worse than a draught of dry cider, and would we take him in a jar along with a fresh loaf, and a pot of mustard—'

'—for which Evan Evans come up trumps,' said Gabriel. 'Baked it special, sliced it good and thick, wrapped it in a double layer of clean towels to hold in the heat—'

'—and I put my foot down,' said Mike Binns, part-time taxi driver. 'Gabriel jumped out while I parked, and he run upstairs with a knife in his pocket and Sandy's particular mug from the Pig – Tom Tucker give it him straight away – and that man was having the time of his life until the ward sister come by and began screeching.'

'I've seldom known a female say so much to my detriment without the use of strong language,' said Gabriel thoughtfully. 'Unless, o'course, she was using medical talk, which the likes of us wouldn have understood.'

He and his brother-in-law exchanged happy, self-satisfied grins.

'A regular performance, that woman gave,' agreed Mike with pride. 'Chased us both from there in a twink – and forbidden to come back until we'd learned proper sense.'

Andy Marsh glanced from one bearded face to the other. She saw the mischief in four bright eyes daring her to ask the obvious question; she could feel the rest of the audience egging her on.

She knew her duty.

She put the question.

Chapter Nine

'So you could never go back?'

'The imperence of the girl!' Gabriel was delighted. 'I take that very kindly, midear.' He bowed to Andy over his mug. 'Yes, I reckon it's greatly to our credit we never gived in to that woman telling us how to behave – and us both of an age to be her father!' He tapped the side of his nose, and winked. 'We had sense enough, mark you, to find out the times she'd be on duty, and only visit Sandy when she wadn.'

'So when he asked us for help – there we were,' said Mike.

'Is that what you meant by the great escape? Miriam told me—'

'Ah, Miriam wouldn know all the ins and outs,' said Gabriel, 'but twouldn be so far off. See, Sandy never did pay that much heed to paperwork, not after his liddle run-in with the taxman having wrote him he owed nought pounds and nought pence and he was to pay up immediate or risk prosecution.' He banged his mug on the table. 'Now there's an example of *proper sense* if you like!'

'Computer says no.' Mike Binns was pleased with this up-to-date jargon.

'So as anyone would, with proper sense, Sandy took no notice. They wrote again, more forceful but the self-same thing – pay us no money, or we'll have you in court.' Gabriel winked at Andy. 'Crazy? You ent in the same league, midear.'

'The Inland Revenue's certainly a law unto itself.' Not a voice was raised against her. 'So what happened in the end?'

It was Mike who answered. 'Sandy still had a business to run, though part retired and not earning so much, and he wouldn waste his time waiting on the telephone to speak with a proper human, or waste money on a stamp' – he tipped an invisible hat to Mr Christmas – 'sending a letter he knew they'd ignore.' Just as Barney pointedly ignored him.

'So he got out his chequebook—' said Gabriel.

'—and wrote a cheque to the Revenue for the 'dentical sum, and sent it recorded delivery so they'd have to sign for it—'

'—and got my grandson Chris,' concluded Gabriel, 'to make a film of him doing it!'

'That's cool.' Andy thought of prawns, and kippers. 'I wish I'd met your friend Sandy. My kind of guy. But I don't quite see where the escape comes in?'

'Ah, that was once he'd started bettering.' Mike wagged his head. 'I still say 'twas the cider helped him turn the corner – but, whatever the truth of it, that woman seemed to have a grudge against poor Sandy from then on. Got his bed moved up the ward where she could watch him every minute – and so she did! He told us prison would've bin easier. O'course we offered to move the bed back, but he fretted she'd keep an even closer eye on him if we did, so we didn.'

'Being fair,' put in Gabriel, grudging the effort, 'he did go on bettering, with her having took charge. Even if the food wadn worth the eating,' he added quickly.

'Ye-es,' said Mike, 'but I reckon he'd have bettered faster yet, had they only let him come home – which she kept telling him couldn be done until he'd got his discharge letter, and for one reason or another he kept not getting it.'

'But he had his suspicions.' Gabriel was grim. 'As did we all. Couldn't wait to be away from there, but the computer said no – and so it went on, every day more and more under that woman's thumb and wanting more and more to go home, and not allowed.'

'Bed-blocking.' Every head turned to stare at the interruption from Barney Christmas. He shrugged, caught the eye of Jasper Merton, and grinned.

'Bed-blocking,' echoed Gabriel, undeterred. 'So in the end me and Mike smuggled him in some clothes, and away goes Sandy to a place he'd not be interrupted unless he pulled the red string, and back he comes with his nightshirt packed away all ready for the off – and off we went. Though not,' he added, 'until after he'd kissed goodbye and thanks to all the good-lookingest nurses.'

'There were so many we had to help him,' said Mike Binns happily. His son shook his head; his prospective daughter-in-law openly laughed. 'To be sure of getting Sandy out of the place in time,' elaborated the elder Binns, innocence in every syllable. 'You only get so long on the parking, see, and we didn't want having to pay extra.' He winked at Barney.

'Sandy was in such a rush to get home, and then – well.' Gabriel contrived to sound mournful. 'A cruel disappointment it was, when we arrived back to find the place a-flutter and crawling with moths, and we had to lend some hens from Miriam Evans and wait in the Pig while the problem was sorted...'

'But Sandy Joy never got his letter from that day to this,' said Mike.

'Nor did they speak of it when he went back this last time.' Gabriel sighed. 'He'd looked forward to a real good laugh, telling 'em he'd a bed all ready and waiting, seeing as how they hadn't signed him free before—'

'—only by then the poor old chap was pretty bad, and never felt able for it.'

As Mike finished the story, there was a respectful silence.

To the surprise of all it was Barney Christmas who broke it. 'Thomas Joy lived to a grand age, considering. I recall his mother was ever a pale, queechy piece – and they say he'd been threaded' – with a nod for Andy – 'inside a week o' being born, nor the last time it had to be done.' Another nod for Susan. 'You'll know better about that, Mrs-Mickey-Binns-to-be. You tell Miss Handy Andy what I mean.'

Andy met Barney's knowing smile with a start of surprise. Susan didn't notice the byplay. The celebrated author glanced around the table, but saw nobody denying her the second chance to explain a local superstition. 'Well, it used to be thought that if you tied a long string, or a piece of thread, to a sick child's finger and held it over a stream, the current would drag the thread away and take the sickness with it.'

'Hence the Threading Pool, upalong to Ploverton.' Gabriel got this in just ahead of Barney. 'With the Chole being wider down here in Tollbridge, and easier reaching, we've no need of such a place – though not ezackly a pool in Ploverton so much as a scoop took out o' the bank, and a couple of steps down. And still there, for any minded to try it after these many years.'

Mike grinned. 'Worked, didn it? Well over six foot was old Sandy in his prime.'

Gabriel recognised his cue. 'Ah, but the man walked everywhere through his whole life, didn he? Wore hisself down with so much walking over the years.' He fixed Andy firmly in the eye, daring her to disbelieve him. 'By the end, Sandy Joy wadn no more than five-foot-eight, I tell you straight.'

Andy saw the grin spread across Sam Farley's face; it was a grin of sympathy; she felt emboldened. 'But Miriam told me he made his own coffin, and I've always understood they must be made to measure. So – which measurements did Sandy use?'

'A drink on the house for your friend here, Angela!' Jan Ridd, laughing with the rest, gestured to his barmaid as the room finally settled down. Andromeda Marsh had won her Tollbridge spurs. Nobody could remember the last time they'd seen Gabriel – or Mike, or any of the gang – so lost for a smart answer.

They all raised mugs or glasses in a toast. Barney followed this up by telling Andy to 'come and see me tomorrow, not too early, but I've a job in mind for you if you'd be interested,' with another private grin for Jasper, who grinned back.

'They'll no doubt put pillows or similar inside if the coffin's too big.' Mike Binns chose to take the question seriously. 'Sandy made it same as he'd of wanted for Tommy, only with the shock he couldn bring himself to do so at the time.' He cleared his throat. 'Poor chap. Ever afterwards he felt the shame he'd bin unable to give his only son the send-off the lad deserved. A hero, that boy.' He buried his nose in his mug to hide a genuine emotion.

Gabriel came to the rescue. 'You forget the wreath he made hisself along of the coffin. You've heard tell of the goats in these parts, midear?'

Andy nodded. She'd been puzzled on first seeing the sturdy gates at each end of the new fibreglass clam, or footbridge, Jane and Jasper Merton had built across 'their' part of the River Chole to allow them to reach the old hemp garden on the opposite bank.

'Goats,' Jasper had explained. 'The local troop will eat almost anything, and they jump and climb like fiends. You really can't keep them out if they're hell-bent on getting in, but if you want to grow something special, a gate's better than nothing.'

'They've a stone wall,' said Gabriel now, 'round Ploverton's burial ground, and in a general way the goats show proper respect, only, come a funeral all it takes is for someone to forget closing the gate and in they go, rampaging after every flower in sight. Tidn respectful. From a very young chap Sandy had it in mind one day he'd teach 'em a lesson, so he carved hisself a wreath o' flowers from oak. You know how the older oak is, the harder?'

Andy nodded again. 'I've done a few jobs in old houses, yes.'

Gabriel was gleeful. 'That wreath must be rock-hard by now. Sandy'll have a proper laugh, wherever he might be, watching they goats try to take a mouthful of his wreath!'

As another burst of mirth died down, Barney sounded a warning note. 'We'll hope so; only, with the goats in these parts having th'Old Gooseberry bred so deep in their bones, it's more likely he'll watch 'em chew it all to flitters.' He shook his head. 'A sad waste, leaving a fine piece o' craftsmanship on his grave to be et by goats and lost to the world. When they devils have their minds set on mischief there's no stopping them.'

'Hence our gates,' Jasper reminded Andy. 'Though I don't believe they've tried to jump them or eat 'em – yet,' he added hastily, tapping the wood of the table before him. 'But if we have a hard winter, who knows?'

The conversation became general, topics ranging from further examples of Sandy Joy's woodworking genius to detailed witness statements on the devilry of the goats. A great pity (some said) 'that such spirit idn of a nature to be bottled. There's folk would pay a goodish amount for a drink warranted to send 'em skippiting like the goats through life with no care in the world beyond theirselves!'

'Cider's always bin good enough for most folk.' Gabriel returned from the bar with yet another refill. 'For generations – and invented in these parts, right, Susan?'

'Well,' she demurred. 'In other apple-growing areas too, of course.' She caught the challenge in his eye. 'But each area's cider is certainly unique to each area, because every local apple is different. And the tradition – the skill – certainly goes back a very long way: even further back than wassailing the apple trees on Old Twelfth Night.'

'Well done, midear.' Mickey patted her hand and gave it a quick squeeze as the old man took the bait, beginning to discourse on shotguns, squibs and buttered toast. Sandy Joy's mourners had mourned him well: some could be nearing the quarrelsome stage. Tact was essential.

'Only in January, though,' said Mike Binns. 'Not sufficient to bring visitors spending money all year round, is it?' Mike, like Gabriel, relished an audience – and the tips, which the two friends shared after each public display of their practised double act.

'We've no cider orchards in Tollbridge,' said Barney Christmas, businessman and realist. 'There's a few upalong to Ploverton still, but who'd come here to buy Ploverton cider when they could go dreckly to Ploverton and buy it from the Pig?'

'As many do.' Gabriel, too, regretted lost opportunities, and had reached the contemplative stage of drink. 'There's not nearly enough folk come visiting Tollbridge and linger for sufficient length of time to benefit fully from the experience.' Again his eye turned to Susan, this time with a hint of gratitude. The speed-reading researcher was always glad to help if her friends wished to brighten their anecdotes and legends with ever more imaginative details. 'For all this modern hankering after exercise and fresh air, there's not nearly enough folk willing to park upalong to the headland and climb Coastguard Steps to get back; and them that parks down on the chezell worry about the tide, against every assurance it never rises so far – as they could see for theirselves by the state o' the beach, only being from the town they can't, having lost their connection with nature.'

Mike sighed. 'If we had a water-powered railway in Tollbridge same as Lynton, that would be a great encouragement. Well worth coming to see.' He permitted himself a brief, beatific vision of the man in charge of the funicular railway: Michael Binns, Senior, wearing a smart uniform, selling tickets, directing the flow of water from tank to river with the flick of a switch, ringing the bell that commanded all movement of the twin counterweighted cars up and down the face of the half-mile cliff.

Mickey smiled kindly at him. 'You'd like a chance at that, hey, Dad? But gadgets and a spot of tinkering such as we enjoy is one thing. The Chole's in the wrong place for even the best engineer to emulate the setup over to Lynmouth. No, I fear it's either climb the steps to Watchfield Point or park on the chezell – and choosing between.'

'As for the chezell…' Gabriel nodded to Barney. 'This talk of Ploverton's put me in mind it's high time one of 'em should be on his way down with a tractor to scuffle the beach-parking level again. Half-a-dozen motors on manoeuvres and a tricksy tide or two, and the place more resembles a pot boiled over than anywhere flat enough to leave a car.'

Barney nodded back. 'I saw Jan Safe not long since, being due his turn for the job. He says he'll be down when he's the time; but he've a farm to work, remember, and a livelihood to earn. Levelling Tollbridge beach is rather the kindness of cousins, one to another.'

'There's more to life than making money, Barnaby Christmas!'

'A good deed in a naughty world,' broke in Jasper. Gabriel might be joking, but cider could make tempers uncertain. 'It's a shame the law won't let us clear some of that chezell out of the way for good. Before we came here I thought we might set up a small jewellery business – local pebbles in a wind-powered polisher, environmentally friendly – but when I checked the legal position, we can't. We can take them from the riverbed, but the Chole's far too fast and cold for anyone to go paddling in comfort or safety.'

Jane seconded his peacemaking efforts. 'And I had wondered about painting pictures on the larger stones, but it's the same problem. The law says you mustn't take anything from the beach, even though you can move bits of it around – but you, and the bits you want to play with, have to stay right there while you play.'

Mike laughed. 'If you didn't, kids making sandcastles would have a poor time of it!'

'Who makes sandcastles in Tollbridge?' demanded Gabriel.

'True,' conceded Mike. 'No castles in Tollbridge, where we've no sand to speak of. But stone pillars I've built here myself – the same like you have, and don't you deny it.'

'Who's denying?'

'Nobody – no more than we're saying there's no moving bits of the beach around for that building. Just don't take 'em away.' He looked at Jasper, of Packlemerton's Publicity. 'Shows how much opportunity there could be in chezell,' he prompted, 'if 'twas known how best to take rightful advantage. Building the tallest pillar?'

'Needs years of practice, building with rounded stones.' Barney Christmas knew better than most how rounded local stones could be. As a child, forced to support his family, he'd spent illicit hours off school scouring the beach for matching sets of knucklebones, which he sold to his friends. White alabaster pebbles commanded the highest price of all.

'What about skimming?' enquired Gabriel, as everyone considered the best way to take advantage of the chezell in these less impoverished times.

'Sea needs to be calm.' Mickey had been a noted skimmer in his youth. 'Which too often, it's not. And do you count the number of bumps, as to which there's often disagreement, or the distance bumped over?'

'You'd never measure it right,' said Gabriel. 'Nor safely. Sit out there waiting in a rowboat with a spyglass and a dan-buoy, and some tarnation fool would be sure to take another skim afore you'd dropped the dan to mark the first spot, and then overboard you'd go, out cold, and most likely drown.'

This seemed at first a pessimistic view, but the modern world did seem to feature more fools than before; or maybe the fools were more in evidence than in the good old days when people didn't know they didn't know but had common sense, and used it. These days, even in an electronic not-spot like Tollbridge, news would eventually filter through from the outside world. As there were more opportunities to collect it, so there must be more of it than once there was; and folly always makes a better story than any amount of common sense.

'The Chezell Challenge!' suddenly burst from Jane. She smiled at Mike. 'Remember you told me once, and I said what a good title, only we'd need to find something better than racing model cars on the beach when they kept tipping over?' He had almost forgotten, but was pleased to be reminded: at least some folk appreciated his good ideas!

Her eyes were bright. 'We could have a handicap race – for humans, not cars – all ages and sizes. Small ones to carry seaside pails; medium-sized, buckets; big, tough types, sacks over their shoulders or a bucket in each hand. Make it a circular route, then they can empty the pebbles out more or less where they were collected. We could have the Pebble Dash, on the flat to the end of Harbour Path and back—'

'—with the turning point at Trendle Cottage,' Mike broke in, 'where they'd have to ring the bell as proof they'd reached it—'

'—and a general issue of ear plugs,' growled Barney, who owned and rented out on a short-term basis the aforementioned cottage, its bell-pull being an elaborate rope braid worked with great skill by Mike Binns in earlier days.

'Rocks Around the Clock!' Mickey had seized on Jane's idea. 'Straight up Stickle Street and round the church – not widdershins, o'course, we'd have arrows pointing folk in the right direction – and down again.'

'Maybe the ding-dong will be fixed by then.' Andy Marsh had heard from more than one person about this, and had explained politely but firmly that she was not willing to climb, even on scaffolding, through a very small window into a shadowy church tower in an attempt to fix a mechanism of which she had no previous experience. There were local experts, she knew: far more sensible to ask them!

'Fixing costs money.' Barney shook his head at her, then smiled. 'Regarding which, you've not forgot you're coming to see me tomorrow? Good. I'm for my bed now. Not so young as once I was.'

As he rose from his chair he shot a quick at Mike Binns, whose pathetic best line this so often was. Mike, however, missed the infringement of copyright. He was listening to Mickey and Susan insisting, yet again, that nobody should worry about the clock on their behalf. Wedding, blessing, or funeral – if the vicar was happy to wait for the hour to change in October, so were they.

'And,' finished Mickey, with another hug for Susan, 'if it's a christening has to happen first, tidn nothing to do with us!'

Chapter Ten

Town-bred Andy had taken Barney's 'not too early' to mean 'not before ten', but even so she found the old man on the lookout at his front window. He was opening the door as her fingers still reached for the knocker, which like so many in seafaring Tollbridge was a fouled anchor, in brass.

'First week's wages,' the tycoon advised as he ushered her inside, 'you buy yourself a real alarm clock. The sort to wind up, with no batteries going flat just when they shouldn't.'

'Next time you make an appointment, be exact about the time,' returned Andy, then wondered if she'd gone too far.

He grunted; then he grinned. She hadn't. Barney liked people who stood up for themselves: they knew what was what. Starting out in business he had met far too many who didn't understand their own worth, and allowed others to take advantage. They had failed to prosper. Barney had observed, had learned – and had prospered.

'Fair enough.' He waved to a chair. 'Sit down. You've some skill in working wood, they tell me?'

'Some. More than many, but it all depends on the job; and the wood, of course.'

'How about metal?'

'I can use a soldering iron, braze, a little, but heavy welding's not my thing. And if you want wrought iron, you'd better find a blacksmith.'

A pause. 'You know the old tin tabernacle being set to rights for the museum?'

Andy laughed. 'I do! One weekend I was down here, Ange had me shifting tea chests straight after breakfast to make tables for sorting stuff. I hope you're not asking me to fix that roof. Thatching's every bit as skilled a job as blacksmithing.'

'I know that full well, so no, I'm not. Tollbridge has a community fund, and Prue Budd whose name's to be on the museum left her money there for just such requirements.' Barney sighed. 'Prue was born a Christmas, and I'm near enough her last living relative. I like to keep an eye on things. Show due respect to her memory.'

Andy murmured something. There was another pause.

'Any building,' said Barney, 'needs watching and repair as necessary, with maintenance at regular intervals; and the older the building, the more regular.' He wagged a wise finger. 'What's also needed is money to pay for such – which, until Prue's affairs are fully settled, idn so easily done without a cartload of discussion and maybe-'twould-be-better and similar nonsense, committees being all of a muchness no matter what their purpose. Now, I like doing things without fuss. That's how things get done.'

Andy nodded. 'The direct approach. Me, too, where I can.'

'Good.' He leaned forward. 'Now you've no call to mention my name to any not dreckly involved, unless they should dreckly ask; but I was walking past the tabernacle down Hempen Row, as from time to time anyone might. Visiting, we'll say. Not checking up or spying.' Andy nodded again: she knew he and Jasper Merton had some mystery project in hand; and Jasper lived at the far end of Hempen Row even if (from what she'd heard) it was Jasper who would go to visit Barney Christmas, and seldom the other way around.

'I didn much care,' Barney went on, 'for the general state of access. The handrail to the steps is like to become a reg'lar rattle-trap concern, if not sorted afore the winter.'

Andy was surprised. 'The steps didn't seem too bad last time I was there. Ange and I were going up and down carrying all sorts of stuff in and out, and—'

'Aha!' The finger wagged again. 'Carrying in both hands, no doubt!'

'Well – yes, I suppose we were.'

'Not able or needing to hold the rail, then, and it's the rail I noticed was in somewhat of a broke-back condition, though the wood o' the steps will likewise need attention before long. You, Miss Handy Andy, and Angela are' – he gestured vaguely – 'young.' Barney let out a long, pathetic sigh. 'Like Mike Binns, and Gabe Hockaday, and Thomas Joy whose loss we've so recently seen, I'm a very old man.'

Andy, like everyone in Tollbridge, knew that Barney carried his walking stick as a mark of distinction rather than an essential. She did her best, however, to appear sympathetic to the frailty of her host; and she certainly couldn't deny his claim to being a very old man. 'So you'd like me to carry out a quick inspection of the steps, with special emphasis on the handrail? With a view to replacing both if they can't be repaired? If you'd rather I didn't even tell Ange, I could say I'm doing it pro bono: she knows that's how I used to work for the women's shelter in Town. I could tell her I'd like to give something back to the community while I look round for a full-time job. That okay?'

Barney was pleased. He prided himself on being a shrewd judge of character: you don't make millions if you make too many mistakes. 'Fix them steps to my satisfaction and you've a full-time job with me, missie. Anyone will tell you old Christmas have property of a wide and varied nature in Tollbridge and beyond, requiring to be maintained. A wide and varied nature,' he repeated, smiling to himself before continuing:

'And never enough time nor people to fix problems so soon as they occur, which is the best way to deal with them. You and that motorbike should suit my purpose very well. Skilled workman's rate for the rail and the steps, then we'll see. Shake?' He shot out his hand, grinning as he echoed her words back to her. 'That okay?'

'Shake!' Andy rose to her feet. 'I'll fetch my toolbox – oh.' She turned back. 'Do you know if there are any preservation orders on the building? It's kind of ancient.' She saw the glint in his eye: another test, she supposed. 'Okay, Ange has never said anything about it, so I'll assume that like-for-like replacement shouldn't cause any bother. It's the sort of thing she's bound to know—'

'—and if she don't, her mother's the one to find out.' Barney chuckled. 'Good at that, our Susan Jones-for-not-much-longer. Still thinking out a new name for the new books she plans, they say.' He shook his head. 'Remarkable how she can find out almost anything for anyone else, but not for herself.'

'It's a funny old world,' said Andy.

Barney was still chuckling as she took her leave.

Angela was gone from The Old Printery by the time Andy returned, but the spare key was useful. Soon the toolbox was jogging on its way down Meazel Cleeve – Andy waved in case Miriam was watching – and along Harbour Path towards Stickle Street.

An elegantly plump but efficient female form was ahead of her, walking in no apparent hurry, but with steady purpose, up the hill. At her side she carried one of Angela's distinctive totes. The jogger put on a quick burst of speed to join her.

'Susan, hi! Lovely morning!'

Susan agreed it was, adding that after last night's celebration she felt a little exercise might help to clear the brain before she started work. She glanced at the toolbox. 'Do I take it you feel the same way?'

Andy recalled her promise to Barney. Could Susan Jones be considered 'directly involved' in the Budd Memorial Museum because her daughter was the part-time curator? 'I thought I might pop along to ask old Ange if she'd any odd jobs for me,' she temporised. 'Sort of keep my hand in while I look around. Someone said something about the handrail to the steps looking shaky, and I might be able to fix it.'

Susan smiled. 'Beautifully put: nice and non-committal! Barney Christmas loves acting the curmudgeon, but it doesn't fool anyone who knows him. Odd how a man who's normally so sharp never realises that.' Andy hid her own smile at hearing her friend voice a similar view of Barney to the view Barney held of her.

'But I won't breathe a word,' promised the world-famous author. 'Why spoil his fun? It amuses him and, fair enough, he's earned it over the years – though he's not normally so careless. The scrumpy must have gone to his head rather faster than usual, otherwise he wouldn't have let us all hear him invite you for interview as he did. The museum handrail will be a test piece, I imagine.'

Andy burst out laughing, but wouldn't commit herself. She felt she owed Barney that much discretion, in the same spirit as Tollbridge currently allowed Mike Binns to play the pitiful old widower whose only son was shortly to abandon him to the life solitary once he married and left home.

'So how's the house-hunting?' Andy enquired. 'Mickey moves in with you in the short term, I know, but I remember how quickly you and Ange got on each other's nerves. She says you might end up living in Boatshed Row and keep Corner Glim just for an office.'

'We're still discussing various options. At least with a husband I won't have to worry about a second bedroom.' Susan faltered briefly in her stride, then walked on. 'You know Angela pretty well, Andy. She… doesn't hold it against me, does she?'

'Not now she's turned her life round,' came the only honest reply. 'And you know she wasn't herself at all, early on, when she might have done – and even then she didn't, not very much, once she started to calm down. Which you know was pretty quickly, once she moved to The Old Printery.' Andy stopped, solemnly raising her right hand. 'May the Mad Dentist of Ploverton use my hammer-drill on my wisdoms if I lie!'

A writer will always appreciate a neatly turned phrase; Susan laughed heartily. 'The Tollbridge dentist might be just as mad, of course. Why Ploverton in particular?'

'I didn't think you had a doctor, let alone a dentist. I know this isn't the most up to date of villages, but surely even here they've moved beyond barber-surgeons – hey! Lightbulb!' Andy rattled the toolbox. 'If there's not enough work for an extra pair of handyman hands, I could specialise in tooth-pulling and make a fortune!'

They arrived at the entrance to Hempen Lane, where Andy was about to say that here she turned off, when Susan said:

'I'll come with you to the museum.' She waved the tote. 'When Angela had the first big sort-out, someone unearthed the local Friendly Society daybook and it sparked the germ of the idea for my Vesta Tilley series.' She smiled in fond recollection of the happy result of her research trip to Bristol in the taxi driven by Mickey Binns.

She laughed again. 'You know Angela! I was only allowed to borrow the daybook if I promised faithfully to repair the broken spine for her, and tidy up the loose pages. Of course I said I would, but you know how it is when you're working – and she's been dropping hints about overdue books and lost property, and last night when I was buying drinks she gave me one of her looks. You know?'

'I know. The old Ange is back with a vengeance, Susan: I'd say there's no need for you to worry about her any more. If only she'd seen through Paul the same way – but there, love is blind.'

Andy giggled. 'Sorry. Maybe not the most suitable subject in present circs.'

Susan wasn't offended, giggling with her as they approached the one-time meeting hall of the long disbanded Brethren of the Doubly Seceding Little Emmanuel. 'Mickey and I have known each other some time now. We're past the stars-in-the-eyes stage, if we were ever in it.' Then she hesitated; for once, the wordsmith was lost for words. 'I suppose, over the years, we just sort of... grew together in the same direction, only it took me longer to notice we'd got there than it took him. And here we are!' she ended in triumphant ambiguity.

They had passed an open window en route to the small side porch that, unlike the main tabernacle with its replacement thatch, retained the original corrugated iron roof. Three grey and weathered wooden steps rose to the porch door. Andy regarded these with professional interest: they seemed just as she remembered them. As Susan reached for the handrail (Andy watched to see if it wobbled) the door opened.

'I thought I heard voices. Hello!' Angela's gaze went at once to Susan's tote. 'You've brought the daybook back, Mother? Good. Better late than never, I suppose – but just think if your cottage had burned down while you and Mickey were on your honeymoon! At least if this place catches fire it's right on the spot for the Octopus pump, and the people who know how to use it. Andy, why have you brought – no, don't tell me.'

She exchanged a knowing smile with her mother, who, shrugging slightly, smiled back. Angela pointed to the toolbox. 'Let's see – Barney Christmas thinks our wiring is dangerous, so he's paying you to check it out with a view to full replacement under some obscure clause in the covenant nobody but he can understand. The committee will automatically tell him to carry on, and he'll end up paying for it out of his own pocket while publicly grumbling to his heart's content about the waste of community funds. Right?'

Andy knew dissimulation was pointless. 'Well, don't let on I told you – but you're wrong about the electrics: it's the steps, or rather the handrail.' She frowned. 'Look here, though. If you think the wiring's dodgy, I really ought to check that for you first. Have you spotted any crackling? Sparks? Singed paint or plaster near any of the sockets?'

'Sockets?' Angela chuckled. 'I'm sorry, of course you won't have noticed. Because it's still summer I've hardly switched on an electric light since I've worked here; and as the weather's been generally kind, with all the rushing around I haven't felt the need for an electric fire. Which is just as well, because there aren't any sockets. No mains, no heating of any kind, just a prehistoric lighting circuit – and I do agree it might be an idea to check that out. I'll bet the Brethren did some heavy soul-searching before they had it installed, all those years ago.'

'They preferred candles?' Andy gazed round for suitable sconces, brackets or candlesticks. She saw no sign of any such.

'Too churchy: altars and priests – shock, horror!' Angela glanced at Susan, who nodded at her daughter to carry on. 'Mother looked them up – the Brethren, I mean. They used oil lamps: wise virgins, you know? I found a whole lot in one of the cupboards. Fish oil, from the smell.' Her nose wrinkled. 'At least it won't have cost too much.'

'The wicks were plaited from locally grown hemp,' said Susan. 'They were very big on the purity of the community and not diminishing their moral strength by letting anything from outside come in, unless they absolutely had to.'

'They were great ones for moral strength.' Angela rolled her eyes. 'No way were they going to pander to basic human weakness – more outside influence, you see. That's why there's no heating of any kind. They didn't even allow hassocks to save their knees from the floor, just in case you dared rest your feet on them out of the draught.'

'Spartan, or what,' agreed Andy.

Susan nodded. 'Spare the frostbite and spoil the immortal soul – but they were an interesting bunch. Dickens thought them worth a mention in one of his Christmas stories – nothing to do with Barney's family – and I suppose in the heyday of the Brethren, all the Sisters would expect to wear their best clothes to meeting: wool next to the skin, umpteen flannel petticoats to their ankles, thick knitted stockings. Very Victorian and correct – and warm. As for the men, you know about the Tollbridge jumper, don't you?' Andy did. 'Well,' said Susan, 'even now they use oiled wool to knit them. It retains a surprising amount of body-heat, Gabriel says; as does Mike, though he prefers to make a beanie, when he knits anything. He says it's quicker.'

'And what does Mickey prefer?'

Angela choked something back, and tried not to grin. Susan ignored her.

'Mickey can knit – he and his cousins all learned from Gabriel – though he's far better at ropework,' said Mickey's betrothed firmly. 'Mike taught him his knots, and *he* was taught by his foster-father, old Ralph Ornedge.' She chuckled. 'Mike's far more of a purist than any local born and bred: that's so often the way, isn't it? He really doesn't approve when Mickey experiments with different patterns from the traditional – hates even using coloured yarn; if Mickey ever did want a new jumper, he wouldn't dare be the one to knit it.'

Angela quivered quietly, and looked away. 'And I,' said Susan, 'am no keener on knitting than on cookery, as my darling daughter is restraining herself from telling you. I can cope well enough with the basics, and that's as far as I'm prepared to go.'

'P-penny Scott,' came a smothered wail from Angela. 'I was only a kid, Mother – and I honestly wasn't c-casting n-nasturtiums!' Her voice broke. Once more she quivered.

'Before I got lucky with the writing,' said the best-seller – who, like her darling daughter, was trying not to laugh – 'we relied to some extent on family and friends, though I naturally tried to be independent and people respected that. My mother-in-law, bless her, found a knitting pattern for a child's sweater she thought even I could manage; my mother gave me the wool, and I tried – and I could.' She glared at Angela. 'I made this child a gorgeous blue one, and she loved it, and by the time she'd grown out of it I'd knitted a green one to fit. Naturally she went on growing, and I – I had a red one in reserve…' Now it was Susan's turn to choke.

Angela took up the tale. 'The first day I wore it to school my friend Penny took just one look and said, *Oh, Angela, you've got another sweater the same as all the others* and when I came home, I t-told Mother what Penny had said…'

Susan recovered herself. 'I have never,' she informed the grinning Andy in a lofty tone, 'knitted my daughter a sweater from that day to this. And if Michael Ornedge Binns wants anything knitted – anything at all – he can ask his uncle Gabriel!'

Chapter Eleven

Andromeda Marsh was making a detailed inspection of three wooden steps and their handrail. She had already given the lighting system an even more detailed inspection and, to her surprise, found it safe, though in need of updating. 'Once the clocks go back and you want to look for things in corners you'll need a torch on every shelf, or one of the headband sort I wear when I know I'll need both hands and there's nowhere to prop a flashlight. Would the funds stretch to a headband torch?' Andy grinned. 'Would you wear it, if they did? It's the very latest thing!'

Angela looked at her friend. 'A complete overhaul of the lighting would be the best solution,' she said firmly. 'The funds will certainly stretch that far, I've been told, but first I must work out where the exhibits should go, and how they'll be displayed. Until then, what we've already got will have to do.'

'As it will.' Andy was still surprised at this. 'We must hope your steps will do as well!' And away she'd hurried to find out if they did.

Angela was leafing with care and an eagle eye through the pages of the Tollbridge and Ploverton Friendly Society's daybook, repaired by Susan in exchange for permission to take it for home study. Now her daughter's scrutiny could find not a single unattached folio, even if some were still loose where the paper had stretched; the stitches were neat, the creases gently flattened. The binding did not ripple or flake as before, although Susan had made no attempt to find matching cloth for the rubbed and bald patches on the cover.

'We agreed it should stay as authentic as possible,' she reminded her daughter, as the former librarian closed the old ledger and nodded her approval.

'We did, and it is. You've made a pretty good job of it, Mother; thanks again. I'd have had to fix it myself, or send it away, sooner or later, and you've either saved me some work, or the museum some money. Maybe both.' Angela contemplated again the safely returned treasure. 'I'd say almost as good a job as I might have done myself.'

'Almost?' Susan laughed. 'Modified rapture! But I must thank you again for letting me borrow it. It wasn't just a fascinating read, and the basic inspiration for Vesta Investigates, but it gave me my first plot – though I'd rather not talk about that, except to say: mystery yes, murder no. Why must it always be murder? Why not blackmail, or fraud, or stolen jewels? How many actual murders did Sherlock Holmes investigate?'

'No idea.' Angela had opened the daybook at random. 'It's the elegant copperplate that impresses me most: one of those skills they don't seem to teach any more, but a century ago it was obviously the go-to handwriting. Even with so many different entries over the years it all looks so... uniform. Really neat and tidy,' finished the former librarian as she continued to leaf gently through the restored prize exhibit.

'We were taught a style called Marion Richardson,' her mother reminisced. 'There was a new girl, Anne Something-or-other, who came from another school where they'd taught her italic. It impressed us girls no end, but she was marked down in a handwriting test because hers wasn't the same as everyone else's.' Susan laughed. 'It was neater, but it wasn't our official Marion Richardson, so...' She shrugged. 'It's a funny old world.'

'That's not fair!' Angela was indignant on behalf of Anne Something.

'Life often isn't: never really was. Anne, and the rest of our class, just learned the lesson earlier than many children do. And we could have had it worse. Do you know the youngest member of that Friendly Society was signed up on his twelfth birthday, when he officially started full-time work? He'd been working part-time for ages before then, work being something like work in the good old days of Victoria the Great.' The irony in Susan's tone wasn't lost on Angela. 'Some of the local lace-makers started at five years old with a twelve-hour day, hunched over their pillows putting in pins and twisting thread until their eyes gave out; one candle and a water-glass lens shared between half-a-dozen kids who'd end up dying of lung disease because they could never stretch and breathe properly – or from internal complications even worse than fashion-plate women being squashed into corsets, which was just as unpleasant for them but was their own stupid choice, not from – from desperate financial necessity.'

Angela knew what her mother meant. Susan had never been a dedicated follower of fashion. 'Louise and Olive had it easy, then. Have they let you see anything yet?'

'Not until the day before, I've been told – more than once! All I know is, they're each making me something to carry with my flowers. If I plan to throw the bouquet I must remember to remove the lace to keep, before I throw it.' She hesitated, then decided to risk it: she smiled at her daughter. 'As you aren't going to be a bridesmaid, would you like to have my flowers instead?'

Angela gave her a look.

Susan's heart gave a little skip: so even a hint about Rodney Longstone remained off-limits. 'Or Andy, perhaps,' she hurried on, nodding towards the half-open door. 'You count as local now, but she's only been here five minutes. Call it a welcoming gesture.'

Angela accepted the olive branch with a cool smile. 'The way you throw, and I catch, Andy's definitely your best bet. She's better coordinated than either of us. I should imagine it's seriously bad luck to drop a wedding bouquet, isn't it?'

'No idea. I could look it up, of course, when I had the time – only I haven't. Now I've brought back the daybook, I really must finish organising my notes. I want them in some kind of order before the wedding, or I'll spend most of the time *thinking* – you know how it is.' She sighed; so did her daughter, who knew it all too well. 'I want to be able to switch right off for a few days with a clear conscience – so now I'll leave you and Andy to your morning's work, and go and get on with mine.'

The handywoman sat on the bottom step, a small heap of ragged weeds to one side. She was working a battered screwdriver in and around the rocky soil at the base of the metal handrail, from time to time tapping it thoughtfully.

'Is it okay to come down?' enquired Susan from above. 'Or have you found the steps riddled with killer woodworm and I'm likely to break my neck?'

'Mickey won't be pleased if she does,' warned Angela.

'Oh, the steps as steps will do fine.' Andy rose to her feet, and pointed with the screwdriver. 'At first I thought the handrail would be okay too, but when you poke about down there it's more corroded than I'd expected, where it's fastened to the wood. The salt in the air doesn't help, of course, but some idiot's gone and used brass screws on a bracket made of steel.' She shook her head. 'The original fitter can't have been that stupid: it would have fallen to bits centuries ago, if he was. Anyone living near the sea knows the risks.'

Her friends were looking puzzled. 'Sorry! Didn't mean to blind you with science, but it's a fact: you don't go mixing metals, especially at the seaside, not if you want outdoor fixtures and fittings to last. Even your basic carbon steel nuts with stainless steel bolts – okay, both of 'em steel, but there are times when they're seriously bad company for each other. Funny. I wonder why whoever must have replaced the original screws forgot that.'

'But brass doesn't rust,' said Angela. 'Does it? I thought that was why boats all have brass screws and fittings, not just to look smart.'

'Why Nelson's sailors used to share their polishing kit and "part brass rags" when they quarrelled,' offered Susan of the serendipity reading habit.

'The more brass the merrier,' agreed Andy. 'Which is what Mr Replacement must have thought, forgetting about galvanic corrosion – seaside rust, if you want a loose translation, though it can happen anywhere. Still, in the short term it makes my job easy. I can fit a new steel bracket to the downpipe and fix it to the step with steel screws, but perhaps in the long term the museum would prefer a smart new wooden rail to match the steps.'

'Which in themselves are safe to walk up and down,' said Susan, duly walking down them, avoiding the handrail. Standing by Andy she gave the metal upright a cautious wiggle. 'I see what you mean.' She bent to peer at the guilty fixture. 'Galvanic corrosion…'

Angela could see the creative wheels trying to turn. 'Maybe Vesta Tilley had a steam yacht,' she suggested. 'Weren't they all the rage for rich Edwardians?'

Susan didn't hear her. She took the screwdriver from Andy, smiled vague thanks, and bent again to peer at the rust she was rubbing away from what remained of the fastening bracket. 'Is this the original bracket? Would the replacement screws be bigger?'

'I think so – and probably. I can imagine one of the Brethren bodging things together to stop them getting worse, and forgetting to come back and do a proper job.'

'Or dying out before he could,' said Susan, sadly.

There was a respectful silence in memory of the long departed.

'This isn't getting things done!' Susan gave the screwdriver a last forceful poke into the rocky ground and jerked upright, shaking her wrist. 'Jarred it on a stone,' she muttered, flexing her fingers. 'Tingles a bit.'

'Not a stone.' Andy's motorbike excursions hadn't yet done serious damage to her hearing. 'Metal, it sounded like. Some sort of spreader plate, I guess, though on soil like this I wouldn't have thought... Let's have the whatsit back, please, Susan.'

Forewarned, Andy poked and tapped with more caution than Susan, moving in a wary spiral from the outer edge of the weed-cleared area towards its centre, going shallow at first, then deeper. Undersoil clinks and the occasional clatter didn't greatly hinder her progress: a deft wiggle of the screwdriver, a spray of pebbled earth, and she worked on—

—until she hit the same obstacle encountered by Susan. 'Metal, I think.' She twisted the screwdriver to and fro, tapping as she went. 'But not a spreader plate: it goes out too far from the business end where the steps finish, and I can't get underneath it the way I'd be able to with anything flat. Look' – she demonstrated – 'it's solid. Goes up and down.'

Susan's tingling wrist was forgotten: her imagination had been caught. 'What we need is a geophysics machine, if there's one small enough to fit this narrow entrance.' Doorways, entrances, thresholds: weren't they all special places for household spirits? Lares, Penates: she could never remember which was which; but had the Doubly Seceding Brethren by some fortunate chance erected their meeting house on a spot already sacred from Roman times? Had the Romans been some of the earliest visitors to Combe Tollbridge?

Her daughter's voice brought her back from the past. 'A spade or a crowbar would be cheaper. The museum's not made of money. If you think it's worth bothering we can always ask Mike or Gabriel; they both live closer than Clammer Cottage, and anyway I don't think Jasper's done much about his plans for the old hemp garden apart from making some, and then getting distracted by a new job that's more likely to bring in the hard cash.'

Andy, starting a cautious excavation directly over the possibly metallic mystery, heard only part of this. 'A garden fork and shovel would be better than nothing. Got a bucket, Ange? To clear away enough to see if we've just unearthed the missing treasure chest of Blackbeard Hockaday, Terror of the Severn Sea – uh, no,' as a vision of Gabriel's Father Christmas whiskers flashed across her inward eye. 'But Whitebeard Hockaday doesn't sound nearly as good.' She dug on, warily. 'Blackbeard Binns?' She looked up. 'Didn't Mickey's mother have Spanish ancestors?'

'Mike likes to think so.' Susan laughed. 'He's a romantic.'

'He certainly likes to tell the tale,' said Angela.

It was a good exit line, clearly intended as such by her prompt withdrawal indoors.

'Mike draws an efficient longbow,' was Susan's compromise, 'and Gabriel's happy to play along, even if Mickey's not always so keen. He says the Jeromes, his mother's family, were originally from France: Huguenot refugees expelled by Louis the Something in the seventeenth century. Mike, the old rascal, loves telling people that one of the Armada ships was wrecked along this shore, and those few survivors who weren't drowned, or massacred by the locals, turned Church of England and married all the prettiest girls – of course – and in the end became ordinary fishermen.'

'It must be a great disappointment to him that his beard's the wrong colour for a pirate.' Andy coughed. 'That magnificent auburn, at his age... I don't suppose—'

'And I don't, either,' broke in Susan. Then she laughed. 'Anyway, you're wrong. In the sixteenth-century Mediterranean there was a genuine terror of the seas called Barbarossa, otherwise Redbeard – but perhaps we'd better not tell Mike,' she added, as Andy continued to excavate. 'He doesn't need any more encouragement.'

'Mike Binns?' Angela reappeared with a plastic bucket left behind after the first great museum sort-out. 'A bit flimsy, sorry, but the best I can do – and he certainly doesn't.' She set down her trophy beside Andy, and joined Susan to supervise proceedings.

'This… galvanised rust of yours,' ventured Susan after a while.

Andy hesitated, gave up further education as a bad job, and murmured in neutral as, with gloved hands, she continued to scoop loosened earth into the bucket.

'You said everyone who lives by the sea knows all about it,' said Susan at last.

'They might not know what it's called' – she had to speak – 'and it's galvanic corrosion, remember – but I'd say everyone must know that it happens. I mean, how could you miss it when you got it wrong? Sooner or later, rusty stuff would just fall to pieces.'

'Sooner or later, someone would notice?'

Andy, once more digging, answered with a nod: she'd had her suspicions, and now…

Angela contemplated her mother from beneath frowning brows. She had worried before that Susan's mental state was rather less sharp than it used to be: was this further proof – or wedding nerves – or (to give the benefit of the doubt) a simple misunderstanding?

The author spoke, her imagination in overdrive. 'Perhaps that might be what he wanted. What he planned. It wasn't ignorance – a mistake: it was deliberate.'

'But why would anyone—?' began Angela.

Andy broke in. 'You're right, it must have been. It was!' By now she'd cleared enough soil to be sure. 'It's a box!'

'It really is!' Susan was thrilled. Angela stared.

Andy picked up the screwdriver. Once more she tapped the surface that, until now, had been hidden from view for – who knew how long? 'Metal,' she said. 'With a handle.'

'It looks like an old-fashioned cash box,' breathed Susan.

'It can't be buried treasure.' Angela tried not to get carried away by the other two. 'It makes no sense to bury valuables so near the surface that anyone might find them. Surely?' Her doubt had now started to doubt itself.

'Well,' said Andy, 'nobody seems to have found it for half a century at least, from the looks of it. The enamel's bashed about a bit, and blistered, but nothing's rusted through.' She slipped her screwdriver under the handle and slowly raised it, to the accompanying graunch of long-motionless metal.

'We need photos before we go any further,' cried Susan. 'We should have thought of it before, only to be honest I didn't really think there was anything there.'

'Me neither.' Andy looked at Angela: once a librarian, always a born organiser.

'My phone's inside,' said Angela. 'I'll get it.' On the point of departure, she paused to pay belated tribute. 'Well done, Mother; Andy, too. You've hit the jackpot – maybe.'

'Amethysts,' said Susan dreamily. 'Topazes, and cinnamon, and gold moidores.'

Andy, who'd never had to learn poetry by heart, stared at Susan in the same puzzled manner as her daughter. 'Cinnamon? I don't know any spices with a shelf-life of more than a year, let alone a hundred – but Ange is the cookery expert. Maybe cinnamon's the exception that proves the rule.'

'Cinnamon?' Angela was back with her phone. 'Cinnamon buns, you mean? What about your diet, Mother!'

The explanation was made, the laughter died away; photos were taken, and Andy was at last able to lift the enamelled metal box into a daylight to which it had not been exposed for many years. Everyone saw the initials painted on the front of the box: D.S.L.E.

'Doubly Seceding Little Emmanuel.' Susan was still dreaming. 'The very last Brother buried the box after he'd locked the door of the meeting hall for the very last time. The Brethren had all died out. There was nobody left who could be trusted to take care of – of whatever's in the box, so he left it for posterity – for us – to find.' Again her eyes gleamed. 'I said it must be deliberate! He moved the handrail and dug the hole and fitted the wrong screws to the bracket because he knew that, sooner or later, someone would repair it. And he trusted them – us – to do what he wanted.'

'Whatever that was,' put in Angela.

'Take care of the box, obvs.' Andy was brisk. 'He had no idea this place was going to end up a museum, of course. I'd say that man got lucky.'

'The Victorians were great ones for commemoration at all levels.' Susan grimaced. 'Only think of the Albert Memorial!'

Andy laughed back at the thought. 'I'd rather not, thanks.'

Angela weakened. 'I'd rather find out what's in the box. Does it rattle?'

'It's not heavy.' Gently, Andy shook it. 'No, it sort of… slithers, and bumps.'

Susan spoke eagerly. 'After we've taken such trouble – we've got to know!'

'But,' said Angela, 'he'll have locked it, you bet. And where's the key? There's a bunch of odds and ends indoors we can try, but if none of them works…'

As one, she and her mother turned hopeful eyes towards Andromeda Marsh, whose face wore a quiet, gratified smile.

Chapter Twelve

'With a modern box that didn't matter,' said Andy, 'I'd just drill the rivets out of the hinges, and open it from the back, but something this old needs a heavy dose of TLC. In due course we'll try what a couple of paper clips and some pliers can do – but I wonder if...'

They were back inside the museum, after a search of the ground by the steps failed to unearth a key. 'Worried about rust,' Andy had suggested. 'Probably thought oilskin wouldn't survive too well underground, with him having no idea how long it would be before anyone dug the box up again.'

'In some ways a second box for the key would have been sensible.' Angela approved of common sense. 'But there's not a lot of space out here; he might have worried it was risky to dig too many holes too close together. Someone might have wanted to know why, and started poking about sooner than he meant.'

'I wonder how long he thought it might be before anyone did.' Susan had appealed to Andy. 'Does this galvanic corrosion happen at a – a predictable rate?'

'Sorry, no idea.'

'And he might not have known, either. Hmm.' As both her daughter and Andy knew she would, the author was considering future plot possibilities.

'So we do it the hard way.' Andy led them back inside, where Angela spread sheets of newspaper on a table and her friend carefully set down their new-found prize. They settled themselves around it for some quiet contemplation. All thought of Susan's neglected home research, and Angela's urge to sort and catalogue, were forgotten. Logic told everyone the box could contain nothing of financial value, but they knew the historical profit from this rediscovery of Tollbridge's past might be invaluable.

Andy's toolbox supplied goggles, and a stiff-bristled brush that she used on every surface of the antique box, paying special attention to keyhole and clips. Shaking the debris in the bucket she sat down again while Angela produced a bunch of miscellaneous keys tied with what Gabriel and Mike had, more than once, assured her was locally produced hempen string. Angela suspected a leg-pull, but with no plans to put the keys on display it didn't matter – though it would be a matter for concern if any damage should be suffered by the lock of the Brethren's long-buried box. 'Probably,' she apologised, 'none of these will fit, but they're all we've got and they do at least look old enough.'

Andy glanced at the keys. 'To paraphrase old Barney, I'd say they're worth a try.'

Susan and Angela watched as, with a small torch, she squinted into the lock. 'Nothing doing: I was afraid of that. Clogged to the eyeballs with a century of rust, soil, whatever. We need to clear this gunge before I can even think of trying those keys.' The screwdriver used outside had a daintier sibling with which she poked, probed and scraped at the keyhole. A few unidentifiable crumbs dropped on the newspaper. 'Worse than concrete,' muttered Andy. 'Water might damage what's inside... So, oil.' She took a small can and snapped the cap from the nozzle. 'Pay attention, Ange!' She tilted the box and let three drops of oil drip into the keyhole. 'This could take a while.' She poked and scraped again. A few larger crumbs fell on the paper. 'Repeat at regular intervals, okay? I must hunt down a bracket for the handrail. Does the post office keep that sort of thing?'

Mother and daughter said they didn't know, Susan adding that it was always 'worth a try'. Angela gave her a look. Susan winked at Andy.

Andy said that Barney Christmas was a wise old bird, and often got it just right. 'Like you with this box, Ange. Not too heavy with the oil: say, every half-hour or so till I'm back. If Farley's lets me down I'll try Ploverton, and I may have to look even farther afield – which at least is good for the bike. Don't wait up for me! Don't make too much of a thing about the oil: as long as it doesn't dry out we can take days over the job, if that's what it takes. Be seeing you!'

She was gone, leaving Angela in charge of the oil and Susan preparing, at last, to head for home and her working notes.

The three had been so occupied with the mystery box they had paid little heed to the noises from outside. As Andy emerged from Hempen Row into Stickle Street, however, after a few yards she stopped to indulge in a fit of quiet laughter.

She was soon joined by Susan. The road near the old school was once more blocked by a council lorry, the area coned off. A work gang stamped about in hi-vis jackets, busily wielding industrial-strength burners to remove all the yellow lines, letters and zigzags they'd been at such pains to put down only a few days before.

'They won't recognise me without the bike,' prophesied Andy.

'They'll take no notice of me.' Middle-aged Susan was a realist.

Stifling their mirth the two strolled innocently past the school entrance, the grumpy workmen and the pungent smell of singed tarmac.

On a revolving display stand in Farley's General Stores Andy found a pleasing selection of brackets and similar hardware, but nothing of quite the right size.

'Bin metric I dunno how many years,' said Debbie Tucker. 'So with no great call for proper-measured stuff, tidn made, on account of most people wanting it will size it for theirselves, where they can. Can you do that, midear?'

Andy could. She chose the closest match to what she needed, adding to her loot a pack of sandwiches and two bars of chocolate.

'Working lunch,' she explained as she paid. 'No time to waste.'

'Not so great a pinch-fart as he likes to make out, idn Barney,' Debbie said, handing the change. 'So long as you do a good job, you'll be all right with him.'

Andy wondered how anyone kept a secret in Combe Tollbridge. She was tempted to ask if Mrs Tucker knew the patterns of Susan's wedding lace, then remembered that one of the lace makers was Debbie's mother Olive. Of course she knew! Louise Hockaday was some kind of aunt, or distant cousin. No need to wonder about keeping secrets in Combe Tollbridge. Why would anyone bother even to try?

Andy returned to the museum. Stickle Street was no longer blocked. The council lorry, the gang, and the equipment were all gone.

They had gone up the Chole valley to Combe Ploverton.

This time they found the correct school outside which to paint the warning message, the zigzags and the double yellow lines – but they weren't starting work just yet.

'Even so high up as here the signal idn no bloody good.' The foreman stood muttering over his mobile phone, a clipboard in the other hand. 'Do I trust the paperwork?' He waved the clipboard in the air. 'What they gived us last time was wrong, and we've wasted half the day putting things to rights downalong – so no, I bloody don't!'

Viciously, he flourished the offending phone. 'Nor I don't want wasting no more time if they've told us wrong again. I'll speak direct to that [epithet] in the office for double-checking the job code and confirming on the map, or not one blasted inch gets painted on that road today! Nor yet the next, if he don't answer quick. And if,' he added through gritted teeth, 'that plaguey computer female tells me just once more my call's important but the lines are busy and not to hang up, I swear I'll – ah!'

When at last he managed to address his complaint to the epithet in the office, he received (to his surprise) a helpful response. Papers were duly checked, boxes were ticked, and the conversation closed with the foreman's temper reduced from slow-burning fury to the habitual scorn of the manual worker towards those who sat behind a desk all day.

'So why are you lot stood about gapesing with your fool eyes out on stalks and work to be done?' he demanded of his underlings. 'Jump to it!'

They jumped.

This time the foreman resolved that things should be done by the book. The Tollbridge error – which, he maintained, was none of his – had deeply harrowed his soul: not so much for the ear-bashing he'd received after Barney Christmas went right to the top to ask why unexpected, costly and inappropriate traffic restrictions had appeared outside his property, and as he didn't ask for them he refused to pay for them… but because everyone else had sniggered, and made comments behind their hands, and left large-scale maps marked up in coloured ink sticky-taped to the door of his locker.

'First we set out the preliminary cones, as per health and safety.' The foreman consulted his clipboard. 'A quiet road, this: no call for lights. So, then we measure. Then we put the cones in their proper places – then we measure again from the other direction. Then we spray-mark where the markings should go. And then we unload all the gear!'

It was indeed a quiet road: so quiet that the footpath ran to one side only, and wasn't in the best of repair; but nobody cared. Local children walked to school by themselves or with friends, rather than needing the escort of adults. A lucky infant might arrive on a scooter with musical wheels; taller, older, stronger children might use rollerblades, or bicycles. If at busy times a farm vehicle, with due caution, drove by the school the pupils, locals all, had the sense to keep out of the way...

Yet the health and safety powers had decreed that a school entrance must be marked, and marked it was going to be – and the council foreman would do it by the book.

The book said among other things that, after a certain hour, overtime rates must apply. The gang began to feel hopeful. The foreman glared first at them, then at his watch. 'We've wasted time enough this day. Time's money.' He feared it was his pay that might be docked if he didn't stand firm. 'We leave this lot now and come back on the dot in the morning – at the normal rates. All right?'

Nobody dared to say it wasn't.

They climbed in the lorry and departed, leaving spray marks on the road and a parade of cones to warn pedestrians not to scuff them. A squat red block of interlockable plastic barriers was piled, unlocked, in the gutter – 'They'll moan if we crowd one inch o' that blasted path' – in expectation of tomorrow's locking. The efficiency and economy shown by the foreman would have gratified even Barney Christmas, had he but known...

But Barney had other matters on his mind.

Once he'd heard of the vanished yellow lines, he stumped his way up Stickle Street to inspect that part of it outside the old school. He peered at the surface, prodded with his stick, and sniffed. He stumped into Hempen Row and inspected Andy's repairs to the steps at the museum. The handrail no longer wobbled. She'd done a neat, efficient job.

The old gentleman returned home to Boatshed Row and began making telephone calls.

The Tollbridge grapevine quickly spread the word. That night the Anchor was crowded. At long last Barney Christmas, Jasper Merton, and the Ploverton doctors would announce their plans for the old school, with or without the yellow zigzag lines.

Those lines – their unforeseen arrival, their belated disappearance – had perplexed from the start. Barney had ignored every hint and dismissed all direct questions. Jasper agreed that he could make an educated guess, but if his client Mr Christmas wanted nothing said then nothing was what, in a professional sense, he must say.

Galahad Potter-Carey laughed at his patients if they made enquiry. 'All in good time! You leave everything to Doctor Gally!'

His partner, Sterndale Bennett, used a similar tactic but laughed rather less. While not blood relations he and Gally might almost be brothers: both of medium height and plump; both with pink faces, dark brows and thick white hair – save that Stan, five years Gally's junior, had a bald patch he'd always hoped nobody noticed. That very week, however, he'd been betrayed by a gust of wind that disturbed his comb-over, even as it blew the morning's mist away. He would have to start wearing a hat! It was enough to drive anyone to more cider than by rights he ought to drink.

'The man o' the moment be with us at last!' cried Gabriel, as Barney appeared with Jasper in attendance. 'Two men,' he amended. 'But no doctors?'

'Apologies sent,' said Mr Christmas. He pulled out a chair and sat down, folding his arms and frowning.

'We had planned to announce something next week,' said Jasper, as it became clear his employer would say no more. 'But when the workmen turned up again it did seem best to put an end to the speculation. Doctor Gally's doing late-night surgery, though he'll try to come down later – and Doctor Stan's gone as reserve with the Pig's skittles team.'

All was understood.

'Away match tonight,' said Mike Binns.

'And my Jerry driving the minibus,' said Gabriel, 'which is for why he idn here neither.' It pleased the patriarch that he would be the first in his family to have the puzzle solved – unless Jerry somehow contrived to wheedle it from Sterndale Bennett. Gabriel wasn't sure how well the good doctor was able to hold his liquor, even if his senior partner was locally renowned for his capacity. 'Us had best be getting on.'

He clattered his empty mug on the table to call the meeting to order, and fixed Barney with a resolute eye. 'We'll have no nonsense, now!'

'I never talk nonsense.' Barney was equally resolute. 'Not in business.' He gazed thoughtfully at Gabriel's two-handled mug. 'But there, business talk among folk with little understanding o' the matter can proper fatigate a man. He might finish so dry with explanations, he couldn't spit sixpence.'

Mickey Binns saw Susan make a mental note, relishing the turn of phrase. Her obvious pleasure pleased him. 'I'm buying,' he offered, adding quickly: 'For the sixpence-spitters, that is – otherwise each for himself, as usual. Gabriel? Barney? Don't make the great revelation before I'm back, will 'ee?'

Barney took his time over the first few mouthfuls, wondering how far he could prolong the suspense. It wasn't often he allowed himself to be the centre of attention. When he was, he preferred to choose his own terms.

Jasper shook his head slightly.

Barney grinned, and swallowed one more gulp.

He set down his mug. 'Planning permission,' he began. 'Applied for in outline, eight years since. Never lapsed, no matter what the economic climate: renewed again not so long back, and doubtless the cause o' they ziggle-zags, some fool at the council having misread the renewal form to think I'd a wish to bring the old school back to life, when all our chillern go upalong to Ploverton, as the council should know. But I've put 'em right! Said I'd not pay one penny towards the job, my original intention as clearly stated on the forms having bin for holiday apartments, not for updating any school.'

Nobody disputed this.

'But there's apartments, and apartments. These days folk seem to want a lot more, having discovered all the possibilities with internetting' – he gestured vaguely – 'and holiday programmes on television.' He drank more cider. 'Now, a man can't ever be sure he've found the best use for a building – but there's two sure certainties in this life, one being taxes and t'other... what we all know.'

His audience was growing restive.

'So, what comes before death? Old age, frailty, illness – and none o' them cause to kill us all off afore our time!' Barney drank again, for longer than his hearers would like. Most tried to hold back their questions, but there's always one who weakens.

'So the doctors are to set up a surgery for Tollbridge where at present we've none?'

The non-weakeners glared. No sense encouraging the man, who was making far too great a piece of work about his intentions and would draw the matter out all night, given half the chance, just to make himself more important.

'Might have bin an idea at one time,' conceded Mr Christmas, 'but no. Too late for that now. One surgery shared with Ploverton have worked well enough for us down here, save when the weather's real bad – and how often does that happen? No, a new surgery, new equipment – and folk to work it – costs money, which these days is hard to find – so tidn that,' he finished, as once more Jasper gently shook his head.

Barney gazed about him. 'To be short, then! You'll agree that if a visit to the doctor can settle most, there's always a few too poorly for that, and sent to hospital – and get better, and come out again – but not so keen on going straight home, should there be none to take care of 'em beyond a neighbour pops in every day for shopping, and the district nurse to change a bandage, or make you take exercise.'

He looked towards Sam Farley, sitting by Andy Marsh. 'Your cousin Olive's knees, remember? The nurse showed the girls how to help their mother, and so they did, though twadn so good a result as hoped because she'd left it too long – but there was no blame to the nursing, nor the exercises. Now, Olive was lucky having someone always on hand. Not everyone is so fortunate.' The more serious became the topic, the less local grew Barney's speech. Tollbridge began to understand how he had managed to hold his own, and make his money, in the cut-and-thrust world of big business.

'So, the hospital cures them and discharges them to free up the beds for others, which is fair enough – only, it's of concern to those being set free should they not yet be ready to stay on their own. What they need for a while is a safe place, halfway between hospital and home, for proper convalescence under medical supervision – and that's what the old school is going to become.' He beamed at Jasper Merton.

'The Halfway Home Convalescent Hotel!'

Chapter Thirteen

To her surprise, his next smile was for Andy Marsh. 'Now I won't deny how the benefits of such an establishment in this part o' the world, where so many folk choose to retire, were already forming in my mind, knowing Thomas Joy as I did, and others equally inconvenienced by this present fear of bed-blocking. Well, a convalescent home's a rare find these days; and when did anyone last hear of a cottage hospital? Seemed to me high time they were brought back, but with a touch or two of today's world about them; and Barney Christmas is as good to bring 'em back as anyone else. And we may say the name I've chosen is all thanks to you, midear, and that motorbike of yours.'

Andy stared at him. Sam Farley smiled at her.

'Young Jasper, too.' Barney was enjoying the sensation this new puzzle had caused, slowly reverting to his usual brogue. 'You'll recall, missie, there was a time you achieved a notable success along to Clammer Cottage, when you cleared the chimley of a mass o' soot burned on so cloggy as treacle. Jasper here' – he nodded to his associate – 'mentioned how, for all you'd no great liking for ladders, you did wonders with metal rods, and a rope down the roof, and organising folk to pull a half-sack of chezell scraping all up and down the inside to clear it.'

'With dust sheets and brooms to follow,' Andy added, 'and with more than a little help from my friends! After all, it was their chimney.'

Jasper, rubbing the small of his back, laughed. 'After which we had the fun of returning the pebbles to the same bit of beach we found 'em, as per the 1949 Coastal Protection Act. We even took photos to be sure we got the right place! A great pity you can't wheel a wheelbarrow over chezell. Half a sack weighs far more than you'd expect, and we hadn't enough buckets to share out the load.' Again he rubbed his back, and made a comical grimace. 'A memorable experience, clearing that chimney!'

Barney laughed with him. 'Poor lad, he told me the sorry tale when I asked the cause of his twitching shoulders. You worked everyone hard, he said, but the job was done and very glad of your advice: which gave rise to my first thought Miss Handy Andy could be a handy person to know.' He twinkled at her across the table. 'He told me, as we talked, how with that bike you'd be half your way home at the very least; then we spoke of other things; yet for all he thought it no more than idle tattering, I didn't forget, and not just the name, Halfway Home. I kept you ever at the back o' my mind, along with others I'd thought to employ once the paperwork was settled and the final plans agreed: so, when I heard you'd left the city to live here – well, you come rather more to the front.'

'The museum steps.' Susan Jones nodded. 'I thought so.'

'I'm never one to pay for a pig in a poke.' None of Barney's acquaintance would argue. 'I've my wits about me and eyes in my head – and a good nose, too.' He tapped this trusty organ with a mischievous forefinger. 'No hopes to play the prawn trick on me and get away with it! But I heard how you'd done some smart woodworking to conceal the evidence, so I thought, I'll take a look for myself at what the girl can do. So I did.' He nodded to Andy, and to the rest of his audience. 'There's a job waiting for you when you want it, midear, same as for others of a similar persuasion once the project's up and properly running. First 'twill be builders, making good and altering as needful; then plumbers and electricals; then painting, decorating, fixtures and fittings and all the fancy finishes and equipment.' He forestalled questions by adding: 'It's the doctors, o'course, who'll look to that side o' things. They know ezackly what they want, though mostly leaving the rest of it to me.'

Then he turned to Mickey Binns. 'My one regret is that it's took so long for all involved to reach an acceptable conclusion, authority seeming to find the idea strange for a hotel to be combined with recuperation, and raising all manner of unnecessary questions – but what is a sauna or a gymnasium in an ordinary hotel but good health for guests? They saw sense in the end, but too late: no chance now of the place being fit for purpose had you and Susan wished for your wedding revel to be the official opening, as I'd hoped once the pair of you finally named the day. So now' – he raised his voice, and waved an empty mug in a sweeping gesture that encompassed the whole room – 'now Jan and Tabitha Ridd must do the best they can in the Anchor, is all. Starting with a fill-up over here!'

The conversation became general, and cheerful. Grumble as he so often did, relishing his public role of miserly malcontent, Barney Christmas couldn't help being seen as a local benefactor. For one reason or another, various schemes for bringing visitors to Tollbridge never really worked, in the long term. The village had for years experienced a slow decline as too many of the younger generation moved away in search of employment, and their elders grew frail. When they died their houses weren't always easy to sell except, perhaps, to the (very) rare weekender, who tended to bring supplies from home and contributed little to the local economy. From time to time Barney would buy up such empty cottages and, with local labour, refurbish them for short-term rental. Local tenants were charged a rather lower rate than outsiders, but Barney welcomed anyone who paid.

Someone asked about his plans for Boatshed Row.

'Ah, yes. We could maybe rename it as Three-Quarters Home.' He chuckled. 'The sheds will be fitted out for true self-catering, thus bringing customers into Farley's shop, but still supervised from upalong to help folk win back the confidence for going home – and cheaper than any hotel, as everyone knows must be the first consideration.' He drained his mug and looked about him. 'The second being, who's to buy the next round? So much talk and planning costs money. I can't afford to waste too much on drink!' He'd been so carried away with explanations, he'd almost forgotten to play up to his reputation.

At closing time everyone dispersed in the best of spirits, though a certain haze in the air warned they could expect to wake next morning wrapped in another muggy white blanket of that dense, clinging mist known locally as a thick wet. It would, everyone knew, burn off as the sun rose at last above the rolling Exmoor cliffs; all hail tomorrow's dawn!

Soon after that morrow had quietly dawned, the quiet was disturbed by a battered, rattling pickup truck that crept down from the moor towards Combe Ploverton. It did not take the direct route. The driver sat hunched over the wheel, peering through swirls of thick wet blanket with only his sidelights switched on. For reasons of discretion he chose not to use fog lamps to assist his crawling advance.

'Can't hardly see a thing,' he kept saying. 'Not a bleedin' thing.'

'Shut up, Fikey.' His companion's response was automatic. 'If you can't see them, they can't see us. It's an ill wind. Keep going!'

'Ill or good, any wind would suit me fine, clearing this lot away,' muttered Fikey.

'So whose idea was it to do the job today? Yours. People waiting, you said. Orders to fill and cash paid, you said. So what *I* say is, shut up and keep going.'

'They could always have waited one more day – and so could you, Robert Miles.'

'You told me you needed the cash.'

'Not that badly.'

Rob Miles scowled. 'Well, I bloody do.' His girlfriend talked of marriage. He'd had no idea how much a wedding dress could cost, never mind the rest of the performance with stag night, hen night, bridesmaids, flowers, music, photographs... 'Not so far off now. You turn somewhere along here – slow down a touch – yes, this is the place. Don't do that!'

He slapped Fikey's hand from the indicator button. With no sympathy for the conditioned reflex, Rob Miles had visions of every window nearby lit by flashes of bright orange – every householder rushing outside to see what was happening. 'Might as well send up rockets, or blow a bloody trumpet!'

'Shut up.' Fikey wasn't going to apologise. 'How much further?'

'Not far.' This wasn't helpful. 'Go slow.'

Fikey continued his cautious crawl.

'There!' Rob Miles pointed. 'Now just back in, nice and slow. Quicker to load and easier to get away—'

'I know, I know! Shut up and let's be doing.' Fikey duly backed, manoeuvred the pickup into position, and switched off the engine.

Rob Miles jumped down from the cab with a crowbar in his hand. Then followed the wrenching sounds of tortured metal, and a sudden muffled clang – after which, both men for some time were very busy.

When the pickup set off again it rattled less than before; instead, it sloshed and gurgled. Its tyres looked flatter on the road, their metal rims closer to the surface. Whatever its liquid cargo, the pickup was far heavier than when it arrived.

'Can see a shade better now, thanks be.' Fikey, still cautious behind the wheel, risked putting on a little speed as the thick wet went on thinning. 'Gordon Bennett!'

He slammed his foot on the brake. The pickup juddered to a halt. Rob Miles, who in the heat of the moment hadn't fastened his seat belt, cursed him roundly.

'Ran across in front of me,' moaned Fikey. 'If we'd hit that bleeder—'

'We didn't.' Rob Miles rubbed his forehead. 'They can move fast when they want.'

'Did it get loose from somewhere? Could be others coming after.' Fikey made a swift and anxious survey of nearby hedges before setting off once more. In low gear.

'Dozens.' Rob Miles fingered the bump that was starting to rise, and swore. 'Hundreds. Who cares?' Suddenly, he brightened. A black eye wouldn't look good in photos. His girlfriend might be persuaded to drop the whole idea. 'Get loose? Well, maybe five hundred years ago. These days them goats don't belong to nobody, so there's nobody keeps track of 'em. They mostly live in the woods.'

'What a place.' Fikey shook his head. 'Wild animals in the fog, hedges high as walls, signposts you can't – what the hell!' Again he braked. The tyres screamed.

If the very last encounter to be expected in this neighbourhood was with an erratic goat, the second last, in late summer, was surely with a snow plough.

Ploverton's oldest-but-one working farmer (his senior being ninety-two) was John Safe, Cousin Jan to most of the upalong village and to many in downalong Tollbridge. After the promptings of Barney Christmas, it had been another Tollbridge relative who reminded the eighty-seven-year-old that the parking chezell was overdue for treatment: it was surely Jan's turn by now if, indeed, it hadn't more likely been the turn before that!

Jan had acknowledged family obligation and again promised to find time when he could. There was always much to be done around a farm: all too often, far too much. For some unknown reason the local goats were in frolicsome mood, having jumped the fence on several recent occasions to fraternise with the sheep and, he feared, trying to teach his mannerly flock the same trick in the other direction. He didn't want any beast, wild or tame, being run into by a car; but fences took time and money to repair.

No, of course he didn't grudge the kindness owed to neighbours! One way or another it would work out fair shares in the end. One morning soon he'd be setting his alarm good and early, and be away down to Tollbridge and back in a twink.

The snow plough was an antique tractor with a vintage bulldozer blade fitted at the front. Farmers never throw anything away. Jan remembered a far-off winter when snow fell and kept falling – and drifted, and froze – not for days but for weeks at a time. Roads were blocked hedge-high, or higher. Farms and communities were cut off from the outside world; emergency supplies were eventually dropped from the air. Birds and animals starved; sheep were dug from drifts. Feeling one life saved to be better than none, the young Jan carried home in his arms a frozen ram to thaw before the kitchen fire. The ram, while losing all its wool, had survived to become the founding father of a replacement flock.

Exmoor never forgot that winter. The equipment, though past its prime, was always kept in good order ready for the next time. Snow, landslip or chezell: Ploverton could cope!

Jan had set the blade so that it wouldn't grind furrows in the road as he drove, but would be easy to drop into position once he'd arrived on the beach. He wanted the job finished so that he could go home to his fences, his sheep – and his breakfast. His wife had promised best back bacon fried with three eggs and supper's leftover potatoes, mashed with salt and pepper: a hardworking farmer can only work hard if beforehand he's been fed good food.

Dreaming of bacon, Jan was so busy negotiating the row of cones and the piled plastic barriers near the school that at first he didn't think to wonder why the unfamiliar pickup truck, loaded with jerrycans and oil drums, seemed so startled to meet him. True, he was blocking the road with his tractor, but surely any fool could see it wouldn't be for long? At this early hour, why not just wait? Easy enough to pull into a gateway and let him safely by; no need to take off in such a fashion, making a U-turn so tight the place was now littered with twigs and branches broken from the hedge on both sides.

'Townies,' muttered farmer Jan with scorn, and rumbled slowly on.

The postman appeared in his little red van. He'd been warned about unexpected hazards in the road outside the school, but it seemed he would manage okay if he took care. He pulled over to where, in a main road, the kerb would have been: here, the pavement was on the other side. The van brushed noisily against the hedge as Jan Safe came closer. The two drivers met and saluted each other; Jan gesticulated to the rear.

'Some fool in a pickup smashing hedges – best watch out!' he bellowed. The postman signalled that he would.

'So,' demanded Fikey, 'which way now?' His panic flight had juddered to another tyre-screaming halt where the road narrowed to a lane meeting two lanes even narrower, by a gnarled and twisted oak to which a signpost had once been nailed. Over the years, as farm vehicles grew larger, all three arms had snapped off without being replaced; even cars were bigger than they used to be, so it was bound to happen again, and signposts cost money. Combe Ploverton held that anyone with legitimate business hereabouts knew full well where they were going – and could always ask, if they didn't.

'Gawd knows. Why the hell did you—?'

'Didn you see that van coming up behind?' Fikey tapped the rear-view mirror. 'They'd soon have clocked us if we'd hung about. Buck up and get the doings on your phone.'

A frantic search. 'Back the way we come, but cut across just before we get there.'

Damn side roads and keeping out of sight! Fikey snarled at his passenger and flung open the door. 'You drive!' He was so fierce that Rob Miles had shuffled across the front seat to take the wheel almost before the former driver's boots had touched the ground.

'Get on with it, then!' The passenger door slammed; the whole cabin shook. Jerrycans rattled and clanged against oil drums. Rob Miles hurled his mobile phone to Fikey, let in the clutch, and started the pickup in a point-turn so elaborate it needed, in the end, seven back-and-forths to get it right, and left bits of hedge all over the road.

'Shut up,' Rob Miles ordered, as at last they were on their way.

'I never—'

'You were thinking it – I heard you! Grinding your bloody teeth—'

'—and why not, you wasting all this time? If that post van comes along—'

'Shut up!' Rob Miles stamped on the accelerator. The pickup picked up speed.

This time it encountered not one – not two – but countless goats. They erupted through the hedge in pursuit of an in-season nanny, who was trying to escape the attentions of billies with blood too hot for even her incontinent tastes.

In one instant Rob Miles braked, swerved and skidded. The jerrycans and oil drums broke loose, and lurched to one side. The pickup truck teetered on two wheels.

It fell over.

Now the passenger door was blocked.

Rob Miles couldn't open the driver's door. Somehow Fikey, stunned but desperate, punched a hole through the windscreen and scrambled out. He reached back in to drag his shocked companion free.

They tried to run. They staggered, dazed and breathless.

They hadn't got far when the nanny goat, panicked into running in circles with her suitors crowding closer, stopped to bleat her defiance directly in front of the men fleeing the overturned pickup. The triumphant billies bounced and leaped.

The two men tripped and fell. They were surrounded.

The pickup truck exploded in flames.

The postman's van came warily round the corner.

Chapter Fourteen

Louise Hockaday, big with news, came to Farley's General Stores in excellent time for her session with Olive. Seven decades of feuding were still, to the surprise of all, on hold. To ensure that Mickey Binns and Susan should have a wedding to remember for only the right reasons, the pair had set firmly to one side their childhood squabbles to design and weave, in almost perfect amity, their butterflies, flowers, and secret motifs. Lace the two were determined Susan should have: she'd ever shown an interest in local craft and, while lacemaking was no longer taught in school, the skill had been handed down by mothers and grandmothers to such little girls as wished to learn. Olive and Louise couldn't recall which of them had first wished to learn, but the second had not been slow to follow her lead!

In the same almost perfect amity they agreed they should work only when together, which made for good company and avoided the risk of private competition 'on account of they bobbins would never stop flying, else – which at our age idn so good for the fingers' and Olive discreetly made no reference to eyes. Olive might have knees, and a hip, and arthritis all over, but she hadn't had her cataracts done, like poor Louise. It would be bad luck to crow and cause ill feeling when they were to weave lace for a special wedding.

Jerry, middle 'pin-horse' of the five Hockaday sons, had brought his mother's lacemaking equipment in the taxi from Hempen Row to the post office, and been at once set by Louise to shift furniture around the small back room where the frenemies were to sit, side by side, working with paper, pins, and pillows on designs that nobody – nobody – was allowed to see until the big day. The cover cloths of linen donated by Amelia Martin were always at hand to be whisked into place if approaching footsteps were heard: Olive's cloth a restful namesake green, Louise favouring the more traditional deep blue. Apart from their butterfly designs it was the only real difference between them.

Tollbridge held its breath as the sudden, unexpected peace continued. When the truce failed (as it was sure to do) the fallout would be worth seeing. Nobody wanted to miss it. Every day the post office and shop did record business as everyone waited…

And to everyone's surprise, and some disappointment, nothing happened.

That is, nothing happened at Farley's General Stores: elsewhere, it was entirely another matter. Before their usual hour for coffee and cake, before sitting down with Olive to the lacework for which clean hands were essential, Louise rushed into the shop and banged her thumbstick for emphasis as she slammed the door shut.

'Such doings upalong to Ploverton!' The bell still clanged and the door shook on its hinges as Louise gazed about her. 'A truck exploded by the school – stolen, most likely – goats capering by the hundred in the middle of the road – flames everywhere – postman Alf a hero, and the police arresting two people!'

All eyes were on her. For once, she was so caught up in the story she took no mental count of her audience, but plunged on regardless.

First she must establish the authenticity of her source for this momentous piece of news. She alone must impart it; interruptions would break the tension. She took a deep breath. 'Now that old Barney have finally come clean over the school, and naturally wanting the job got under way, the builders turned up first thing.' She cleared her throat. 'Paying them double, no doubt.'

With a significant nod she paused, acknowledging laughter all round. Maybe he did, maybe he didn't pay extra, but Barney knew how to keep a secret and required those who worked for him to do the same.

'And so,' she went on, 'hearing their commotion my Gabriel roused Mike, and off they went to learn the cause-for-why – the school gates having bin fastened, remember, after they motorbikes a while since, and Barney putting on a padlock and chain which, after so many months, were in need of oiling, and a chisel.'

Everyone nodded. Rust comes as no surprise in the salt-laden air of the Severn Sea.

'Now for this new job,' Louise continued, 'it seems Barney's carpenter is Sam Wilkins, that's cousin to my Gabriel and likewise Alf Raybrock' – again they nodded: Alf was the local postman – 'so o'course Sam heard from Alf ezackly what happened, him coming late to the event and finding Alf still there rather than delivering letters – for which he's paid, but the police asked him to stay as witness and he said he'd wait a short while – on account of Sam's own van having followed behind the ambulance – or was it the police car? – the last part of the journey. Sam was wishful to know what should be making him late to work rather than come dreckly to Tollbridge, as anyone with sense would have done, being paid for it and knowing Barney Christmas likes his money's worth.' Her sniff showed that Louise might accept the carpenter's argument, but thought it a poor one. She herself could have found far better reasons for such (understandable) curiosity!

They knew her sniff had been for effect; and it was effective. An eager chorus urged her to continue. With a gratified smile, she did.

'Seems the goats had come chasing out from Ploverton woods, you know their way' – further, emphatic nods – 'and stopped the truck across the road lopsided on its wheels, and the load shifting in the back – and,' she finished in triumph, 'what was that load but jerrycans and drums full of oil, catching fire!'

There were exclamations of shock, amazement – and glee. 'Got 'em at last,' was the general view. 'Serve 'em right! Weeks, this raiding of farms have bin going on, fuel being siphoned from outside tanks and the police able to do nothing about it—'

Louise was scornful. 'And small thanks now to the police they were caught! 'Twas all down to Alf Raybrock using his brains to recognise something wadn as it should be, about the flames. Too many and too fierce, he said – so, mindful of what's bin happening hereabouts, when he phoned 999 and they asked which service he said all three, though the fire engine was there almost so soon as he'd phoned, he said. Only to be expected, o'course, and it was under control before there was time for the others to arrive.'

Combe Ploverton, like many isolated rural areas, has a retained fire service crewed by trained locals ready and willing to stop whatever they might be about, the instant the alarm is raised. Combe Tollbridge, with more fishermen at sea than farmers on the land, relies when fire breaks out on amateur goodwill and the Binns/Hockaday Octopus pump, until the official Ploverton pump appears. The arrangement works well, and everyone understands it.

'Better late to catch 'em, whoever did the catching, than never, as with the dine-and-dashers in these parts not so long since. It's an ill wind,' offered a village philosopher.

While others prepared to debate this point, old Hilda Beacon displayed further curiosity. 'Anyone hurt?' she wanted to know: the first to make such enquiry.

Louise had to think back. From the builders, all talking at once, she'd had several different versions of what postman Alf had told his cousin Sam and Sam had told them and kept trying to correct as they repeated it and got it wrong. Louise couldn't now be sure who had told her what, and who (if anyone, according to Sam) had been right. More-and-so, any damage (or not) to a pair of sneaking oil thieves not of the twin villages must of course concern Louise far less than would any damage to the surface of the road, the disruption to the flow of traffic, and the likely harm to the goats.

'None hurt so bad they couldn be took from the ambulance after treatment and talked to by the police,' she said at last. 'Sam said Alf told him he'd bin asked to give a statement, but Alf said he'd waited long enough with letters to deliver and couldn spare any more time. So Sam thought he'd best leave 'em to it, with the fire people hosing down to clear the mess, and the police putting up signs to block the road, and Sam not wanting to be later to work than he was – which is how I come to know, having gone myself to learn what should keep Gabriel from coming home to tell me. He and Mike,' she added darkly, 'are still telling the builders what's what and like to be there half the morning, so I come away without 'em.'

To be first to bring the news, of course; but nobody grudged her the fun, in which they all enthusiastically joined for some minutes, pleasing her greatly.

And then it was not Hilda but her sister Daisy who put another question to make people stop and think. 'I wonder, now. Do this occurrence mean the ill luck – if any – is ended from the ghost ship, in good enough time for the wedding?'

Whereat the debate raged long, hard – and undecided.

On arrival at the old school to investigate the builders, Mike Binns and his brother-in-law had been pleased to find that apart

137

from cousin Sam Wilkins and one other, none could be called local. Locals, Barney had promised, would have a chance to work once the first stage of the project was concluded. At present nobody was employed from Tollbridge, and from Ploverton only carpenter Sam and a fairly recent (seventeen years) incomer, one Jinkins, who'd been recommended to Barney by the doctors and, it was supposed, was to be their unofficial deputy, first among equals. Barney's builders, in short, were an almost new and certainly captive audience for the polished and imaginative anecdotes Mike and Gabriel needed little encouragement to start delivering at the earliest opportunity.

This would come at the first tea break, they knew. They had sense enough not to interrupt the working day – Barney might be along any moment to check on progress – but the British builder is famously powered by frequent and regular infusions of tea, treacle-brown and well sugared. The vacuum flask is a wonderful invention if there's no cheery neighbour with a generous kitchen close at hand.

'You'll be turning the electrics back on, o'course.' Gabriel, observing a small plastic crate with mugs, spoons and other essentials, made conversation. 'This old place havn bin shut so long the wires will be rusted away, so I make no doubt it's all safe to use.'

'So long as Barney have kept paying the bills,' put in Mike.

'Old Christmas pays his dues, never fear,' said Jinkins.

Mike was hurt. 'Did I say he didn't? But, with the building stood empty for so long it could well of slipped the man's mind.' He sighed. 'We'm none of us getting any younger.'

Gabriel seized his cue. He shuddered. 'Younger? I doubt any of us would wish to be young again, having to be schooled in this fearful place!'

'Ah, the good old days.' Mike in his turn shuddered. 'There was a child starved to death – before our time,' hastily, to deflect awkward questions – 'but beaten black and blue by the teacher for no more than mischief. Locked in a cupboard and forgot, as a great storm blew up sudden and the lifeboat put to sea and the teacher among the crew—'

'—and the lifeboat lost. Every man jack o' them drownded,' elaborated Gabriel with relish. 'And the whole village in such shock and mourning, none spared a thought to the missing child... until too late.'

Sam Wilkins regarded his cousin with a sceptical eye. 'Did the child misbehave by any chance at suppertime, that he dared to ask for more?'

This warning shot neatly fired across the two old fishermen's narrative bows, after a few thoughtful moments everyone relaxed. Sam handed Gabriel a mug three-quarters full, and laughed. 'You'll be telling us next to keep our eyes open as we work, for fear we should encounter the skellington o' that poor starveling – him having bin denied burial in church, for some reason we've yet to hear.' He shook his head. 'Or the pair of you time to dream up,' he added, with a look that made Gabriel stroke his beard and Mike Binns chuckle.

'No need for dreaming,' he said happily. 'Real life needs no enhancement. After the ghost ship t'other morning, who's to say what might or might not be happened upon by anyone in this fearful place?'

'Or anywhere else along the coast that saw it.' While others grinned, Jinkins scorned all hint of superstition. 'Tollbridge can't lay sole claim to that mirage, remember.'

'Fata morgana,' said Mike helpfully, but Gabriel was speaking over him.

'There's mirages o' more than one kind, you must know, not just to the eyes. There's a cold shiver felt down the spine: would 'ee call it a ghost? So then, what's that ghost but a hallucination o' the heart?'

'And the groans and clanking chains, a hallucination of the ears,' offered Mike.

139

'Like the bells,' said Gabriel, gravely. 'The church bells, drowned at sea – there's a piece o' true history for you, not just stories in books.' He and Mike exchanged glances: best abandon Dickens, for a while!

'Susan Jones,' said Mike proudly, 'her that's soon to marry my son and knows history and how to find things out for her books, she told us from her computer all about the bells. The first Elizabeth, that's when the tale begins – and, even in them days, a Christmas in the business.' Nobody seemed very surprised. 'Upalong to Ploverton,' said Mike, 'but doubtless the same family as our Barney, Tollbridge having few inhabitants in them far-off times – times of religious upheaval. Church treasure confiscated, congregations fined for trying to hide their precious things – Exeter besieged, the city gates burned – riots, and folk killed – and all the church bells took down by authority to be melted into cannon for the wars against Philip of Spain.'

He hesitated, but decided to omit his Armada story, which didn't quite fit. 'This Christmas, then, he begged for rights in the Ploverton bell clappers and the iron furniture, being no use in gun-making but still worth money – or it may have bin his father, and 'twas the son later tried to make amends for riches acquired in such a fashion – but either way, as times grew less fraught the man eased his conscience by paying for a whole new ring o' bells from Bristol, to come by water' – he waved towards the channel, sluggish but glittering in the late summer sun – 'being easier transport than being drawn on a waggon by oxen or horses over the poor quality roads of long ago, not to mention the steepness of the many hills and valleys on the way. But there was sickness among the crew, and a delay in sailing, and a storm come up while they struggled to escape the shore but with the tide against them, weak from fever and too close to the rocks...'

Again he gestured seawards. 'Well, on the turn o' the tide they broke free at last, only too late, and the ship was lost with all hands – and with the bells.' He nodded slowly. 'The bells,' he said again, directing a deep, portentous sigh towards his brother-in-law.

Gabriel was about to seize his cue when Jinkins snatched it away. 'And the bells are still heard to ring a warning peal when there's danger or disaster ahead. See here, Barney Christmas told us about you two. One ghost ship, true or false, did ought to be enough for anybody. Only Combe Tollbridge dares lay claim to a brace o' such horrid apparitions!'

'Truth is,' said Sam Wilkins, 'he called you a pair of 'nointed old rascals and, for them as don't already know you, not to credit a word either of you said. Sorry.'

Mike and Gabriel looked pleased that their reputation had gone before them. They exchanged grins, and shrugged. 'Worth a try,' said Gabriel.

Even Jinkins had to smile at this, while everyone else chuckled.

'But,' said Mike, 'did Barney warn you, and being serious now, there was the Home Guard here during the war? Gabe and me, we remember it well. School in the daytime, Home Guard every night, and us boys curious to watch what they did, where we could.'

'Training and drill,' said Gabriel. 'Target practice wi' shotguns early on, then Lewis guns and a long metal pipe that pumped hand grenades into the air with steam.' He saw the doubting expressions from most of his audience, and scowled. 'I forget the name, but it's in the history books. You ask Susan Jones!'

'After the wedding,' said Mike hastily. 'But Gabe's right. There was a fishing boat took for the Navy, sunk by a mine afore this special pipe could be installed. A pity it should rust away on the quay, they thought, so, though 'twas never so accurate as a proper gun, our Home Guard borrowed it anyway.'

'Learned other tricks besides borrowing,' said Gabriel, as the doubters were silenced. 'How to set booby traps, and prime grenades – how to fill bottles wi' petrol for Molotov cocktails...

All manner o' fiendish devices they had against invasion, and no joking.

'So take heed, and be careful where you dig. It might be no more than clever photography, but that ghost ship could signify trouble ahead after all!'

Chapter Fifteen

The builders thanked their visitors for the warning, and waited for them to go away and let them get on with the job for which they were being paid. Gabriel and Mike decided to quit while they were ahead. They went. They also recalled that today was a Fish Day, which meant driving up to Ploverton, and the chance for more gossip.

After routine skirmishing it was agreed that Mike should drive the van, an elderly but well-maintained vehicle distinguished from others by the livery it wore with true family pride. The doors and bonnet were a strong sea green; everything else was a clear sky blue except where Jerry Hockaday, fired by creativity, had decorated the sides with two long white banners bearing, in neat black letters, the legend *Ornedge, Binns and Hockaday – Purveyors of Fresh Fish*.

Mike and Gabriel, like Barney Christmas and most of their contemporaries, never willingly admitted to age or physical frailty, but the loss of Sandy Joy had unsettled them. Mike was also aware that, thrilled though he might be at the forthcoming marriage, he would miss his son more than he cared to say. After all, hadn Mickey come back from travelling the world to keep his widowed father company? But Susan Jones-for-not-much-longer, like any bride, wanted a home of her own – and only

143

natural. Mike's Marguerite, gone for so long but brought to mind each time he saw her likeness in her son's features, had felt the same way; her sister Louise had happily agreed to a double wedding, but never to sharing a kitchen! No woman would.

Mike worried that he'd soon be seeing even more of the senior Hockadays, Gabriel and Louise, than ever. He knew this companionship would be kindly meant, but he feared it might encourage folk to think of him as a lonely old man unable to cope by himself, in need of cheering up. Mike Binns in need of cheering: the very thought was an insult!

Then it came to him that Gabriel, too, must be conscious of the passage of time, and looked now for reassurance. The pair had been friends long before they became brothers-in-law, from their schooldays in that same place Barney had set the builders to turning into a hotel. Barney was even older, and had (so far as anyone knew) never been married. Was Barney Christmas a lonely old man? Did anyone dare to think of him as such? Hadn the man friends of all ages? Such as the young incomer Jasper Merton (even if it had begun with a business connection) and his Jane, goddaughter to Miriam Evans – a distant cousin, though never taking advantage of the connection: a young woman welcomed by all when she came with her husband, a Londoner (like Mike himself) to live in the village she had (again like Mike) known from her earliest years.

Jane was not only a friend to Messrs Binns and Hockaday, but treated them with proper deference. The pair had admired, and together laughed over, the sketches she'd shown them of the Ride of the Valkyries and the bearded warriors; Jasper thought the characters might have potential as a comic strip, but Jane would take the matter no further unless the principals were agreeable. They had fully enjoyed the joke and, while not bothered about how they themselves were portrayed (so long as the beards kept their magnificence) their one request was that the goddess Louise should have sympathetic treatment – because (as Gabriel pointed out) young Jane didn't have to live with her, and he did.

'If I'm to be given a hard time by my wife, there's no doubting I'm bound to take it out on someone else, or burst! And, Mike being a convenient scapegoat for her wrath, 'twould be more than a touch unfair when the poor soul's to have troubles enough of his own all too soon, left by his new-wed son to rattle about in that cottage all alone, brooding in sorrow on the many past contentments lost to him for ever.'

Gabriel then sighed, and shook his head. Mike drooped pathetically as his brother-in-law clapped a sympathetic hand on his shoulder and shook his head again, slowly.

It was a splendid performance, which Jane had treated with the respect it deserved.

Right now any rattle was coming from the fish van being driven by the poor, soon-to-be-lonely old man away from Tollbridge's little pier with a load of crates in the back. What remained of last night's catch after Tabitha Ridd and others had made their purchases was to be offered to shoppers up in Ploverton: everything that remained – with one exception.

Mickey Binns wasn't the humourist his father and uncle all too often were, but he could enjoy a joke. When he'd announced that the *Priscilla Ornedge*'s overnight catch included a blue lobster the old gentlemen had duly scoffed – until Mickey produced the evidence, which clung halfway up the side of its pot and glared out with quick, beady black eyes.

'There's such things as pink grasshoppers,' said Mickey, 'for I've seen more than one photo of the genetic mutation; and flamingos will turn pink when they eat the right food, so why not lobsters? Though I believe that's genetics too, not feeding,' he added thoughtfully. 'Susan can look it up later, if she's the time.'

'A blue lobster,' said Gabriel. 'I've heard of such, though never yet seen one till now.' He studied Mickey's captive. A sizeable specimen, it waved long feelers and briefly detached one huge claw from the wickerwork, to open and close with a vicious snap. 'Now, I'd say that's no ordinary creature – and turned up bang on cue, what's more.'

Mike nodded. 'It's an omen, son – a good omen for your wedding. There's the something blue, you can't deny!' Tugging his beard he pondered further possibilities, and thought again about Boatshed Row's place in the Halfway Home schemes of Barney Christmas.

Combe Tollbridge harbour must once have been sufficiently busy to justify construction of the small pier alongside which was currently secured M.V. *Priscilla Ornedge*; but the longshore drift of local chezell – dragged daily to and fro by the mighty tides of the Bristol Channel, shifted and sculpted into banks and shoals by every Atlantic storm – could be kept at bay by only the most financially successful communities. Tollbridge had never enjoyed such success. Barney's sheds were sometimes rented out for storage, but were now so far from the water that everyday use by the fishing community was no serious practical option.

'A whole row of empty buildings,' mused Mike aloud. 'Surely one could be spared by the Half-to-Three-Quarters folk… No! We won't sell that lobster, not for love nor money. We'll build a tank, and keep fresh seawater pumping – and so long as he stays blue,' he added quickly, 'so will the good luck continue in your marriage.'

Gabriel knew the workings of his old friend's mind. Mike was thinking beyond the wedding to the general village benefit. Sacks of chezell raced along Harbour Path; ducks racing down the river – and the relaxing sight, close to, of a marvel of nature! 'The Octopus pump shouldn't be so hard to copy and adapt for the purpose,' he said. 'Easier than buckets carried in, night and morning – and well worth paying to see.'

'True. The spectacle is ever the thing.' Mike's sense of mischief was seldom long suppressed. He winked at Gabriel, and looked sideways at his son. 'I don't suppose Susan would be willing, for added luck, to walk the creature down the aisle on a length o' satin ribbon? Blue, for preference, though of a different shade—'

'White, for contrast,' said Gabriel at once. 'Or silver, mebbe – tied in a bow—'

'No!' Mickey had somehow missed the grins, and the gleam in his father's eye. 'And don't neither of you dare drop so much as a hint! It's to be a solemn blessing in church, not a circus act. My Susan's no – no Geraldine de Nerval to have a lobster on a string, quoting poetry and making a fool of herself!' He drew a deep breath. 'Be warned. Any more nonsense and this pot' – he snatched it up with both hands, and held it high – 'goes over the side the next time old *Priscilla* puts to sea. I mean it!'

Mike and Gabriel exchanged further glances. The groom, it seemed, was growing as nervous as any bride. Best apologise before he got really upset.

'Sorry, son. Just a bit of fun, is all. We didn't seriously think...' Mike shrugged helplessly, and ventured a smile.

Gabriel nodded. 'Got a bit carried away: sorry, boy. Not what you had in mind when you first showed us the creature, I'll be bound. Time may come when it might be a good idea, but...' And he, too, shrugged and smiled.

'But not this time.' Mickey, having made his point, began to calm down and see the funny side. An olive branch occurred: with his booted foot he gave the pot a gentle tap. 'Make a pet of this chap, and he'll need a name, same like any dog or cat. So how about Barney Blue? Who knows, old Christmas might even charge less rent for the shed, if that's where you plan to keep him with your fine new pump and all.'

'Might well charge more,' said Gabriel. 'Knowing Barney, probably will.'

'He can try,' said Mike. 'In which case we tell him the name's "Barnacle" for posh – and let the old devil make what he likes of that!'

The brothers-in-law continued to discuss and embellish various aquarium plans as they drove up Stickle Street, bound for Ploverton. Gabriel's white beard wagged furiously in the passenger seat as he laughed with his fellow conspirator over the wordplay possibilities to be had with the determined claws of a lobster, and the grasping clutch of the miser Barney liked people to believe he was.

The miser's workmen watched the little van approach; recognised the Father Christmas beard; heard the laughter. They saw the open window and, anticipating rural wit, prepared appropriate responses; but they weren't needed. Mike drove by with no more than a fanfare on the horn, and Gabriel made a hand gesture that might or might not have been rude. The van disappeared up the valley towards Ploverton.

In the anti-climactic silence that followed the workmen stared at one another, and shook their heads. Puzzled shrugs were exchanged. Perhaps the way Sam Wilkins had warned off them old devils earlier had gone home. Perhaps they'd accepted twadn no use trying to scare folk any further with ghost stories and warnings of wartime bombs.

'Or perhaps,' said Jinkins, 'there's fresh fish in that van nobody with any sense would wish to be kept too long outside the freezer.'

He had spoken. There was to be no more discussion. There followed a hurried and general resumption of the clearing, tidying, and preliminary exploration on which they'd all been previously engaged.

A rubbish skip had been delivered overnight, and of course the sub-contractors had dumped it in the wrong place. An argument followed this discovery; everyone saw different benefits to different locations and nobody was willing to back down for the convenience of anyone else. Jinkins used stern language, and reminded them that Barney Christmas was sure to be along some time that day to check he was getting his money's worth:

'And the doctors likely not so far behind, having house calls to make in the neighbourhood and only the one road, not to mention natural curiosity being part o' the human condition.'

'And they'm paying, same as Barney,' someone said, 'though busier in real life. That man have little else now to do save count his money and watch how it's spent. So, then...'

Further argument was abandoned as brute force and crowbars were organised, with chains and tow ropes and one or two squashed fingers to manoeuvre the empty skip a compromise three-trucks'-length further to one side of the main gate.

'What's that?' As the skip clanked into position, overgrown weeds were left flattened. Amid the tangle of mangled greenery a long, narrow, unidentifiable shape lay half revealed. Overall a dull brownish grey, at one end it gleamed faintly with a grubby metallic sheen.

'Don't like the look o' that,' someone said at last.

'And they dumped that skip pretty much on top of it,' breathed someone else.

'And us poor bloody fools moving the thing thirty foot at best – and never a thought to the risks we could be taking!'

'We don't know that,' said Sam Wilkins pacifically, as through shaded eyes he tried to make out what the sinister shape might be.

'Nor don't we know about *that*, neither.' Jinkins, too, was trying to identify the metal-ended object towards which nobody, not even Sam, liked to be the first to step. Workmen's boots had steel toecaps and heavy studs. After eighty years just how sensitive to vibration, or a careless spark, might an unused Home Guard weapon, left to deteriorate for decades in the open air, have become?

For some moments there was a thoughtful silence, broken only by an uneasy shuffling. Sam felt that he, as one of the oldest present, should make the first move, but his eyesight wasn't what it once had been. He'd have to get closer than might be wise; and for all he felt he ought to set an example, somehow he couldn't quite set it.

One of the younger workmen, something of a history buff, had an interest in the Second World War: he had believed the basics, at least, of Mike and Gabriel's Home Guard reminiscences. He coughed, and pulled out his mobile phone. 'Looks a bit like a potato masher, only bigger – a stick grenade,' he translated quickly. 'Such hand-held grenades went much farther when thrown than your basic Mills bomb, and them two old devils' – they knew who was meant – 'did say they'd a habit in these parts of – well, borrowing pieces of equipment, given the chance. We could send a photo to the police and ask if this might be something like that Holman projector they told us was borrowed when the boat sank, for pumping hand grenades in the air with steam – only this one for stick-bombs, or bigger. The police would know if the bomb squad should be told – evacuate the nearest houses—'

'Can't send nothing from here, young Huffam,' someone said. 'No signal. A mobile's a total waste of space in Tollbridge, save for photos.'

'Close-up view first.' Jack Huffam brandished his mobile phone. 'And then ask in the pub or post office who's got Wi-Fi to send it if needful.'

Silence once more fell as the workmen waited.

Sam Wilkins watched the camera come into its own. All along he'd felt uneasy; as the photography continued, his uneasiness grew. 'Be sure to bring it really close up,' he said. 'I don't know… We'll raise no alarm until we've checked and double-checked – not that I suspicion it can be aught to do with Mike and Cousin Gabe for all their wild tales. Whatever that thing might be, it's laid in the undergrowth a sight longer than they've had time to make a practical joke of it, but—'

'But it isn't.' Jack peered into his tiny screen, tilting it to and fro as he brought up the clearest possible image. 'The joke's on us, friends. More like a fence post, with creosote or similar colouring the wood and metal on the end protecting it in the ground.' He sighed, regretting the loss of a hitherto unknown experimental weapon; but the sighs of his colleagues as they crowded round were rather from relief they hadn't got carried away and made fools of themselves by reporting a non-existent emergency – and earning the wrath of Barney Christmas when they stopped work and further delayed his project.

Sam Wilkins nodded. 'I did wonder. This place have bin a school two hundred year, give or take, and eighty since the war and the Home Guard activities. Hard to suppose one o' the kids wouldn have uncovered that thing long afore now, and teachers having it cleared away if there was any danger. If we hadn seen Gabriel and Mike just now, we'd doubtless have straightway recognised that post for what it was.' He was brisk and decisive. 'So we'll think no more of them two and their nonsense, but leave 'em to whatever they'm about while we get on with doing what we're paid to!'

The nonsensical two just then were catching up on local events with Tom and Dora Tucker of Ploverton's Slandered Pig, a hostelry famed for its thatched roof and reed 'dolly' on the ridge. This fine example of woven straw commemorates the eponymous porker who, in the fourteenth century, was wrongly described as unfit for human consumption by a neighbour with a grudge that involved a storm-damaged fence, half a row of cabbages and five, possibly six, prize onions. The guilty pig's breeder had made due recompense as soon as possible but later, wrathful at the loss of a sale, was drowning his sorrows when he saw the neighbour enter the alehouse. Words were exchanged. Noses were punched. This time the village court had to impose a modest fine on both men, but local sympathies were very much with the breeder (and with the pig) and the neighbour grumbled all the more. The current pub dates from a later century, but stands on the original site.

Isadora Tucker's tongue, from her birth hung in the middle to wag at both ends, was always busy, except in the kitchen. Dora was proud of serving good pub grub, and raised a better pork pie than most in the West Country: she had a reputation to maintain, and when cooking liked to concentrate. She therefore reserved her chatter for non-culinary moments such as the visits of the fish van from downalong, when she could enjoy a good gossip – although at the back of her mind, despite every assurance of fair treatment, she suspected the Anchor's Tabitha Ridd of having managed, yet again, to buy the choicest specimens ahead of her.

Tom Tucker was less of a gossip and more to the conversational point than his wife. A giant of a man gone to seed (unlike Jan Ridd, who remained mostly muscle) Tom did his best to disguise an age-related tummy with a brown canvas apron whose pockets, over the years, had stretched and billowed to become a kindly camouflage that fooled nobody.

'Yes,' Tom said now, hands deep in his pockets, 'Joe Tuggs be missing old Sandy a sight more than he ever thought, though to me it comes as no surprise. The dog and the bird's company of a kind, but tidn the same, and can't never be—'

'And,' broke in Dora, 'so soon after losing his brother's made it all the worse. Joe and Sandy would always enjoy a laugh together, specially over them teeth, but young Lottie was never one to see the funny side, besides deeming it unhygienic – and now, having that bird laugh back in Sandy's own voice somehow makes it worser still for poor old Joe – which Lottie can't forget, nor seemingly forgive, not even in death, for all old Tuggs hisself would have took it as a joke and laughed every bit so loud as Crusoe. But she'm on and on at Joe all the time for bringing the poor creatures into the house, though she'd accepted 'em well enough on previous occasions – but permanent, she says, idn what she bargained for—'

'Nor feathers,' said Tom, as Dora paused for breath. Everyone chuckled; Gabriel and Mike guffawed. They all remembered the moth infestation and the borrowed chickens and Lottie's irritation at the mess blown over the garden fence.

'That Crusoe,' Tom remarked, 'have an uncommon knowing of words, for a bird, but always polite: you might suppose 'er had swallowed a dictionary. And lively! The tricks and screams and running up and down—'

'—and feathers everywhere,' broke in Dora, 'and laughing. Lottie says she'd take a gag to his beak, if she didn fear pecking.'

'But she can't complain similar of Turk,' said Mike Binns, in some relief. 'That dog haven't a mischievous bone in his body.'

'But he've a thick coat,' said Dora. 'Lottie carried on something cruel about the brushing. In the end she made Joe take the vacuum to him – only the hose bit,' she added hastily, as Mike's jaw dropped, 'wi' the liddle round brush and soft bristles. She says Turk, now he'm accustomed, he almost seems to enjoy it.'

Gabriel laughed. 'I'd like to see her try hoovering the parrot! But they've undertook a serious responsibility, her and her father, for all 'twas done at first with kindness, setting Sandy's mind at rest. Just goes to show how a kindly deed can come back to haunt you.'

There was a thoughtful silence as they pondered this difficult philosophy.

Tom roused himself first to be cheerful. 'Not long to the wedding, now,' he observed. 'You know where they're to honeymoon, Mike?'

'No idea,' said the bridegroom's father, with a grin. 'Mickey said he wadn having me and Gabe turn up wi' confetti and good luck messages piped over the public address system if they told us the name of the hotel.'

'You're going to miss Mickey,' said Dora, 'living together so many years as you have.'

'You'll miss the company,' said Tom. 'Someone to talk to. Thought of a lodger?'

'Maybe,' said Mike, 'young Angela, once the knot's tied, being near enough then her grandfather – or her friend Andy, only people would talk.' He winked. 'And then again, I might take to living on my own. When Mickey was away from home before it never bothered me, and,' as Tom and Dora exchanged looks, 'as for another dog, when I lost Bran all them years back I said I wouldn never have another dog – and I never have.'

Then he laughed. 'More-and-so, my hoover don't have a hose with a brush!'

Chapter Sixteen

The gang currently working at the Halfway Home Convalescent Hotel thought poorly of what had been achieved by those sent ahead to complete Stage One of the project. Far too much that should have been sorted then, they felt, had been left for them to sort.

'The lazy beggars! No more than faffing about with a feather duster!'

'Scarce enough to justify wages!'

'Old Barney would've kept his purse shut if they hadn earned it,' Sam Wilkins pointed out. 'I've not heard anywhere nobody wadn paid. Have anyone?'

'They've done the very leastest they could get away with, then—'

'—and the rest left for us, and not a penny of overtime we'll receive, more than like—'

'—so we'll do what we can,' said Sam, 'in working hours, and think it's lucky for some we'm able to sort their mistakes and do a better job than them.' He unfolded a plan of the site. 'Here's where we bring in the small digger and set the first trench. All right?'

Not even Jinkins cared to say it wasn't. Once work finally began they made slow, but steady, progress; Barney Christmas had his expectations, and if people failed to meet them they didn't work for him again. Sam's gang had known and worked for Barney a long time. He was firm, fair – and unpredictable. At any moment, they knew, the familiar figure might come stumping up the hill to see what they were doing and to demand, if they weren't, why not. He would probably have excused, or at least understood, the fence post delay, but he did like to get his money's worth, for which none could blame him. Worth millions now, wadn he? Only went to show the man had got it right, whatever it was!

Which explains why a shout from the driver of the digger, pausing his bucket and stopping the engine, caused anxious over-shoulder glances on all sides before tools were downed a second time, and everyone again converged upon an unexpected sight.

'What is it now?' Jinkins beat Sam to the question by half a second.

The older man raised his eyebrows at the driver for an explanation. The driver, leaping from his seat, had retreated several yards to point, speechless, at the most recent dump of soil and stones that with the rest made a guard of honour along one bank of the trench, giant molehills on parade. Half in, half out of the apex of the newest rubble hillock stuck a strange rectangular shape. Clods of excavated earth adhered to its surface.

Its metal surface.

'Something clanked in the bucket as didn feel like no stone, then I saw 'twas a touch glinty as I tipped it out.' Speech had returned now that reinforcements were beside – or rather, discreetly behind – the digger driver. 'O'course I thought o' that fence post, but this have altogether a different appearance – and, well...'

His colleagues murmured that indeed there was a difference. They shifted backwards on uneasy feet.

Jinkins looked about to speak, but Sam raised a stern hand. 'That cousin of mine have a deal to answer for – him and Mike

Binns and their Home Guard nonsense! Now listen up, all. Didn Barney remind us afore we started here? Didn I tell them two rascals plain we was awake to their tricks and tales and they laughed and went away? I ask you, did anyone ever see or hear tell of a bomb with corners and straight lines, the like o' that there?'

He turned to the history buff, who shook his head. 'Not as such,' said Jack slowly. 'Streamlined is best for weapons, for easy flight in air or water, but' – renewing earlier hopes shattered by identification of the fence post – 'there's no knowing what might not have bin part of some secret experiment as come to nothing, and that's why nobody's heard of it, which o'course idn to say it never exist—'

'Rubbage!' Jinkins could contain himself no longer. 'Let me but take a pick to the thing and we'll soon see how bloody secret it can be!'

Again Sam cautioned with a stern hand. 'First we take a closer look, soce.' The friendly form of address gave Jinkins pause. Sam nodded. 'We use our brainboxes upon the matter. Now, think. If being dug from the ground and dropped in a heap didn explode that-there thing, if explosion was its original purpose, then us walking careful in our boots should be safe to approach for a looky-see.' He smiled at Jack Huffam. 'And maybe photos, too.' Jack brightened. 'So come on, all!' cried Sam.

It was hardly an enthusiastic stampede, but nobody went in the other direction. With dignity the carpenter led his little party of pressed volunteers towards the mysterious metallic shape. They stood around the heaped-up rubble, and stared at what was on top.

At last: 'Seems there's no great need for your camera,' said Mr Wilkins to Mr Huffam.

Jack was too disappointed at this second anti-climax for any words to come. It was an effort even to sigh, or to force a rueful grin.

'Buried treasure,' said Jinkins in a tone that showed he didn't believe it. 'Looks like one o' them old-time cash boxes, though bigger than most, and hard to be sure – and might be something altogether other, being that size.'

'And might not,' someone said. 'Stands to reason you'd have a box adequate for a large treasure, if a large treasure's what you wish to bury.'

'But for why would anyone want burying a treasure box in the grounds of a village school?' someone else wanted to know.

Jack stirred. 'Might not have bin a school when they did it: buried back in historical times, such as the Civil War or the Monmouth Rebellion, or fear of Napoleon invading. Not the Great War, o'course, nor the Second with Hitler, for this place is Victorian and built long before them eventful days.'

Sam Wilkins was thinking. 'A part of history, none the less, whatever it might be and whenever buried. Remember, Barney means to preserve the general atmosphere, where appropriate. In the public rooms there's to be displays of such mementoes found about the village – writing slates and pencils, school-books, old photos…' It was Sam's proud and skilful hand that would lead the way in designing and assembling the necessary display shelves and cases, once suitable items had been selected and the best locations chosen.

'A cane or two,' suggested Jinkins. 'A leather strap!'

'No, a leather slipper.' Even Jack was starting to see the lighter side.

'Or one o' them blackboard dusters made of wood,' someone said, 'got throwed at you for misbehaving? Talk about stream-lined. Not!'

'Nor wadn a stick o' chalk so much the better,' said Sam, 'but it smarted all the same.'

There was a burst of laughter. Even Jinkins had to smile.

'So, then.' The carpenter brushed his hands. 'We agree this box is no great danger?'

As they fell again to contemplation, a lump of soil broke away and dropped off, revealing more of the metal surface.

'A cash box?' The history buff was doubtful. 'Similar in shape and colour, true – but I dunno.' His eyes gleamed. Maybe, after all…

'Can't judge a book by its cover,' Jinkins reminded him sourly.

'Clanked in my bucket most alarming,' offered the digger driver.

'Unlikely to be buried treasure,' said Sam, 'but we did ought to check.' He frowned at Jinkins. 'Though I can't say I'm happy with the notion of a pickaxe.'

'Nor me,' said Jack. 'But a cold chisel and hammer to the lock shouldn't distress anything overmuch, if carefully applied – you reckon?'

'We-ell,' said Sam. '*Very* carefully applied.' He took pity on the young man. 'I'd say it's you and me, soce; and, your legs being less creaky than mine, it's for you to scramble up top and do the hammering while I pass the tools and catch whatever might be let fall.' He gazed about him. 'Tools?'

Jack was in his element. Having duly scrambled up, and confirmed the find as a large, black enamelled metal box 'wi' the lid soldered tight against air or water' he used his phone to photograph it before taking a stout, cautious stick to clear what remained of debris and soil. If he listened for any clockwork tick, he did not say so. With the stick as a crowbar, tapping with the chisel, he dug half under the box, and with a jerk tumbled it free. The handle rattled as it shook loose – and a yell came from the history buff as he rubbed a trembling finger over the lid and peered down at what was revealed.

'A brush! A brush here, quick!' He flung away the crowbar stick, stuffed hammer and chisel in the cargo pockets of his trousers, and began to drag the cashbox to level ground, at the base of the spoil heap.

'Look at that!' He controlled shaking hands to steady the box, and again whipped out his phone. 'Just look, will 'ee!'

To the faded lid was affixed a metal plate on which a few words and a date had once been engraved, now given back to the light by the rub of a trembling finger.

'Eighteen-seventy... three, mebbe five,' breathed Jack, peering closer. 'A century and half and more this-here box have waited to be found – and we found it!'

Sam Wilkins was offered a brush but shook his head, and yielded privilege to Jack, telling him to busy himself 'on account of there idn a man among us not curious to know what message might be coming down the ages' and then they could all get back to work, for fear Barney Christmas might arrive and find them slacking.

The history buff was for some moments keenly busy; he took more photos and cleared his throat. '*Combe Tollbridge School Official Opening 1875,*' he read aloud. 'Not ezackly buried treasure in general terms, but buried history in a time capsule, and resurrected!' His eyes sparkled. 'Whatever it might be. Items of commemoration, at a guess—'

'—and the property of Barney Christmas,' Jinkins reminded everyone. 'Found on his land, and him paying the wages of them that found it.' He sensed opinion move against him, and added: 'Mark you, after so many years, airtight or no, could be nothing has survived that's worth the effort of breaking it open. Remember, old Barney don't hold with wasting time. Could be our wisest course is to open it up aforehand?'

This was more to his companions' taste. Their curiosity surely deserved satisfaction when, for aught anyone knew, they might have bin risking their lives when that box was first uncovered! Again they contemplated their find in silence. They saw a keyhole, and a padlock to which soil, long dried in lumps, still adhered – and, as Jack had told them, a heavy bead of solder round the lid.

And they saw Jack with, in his pockets, the cold chisel and the hammer he'd been so keen to use, not so very long ago…

But now young Mr Huffam hesitated. Historian first, builder second: or the other way round? Differing interests: one dilemma. 'Backalong,' he said slowly, 'they made things to last. More-and-so, for a time capsule they'd be sure to choose the best.'

'If they could afford it,' said Jinkins.

'Stands to reason they'd make the effort for an official opening. But the worth of buried treasure's… debatable: gold coins or broken pots or an old newspaper, all depends on the interpretation, and who makes it. We should mebbe ask someone with better knowledge of local history than any of us, before we start to interfere.'

'Best leave it to old Barney.' Sam Wilkins had made up his mind. 'As has bin said,' with a nod for Jinkins, 'this-here's his property. His school. His village! I doubt even he'm old enough to have bin present when the box was first committed to the ground' – his workmates chuckled – 'but that man have a right to know ahead of others what's inside, should he so wish – or to leave it unknown; and most of all, to make choice of who's the one best to ask what should be done with the thing.'

Jinkins nodded back to Sam, and even found a smile for Jack. 'Knowing old Barney, I'd remind everyone it likely won't be long afore he's up here watching what we'm about – until which time, I'd now agree the whole business should be set to one side.'

And there, to some relief and some disappointment, the matter was left.

The Tuckers had returned to the Pig, leaving Mike and Gabriel to chat with the fish fanciers of Ploverton and others who just fancied a chat. The thwarting and capture of the oil thieves through the good offices of the goats and the postman was told for the umpteenth time, with appropriate improvements, ending as ever with 'and serve the beggars right!' and roars of laughter. Several people refurbished anecdotes of the late Thomas Joy; the brothers-in-law heard – and savoured – various imaginative twists to the Great Hospital Escape they wished they themselves had thought of at the time.

'Joe Tuggs still takes it hard,' someone said, to a general shaking of heads and the click of sympathetic tongues. 'Misses the man something cruel, coming as it did so soon after losing his brother. A daughter's never the same, no matter how she may try.'

It was pointed out that Miss Charlotte Tuggs was trial enough, the death of her uncle and her father's best friend notwithstanding, being a woman of spirit and strong opinion –

'Bossy,' said a realist.

'Naggy,' said another. 'Oh, she've accepted the dog and the parrot on account of Joe's promise to Sandy, but she don't never let her father forget 'twas a foolish promise to make, given Turk be still in his prime and how long that-there bird could live.'

'A promise is a promise,' said someone else. 'Neighbours since marriage, Joe and Sandy. Always there for talk and sharing a joke, even if Joe's hearing idn now what it was – but they'd bin acquainted so many years it didn matter, on account of each knowing pretty well aforehead what t'other was likely to say.'

'Ah, there's great comfort in a long acquaintance.' Everyone nodded. Gabriel and Mike caught each other glancing sideways and, embarrassed, each looked quickly away. 'You'm in the right of it, a daughter's never the same.'

'Neither's a son,' said someone determined to look on the bright side. 'So what's the latest on the wedding, Mike?'

Mr Binns launched into an update but, in full and enthusiastic flow, sensed the attention of his audience begin to drift. He looked beyond the gathering to observe, heading purposefully towards the van, a gleaming black dog at her side and a wicker basket on her arm, a female form fast ripening into luxuriant plumpness.

He broke off. 'Morning, Lottie! Treating your Turk to shellfish? We've just the one crab left, if he wouldn mind the crunching – which o'course you wouldn, hey, boy?'

As Charlotte Tuggs drew near she let Turk's lead slip, her mouth a-twitch as the dog rushed straight to his friend Mr Binns for fussing. His ears were gently pulled, his noble ruff was stroked and admired; she wasn't even sure Mike heard her as she answered:

'Oh no, he wouldn but, though I'll take the crab at a fair price, the dog gets none of it. A bone after Sunday dinner does for cleaning his teeth. I wouldn waste crab shell on a dog! Makes a nourishing stock, broke small and carefully simmered.' Like many local ladies Miss Tuggs was a fine cook. Her plumpness was not altogether due to heredity.

After making her purchases and chatting with her Ploverton acquaintance, Charlotte remained as others began moving away. She looked thoughtfully towards Gabriel as Mike continued to make a fuss of Turk.

'Seems you pair have finished your business here?' Gabriel agreed that they had. 'So unless you've to rush on otherwheres, I'd take it kindly if you'd both stop by for a visit with Dad. Tidn so much he's in want of cheering, no matter what others may say – but what I say is, he needs some sense talked into him.'

Gabriel blinked; even Mike looked up, and stopped rubbing Turk under his chin. The dog butted his head with force sideways against Mike's knees. Mr Binns resumed his caresses. Gabriel grinned, then sobered as Charlotte went on:

'Dad says a promise is a promise, but it's on me the burden of keeping that promise falls. He idn ezackly in the best of health, never mind advanced in years.' Gabriel said nothing. Mike said nothing. 'And it's getting too much even for me,' said Joe's daughter, 'which is what I can't make him understand. You two might have better luck telling him he idn the only one not so spry as once they were. Oh, tidn that it's on purpose he don't hear me. I'll accept his ears aren't so keen as they were – nor his eyes, meaning he don't recognise how much extra needs doing when there's a dog wants regular brushing brought into the house, not to mention feathers everywhere, and sand kicked from the cage and the tray cleared daily from under the perch. A bird's more of a trial than a dog in so many ways. A dog might wap, or bark, or howl – but not all the time! Dad don't hear the half of what that Crusoe comes out with, beyond thinking it the usual chittery of a bird, which mostly it is. But all the chackling and the laughter and the bell – well, the noise would drive a body mad!'

'Language of character?' Gabriel was surprised. 'Colourful?' He'd always considered Crusoe to be a sprightly but well-mannered bird.

'Blue,' suggested Mike with relish. 'Deep blue, if not purple—'

'Rubbage!' Charlotte glared at them. 'That bird just don't seem willing nor able to keep quiet about the house, and there's a limit to how much rumpus anyone should have to put up with. Nothing wrong with *my* hearing.'

'Throw his night-cloth over the cage,' said Gabriel.

'He pulls it through the bars and chews holes and starts up again, morning and evening regular as a theatre performance – and most o' the rest of the day, likewise.'

'He misses Sandy same like anyone, no doubt,' said Mike. 'Poor Turk, now' – the dog swished a friendly tail – 'he refused his dinner, didn he, the very day the old chap died? And how he could have known is a mystery, but he did, or so I heard.'

Charlotte acknowledged the truth of the tale, adding that it had been only the once. 'And it's certain he've made up for it since! Plenty of tasty scraps, o'course, and don't think we grudge him proper vittles – and he's company around the house, never mind when either of us walks out.' She smiled, a little ruefully.

'I could lose a few pounds and gladly spare them – but you can shut a dog outdoors if needful, which you can't with a parrot on account of their tropical nature. Our place have no room for an aviary even if I was willing to put up with all the mess and confusion – but it's the noise that's the worst.'

'Still laughs in Sandy's own voice, we've heard,' said Gabriel. 'Uncanny listening, I would think, him having bin so close a friend.'

'If he'm able to hear it.' Mike gave Turk's ears a final tug, and straightened.

'Sometimes hears the bell,' said Charlotte, 'though as a rule too high and tinkly for him, he says. But I hear it every time, and know what's to come – which is Sandy Joy laughing his fool head off, out of that parrot's beak! *All hands on deck!* and *Man the guns!* in Sandy's voice after he've climbed to the top and rung the bell, and then he laughs, and sometimes talks poetry, which again Dad don't always hear beyond thinking it general chattery – and he laughs again! You've seen them ladders, and the perches. Such extravagance, for a bird!'

Gabriel nodded. 'Made it himself, didn he? The ladders and the perch and the bell at the top. Proper craftsmanship. Sandy said nothing was too good for that parrot.'

'Belonged to his son,' Mike reminded his friend sadly. 'Keeping the memory green, he said, which is why he made such a rare job of it, for young Tommy's sake.'

There was a respectful pause as they acknowledged the skill of the master carpenter in the grim aftermath of the floating mine.

'Yes,' said Charlotte at last. 'Rare – and worrisome, for fear of breakage. When I want running the hoover across the floor, as with that bird is every day – and with other calls on my time as well' – she looked pointedly at Turk of the thick, glossy black coat – 'then I've a pretty job of it to shift the thing careful without asking for assistance, which with Dad how he is I don't care to do unless I really must.'

Again she looked at Turk, once more urging Mike to pay him attention. 'One or t'other of them I'll let stay,' she said. 'Not both. You two come with me and make Dad see sense: I can't stand much more of this. I mean it.' She played her trump card. 'There's a fruit cake, baked only yesterday.'

'Oh, you'm a temptatious woman, Lottie Tuggs,' said Gabriel.

'She drives a cruel hard bargain,' said Mike. 'But Joe's an old friend—'

'And fruit cake's not to be wasted,' said his brother-in-law happily.

Joe Tuggs was a little dark-faced man with shiny hair, twinkling eyes and a body of very considerable thickness. His daughter greatly resembled him in build: her late mother had been decidedly comfortable in form, and Charlotte was even more decided. Food was there to be enjoyed and, like her father, she enjoyed it.

They found Joe eating pickled salmon with a pocket-knife, a mug of cider on the table before him. 'Not in the mood for sugary stuff,' he explained, as Charlotte began to scold.

'Sugar and spice and all things nice!' cried Crusoe, dancing in welcome up and down an Eiffel Tower lookalike that stood four or five feet high, a lattice of wooden ladders varying in length, cross-tied for stability with a series of perches. Above the parrot's head the bell's brass chain rattled and swung as he jigged, bobbed and bowed. 'Sweets to the sweet! Yo-ho-ho and a bottle of rum! Man the guns! Man the pumps!'

He was a handsome bird with feathers of silvery grey, a black beak, and a red tail which he spread for balance as he suddenly shrieked, flapped his wings and turned upside down. 'Man the guns! Man the pumps! Abandon ship!'

He then emitted a scream of laughter, forcing Mike and Gabriel to clap their hands over their ears. Joe, with a grin, speared another tasty morsel from the pickle jar.

Chapter Seventeen

Sam Farley was entertaining visitors. He hadn't intended this, but in a small community such things sometimes happened and the Coastguard Printery was currently a bustle of coffee mugs, biscuit tins and chatter.

Andromeda Marsh had been the first arrival, bringing for Sam's professional attention the new job-hunting flyer Jane Merton, one night in the pub, had redesigned from Andy's London original. Miss Marsh was still Handy Andy, proud and competent Jill of All Trades; the practical skills on offer remained the same, but instead of dungarees and a baseball cap the cartoon handywoman sported jeans, shirt and a rustic waistcoat. The heavy work-boots were identical. At Andy's request Jane had drawn a second sketch of the young JOAT chewing a thoughtful straw as she held her electric drill 'to show I always focus on the job I'm doing,' said Handy Andy.

She and Sam were debating the relative merits of JOAT with, or without, the straw when Angela arrived, a little pink and slightly puzzled. She wasn't bothered about playing gooseberry: Andy was all business, and so was Sam; but Angela looked – and even spoke – as if she wasn't quite sure why she'd taken time off work to be there.

'But he did say,' she explained, 'that he thought I might be interested – Rodney Longstone, I mean. When I saw him yesterday he told me he was expecting a – a call here on the headland about this time today—'

'Rather later than that now, I suspect.' It was the captain himself who spoke, entering with a brief tap on the printery door and smiling round at everyone, with a nod of apology to his host. Sam nodded back, smiling for a different reason. After so many years in Tollbridge giving little more than the time of day, how that man had come out of his shell since getting to know Susan Jones's daughter! Well done, Angela Lilley!

'Coffee's quicker'n tea,' was all Sam said out loud. 'All right by you, Cap'n? So you expect a call here – on my number, would that be?'

'Coffee would be most kind, thank you, but I wouldn't presume any further on your kindness by tying up your landline with my private – that is, more or less – with my own affairs.' Rodney changed the subject. 'Ginger biscuits!'

He made straight for the tin, hesitated, and sadly shook his head. 'From a packet? Dear me. Angela, what do you think?'

'Words fail me.' Angela helped herself and proceeded to munch.

Talk became general. The captain was asked his opinion on Andy-with-a-straw or Andy-without, but couldn't decide between them because 'I know nothing about art, and wouldn't wish to insult Jane's creativity by preferring one above the other' which made his friends laugh with, not at, him. Sam's inward smile broadened as he saw Angela's public smile, quickly suppressed though it was. And about time, too!

Angela praised to the others the skill of Handy Andy in successfully opening the box of the Doubly Seceding Little Emmanuel, after several sessions of careful oiling.

'Wish I hadn't bothered.' Andy shuddered with exaggerated distaste. 'Grim, or what! I don't know who or what they were seceding from – but I wouldn't blame anyone who wanted to secede from *them*. What a record to leave for posterity!'

Angela sighed. 'The Roll of the Righteous – but very far from your average membership list. A sort of diary of general behaviour, too.'

'List of punishments,' said Andy. 'Talk about sanctimonious! Gloating about how the backsliders and sinners should pay their dues and might, if they paid enough, *might* in time earn forgiveness – for playing football, or singing songs instead of hymns, or reading Dickens on Sunday, or – or stringing acorns to make a necklace! Jewellery's not really my thing, but it made me want to go right out and buy a tiara.'

'It was what they didn't actually say that was worse.' Angela likewise shuddered. 'So-and-so was playing with her little sister, who'd made a daisy chain for her hair: vain adornment, you see; trying to improve on, which means doubt, the wisdom of the Almighty. Baby sister was "publicly rebuked" in the tabernacle – but the older girl was "privately chastised" later, by Brother Something, for not having stopped the poor child falling into sin. Ugh.'

Sam nodded. 'It was ever said they were a hard religion, but they kept theirselves to theirselves so nobody rightly knew – and all so long ago, it's now mostly forgotten. Which is just as well!' He deliberately changed the subject. 'This caller of yours, Cap'n – you've warned him the signal's not always reliable, even so high up as here?'

'That won't be a problem. They've already called me at home to say they'd be late – which explains my own tardiness, as I had meant to be here in good time to let you know to expect' – Rodney smiled – 'company.'

Sam deduced company in the plural, unless the captain was trying not to let on that his guest was female – though they'd all find that out soon enough and, if it was going to upset Angela, why ask either of 'em here in the first place? It was too much for a man to puzzle over; he tried for a non-committal response. 'Then best go easy on the ginger snaps, as I've no more in the larder. Mugs and coffee enough, and sugar, but—'

'Please don't worry about it,' said the captain. He smiled at Angela. 'I doubt if they'll be staying too long – just a flying visit, really – but of interest, I think.'

Angela reminded herself that he'd thought it worth asking her to take the morning off to meet these mysterious not-yet-here flying visitors; and he wasn't bothered by the presence of others. A sudden thought occurred; she felt a blush begin, and her second self-reminder was that she was still anti-man. But she knew the blush was deepening, and she started to giggle. How likely was it – seriously – to be Rodney's parents, looking her over!

'You've explained about parking up here rather than down by the harbour?' Andy did her best to divert attention from her pink-faced friend. 'It's a climb and a half up Coastguard Steps if you're not used to it. Some of 'em might not be too fit.'

'Parking, like biscuits, should be no problem, but you're right. Some of them aren't as fit as others.' He smiled. 'The desk-bound types who enjoy their biscuits rather too much, at a guess! The exercise of the Steps would have done them good.'

'Sounds to be a variable crowd,' said Sam. 'Mixed company?' He would never have put such a question to the captain even a few short months ago.

'Ladies and gentlemen, you mean?' Before today, nobody remembered ever seeing such a twinkle of mischief in Rodney Longstone's eye. 'The – yes, we'll say gentlemen – are coming with one they refer to as Cherry B, and' – he cocked his head to one side – 'here, I believe, they come at last.' He checked his watch. 'Yes, I'm sure that must be them.' They heard a far-off mechanical hum, growing steadily louder. 'Do follow me, if you would care to meet them?' He glanced round at everyone, but his smile was directed mainly at Angela, who smiled back and followed him outside.

The steadily increasing hum turned everyone's attention to a distant airborne object now approaching from the general direction of HMS *Whirlybird*, the stone frigate, otherwise Royal Navy shore establishment, further along the coast, where some of the captain's friends continued in service. The occasional 'buzz' from a high-spirited helicopter pilot wasn't unknown in Combe Tollbridge – but if this new arrival was a helicopter, it was a model unlike any ever seen before.

'That can't be a flying saucer,' said Andy. 'Can it? Rodney, don't say you've arranged a close encounter of the third kind!'

'An encounter, yes, if they land according to plan. Flying, certainly – but as to saucer, all I can say is, have you ever seen a saucer that looked anything like that?'

Nobody had. They watched as the flying not-saucer drew closer, a giant drone with three huge rotors triangularly placed at different heights, with another, far smaller, rotor extended horizontally on a stick-like tail to the rear of the… conveyance, thought Angela. The triplane? She glanced at Rodney, and saw the modest smile that yet held a hint of pride. The early retired captain still drove into Taunton every fortnight for his regular, if unspecified, meeting at the Hydrographic Office; a Tollbridge local had recognised him, or rather his car, enter to a formal salute. One or two questions at the security gate had partly satisfied; guesswork did the rest. It seemed that the… device now heading for Watchfield Point might be a result of those mysterious meetings.

As Angela puzzled, the other two continued to exclaim and discuss. Andy thought the overall design less streamlined than her motorbike; Sam wasn't sure this would have much bearing on efficiency. Andy marvelled at how quiet it was; both agreed that the power of the thing was amazing.

Angela, no mechanic, said that as it clearly stayed up in the air, and was moving well as far as she could judge, she supposed this to be the object of the exercise.

They all looked to Captain Longstone for an official opinion. He nodded.

'Objective achieved – so far; but we'll let her land safely before giving a final verdict on this latest outing for the Cherry B: more formally, the current prototype of the Charybdis helicopter that's to replace our fleet of Maelstroms as they reach the end of their operational life. She's finished the purely experimental stage and is getting ready for public demonstration – as you can see.' The Charybdis had come to a sudden halt, swivelled her tail rotor, and performed a swift vertical figure-of-eight before resuming her steady Watchfield approach.

There were more exclamations of surprise from the non-naval types on the ground.

The captain chuckled. 'I'll uncross my fingers now: that was higher and wider than I've seen her go before. Looping the loop's probably too much to ask, ditto a victory roll, but some impressively complicated manoeuvres have been achieved and of course, in an emergency, you need to be prepared for the unexpected. The number of air-worthiness tests that have surprised us, you wouldn't believe! So when the latest was scheduled it, ah, occurred to one or two colleagues that I might find it of professional interest if' – apologetically, he cleared his throat – 'if they were to pay me a – well, a flying visit.'

His friends emitted appropriate and appreciative groans, but fell silent to gaze upwards and admire as the Charybdis arrived overhead and hovered, slowly rotating in a clockwise direction. Rodney permitted four rotations and then began waving his arms, semaphore fashion. When he'd finished, a bright light flickered in elaborate Morse from the Charybdis; Rodney was laughing even before the message had concluded.

'I wondered if they knew that one! I signalled: *You're making us all dizzy. Please go round the other way* and they sent back *A new broome like me always sweeps clean* – oh, yes, the old ones are the best. Broome with an "e" after Captain Jackie of that ilk, a legend in his own lifetime.' He warmed to his theme, relaxed as few had seen him. 'Jack Broome was a convoy escort commander in the Second World War, being driven mad by an enemy reconnaissance plane that kept circling his ship just outside the reach of even his largest guns. In the end he grabbed a signal lamp and flashed what I've just said about dizziness, and the German flashed back that he'd understood – and did as he was asked, while keeping safely out of range, of course. Now it looks as if they might be landing. We're safe enough here, but – Sam, are your windows closed? I'm sorry, but I've only just thought about downdraft, and papers being disturbed.'

'Thank you, Cap'n, but there's little to fret over at present beyond Andy's leaflets, and they'm only samples so it don't really matter.'

'Oh? It might matter very much, to me.' Andy ignored his grin, and tried to look stern. She failed. 'Okay, okay, it might not, because I saw you leave your notebook on top. Do you always weigh things down like that?'

'Since I moved up here wider open to the four winds than my old place, I do.'

There was less need to raise their voices now because the Charybdis, having tilted back and forth several times as an aeroplane might waggle its wings, had begun moving away from the little group beyond the spot allocated for the Coastal Watch headquarters towards an open patch of ground.

'On the tripod principle, three skids – shock absorbers – give a more stable landing than the usual two,' the captain explained. 'More adjustable than the usual, as well.'

'I do hope,' said Angela, 'you won't feel duty bound to shoot us now you've let us into a state secret.' She was smiling; he was laughing again.

'Didn't I tell you the first public demonstration isn't far off? I should say you're at least reasonably safe from wholesale slaughter.'

'Much safer, when you think about it.' Andy's eyes danced. 'The best marksman in the world could get only one of us at a time, and the other two would naturally rush him – you – and disarm you. And even one dead body would be tricky to get rid of up here, where the ground's near enough solid rock.' ('Don't we know it,' moaned Sam, recalling preliminary excavation work for the Coastal Watch building.) 'Three bodies,' continued Miss Marsh, 'would be kind of obvious if you chucked us from the clifftop for the tide to take away. Far too much of a good thing, that would be. Overkill – and how!'

Their smiles hadn't quite faded as the helicopter found the right spot and gently settled on her three landing skids. A diminishing whine heralded the slowing, then stopping, of the rotors. Everyone looked at Rodney.

'Come on,' he invited; and the little party set off for a close encounter with Charybdis.

The door opened and a young man in naval uniform jumped down, followed by five other nimble uniforms and one male mammoth in civilian dress, who was slower. As this laggard waved a greeting, Captain Longstone stopped in his tracks.

'Good grief! Jonny Doe, in person – after all these years!'

'The one and only – and I've a bone to pick with you, Captain Restronguet,' roared the mammoth as he drew near. The uniforms, staying back, nudged one another and grinned at this joke successfully played on the unsuspecting Longstone.

'Several bones,' John Doe amended in his cheerful bellow. 'You cunning old devil – the sleepless nights you've given me' – and, reaching his friend, with a meaty finger he prodded him in the chest, following this up with a hearty slap across the shoulders.

Rodney Longstone staggered a few steps, then recovered. 'Jonny – everyone' – his gaze embraced the grinning uniforms as well as his friend – 'welcome to Combe Tollbridge and, ah,

174

thanks for dropping in. How was the flight? Oh – my manners. Introductions first.'

These were made. The Tollbridge contingent was at first puzzled that Rodney's John Doe was introduced formally as Commander Jonathan Hynde, naval boffin (retired) 'and former partner in crime of this merry lad here,' enlarged the commander, with another slap for the Longstone shoulders. 'There's been a gallon or two of water flow past the periscope since then – true, Restronguet, you old rascal?'

'Oceans,' agreed Captain Longstone. With a quick and quelling frown he moved across to join the uniforms, plunging into their discussion without missing a technical beat. Commander Doe/Hynde (it didn't take long to work this out) followed him, producing notebook and pencil from one capacious pocket while some of the younger element returned to the Charybdis to retrieve their own clipboards and files.

Tollbridge wondered about making a discreet departure, but the first uniformed figure broke away from the animated group of experts to grin at them. 'Take a look around,' he invited, waving an arm adorned with braid and badges. 'Don't pull any levers or press any buttons, but otherwise, feel free. Make as if you're members of the public at a Navy Day! You'll be good practice for the real thing in a few weeks' time.'

Three members of the public shared expectant glances. 'Captain Longstone did tell us,' began Angela, 'we wouldn't be betraying any state secrets…'

'There you are, then. The wash-up itself shouldn't take long – the debrief,' he translated swiftly, 'the techno talk – but then there's the big reunion. Old Hynde lives somewhere near Hadrian's Wall, and that pair haven't met up, apart from video conferences, since Long John Silver's parrot was an egg.' He grinned again. 'They were in the same term, same ideas, but our Jonny was a well-built lad even then. He would have passed his Perisher fine – got command of a sub – but he banged his swede' – he tapped his head – 'once too often, and decided he'd be happier working somewhere with more elbow room. Still needs it, too! We practically had to shoe-horn him into the cabin with the rest of us, but it was worth it just to see old Rodney's face.' He gestured towards the captain, laughed, and with another airy wave returned to the wash-up.

Angela, Andy and Sam looked at each other. 'Ladies first,' said Sam.

'And nobody touch anything, remember,' said Angela.

'Pity.' Andy's mechanical interest had been thoroughly awakened. She couldn't wait to start looking around. Sam was quite as interested as she, and Angela had no intention of missing out. She guessed it wouldn't be long before other *members of the public* arrived on the headland; too much of a crowd would spoil the fun. The Charybdis must surely be one of the most distinctive vehicles – she hesitated over the term – vessels? No – one of the most distinctive *craft* (neutral, acceptable) ever to visit Combe Tollbridge. The recent ghost ship didn't count, being a mirage visible for miles along the coast; this remarkable three-rotor helicopter was right here, on the spot, a chance not to be missed for adding another legend to the rich Tollbridge store.

If Rodney's logic (mused Angela) hadn't so laughingly dismissed the idea of a flying saucer of this peculiar shape, she could envisage Gabriel and Mike assuring future tourists that alien invaders had come to the village and abducted one or two locals for experimentation, these individuals having made miraculous and high-couraged escapes after which, thwarted, the aliens had beaten a decided and permanent retreat.

Angela smiled still as she hurried after Andy. If Mike and Gabriel were ever to tell such a tale, she wouldn't have to guess at the identities of those high-couraged escapees.

Chapter Eighteen

Setting aside the commemorative box for Barney's personal attention, his workmen returned to work using equipment that made a lot of noise. They wore ear defenders (Mr Christmas might be careful with money, but he also took care of those who earned it for him) and were conscientious employees. This, and the flightpath of the Charybdis from HMS *Whirlybird* having followed the coastal rather than the overland route, meant there were fewer witnesses than might be expected for the activity on Watchfield Point.

Barney, stumping up Stickle Street, paid more attention to the mechanical sounds he heard ahead of him than to any curious hum, whine or rattle that might be heard astern. It was even possible he didn't hear them, but it would be presumptuous to suppose this. Perhaps, mindful of his age, he worried about losing his balance and falling if he turned too quickly to look back, preferring to focus on whatever might (or should) be happening at the old school because he, after all, was paying for it to happen.

When he appeared work was paused while Sam Wilkins detached the history buff from his mates and, with Jinkins adding remarks intended to be helpful, told of the box's discovery as Jack did his best to show the photos. Barney said these were a touch on the small side, but he'd got the general idea and would take young Huffam's word for the rest which, with the box in front of them as proof, should give no cause for argument. 'Found on my property and therefore mine to do with as I think fit – which I suggest is a prime position display case, glass-fronted.' He nodded to the carpenter. 'Another job for you, Sam Wilkins.'

'But should it be opened and the contents examined, or not?' agonised the history buff. 'We did perhaps ought to check with the museum before—'

'Young Angela,' growled Barney, 'is no true historian, as she'll admit if asked. She'm a librarian doing the village a kindness – though being paid for it,' he added, 'if not full-time, to honour Cousin Prue Budd and the family, and the village as a whole.'

'The *county* museum, is what I meant.' Jack had thought about this even as he worked. 'They've the equipment – expert knowledge – degrees, and historical qualifications—'

'And your *qualified* historian, given the chance, is a damsight too keen throwing a spanner in anyone's business that makes enquiry!' Barney spoke with the conviction of bitter experience. 'They either hold back a project long and longer while they make further enquiry – or they'm over hasty to claim keeping what was asked about for their own purposes. What's found in Combe Tollbridge belongs to Tollbridge and should stay here – or,' a grudging concession, 'in Ploverton, being the same family, if distant; only they've no plans for a museum upalong that I've heard, and so would be willing to share. As families do.'

'The county museum,' urged the amateur historian, 'could X-ray the box, or scan it to find what's inside if it might be of value—'

'Anything of value to a county historian's also like to be of value to us – and for once I don't mean value for money.'

Jinkins gaped, Sam gasped, and Barney grinned at the effect of his words. 'Caffender Wilkins here will make a display case, as discussed; and we say nothing to any outsider who might try to stake a claim.' He saw Jack's mouth open. He glared him down. 'Oh, they'll make fine speeches about conservation, and safekeeping, and heritage – the outcome being, we'll never see this box of ours again, or what's inside, without us making a special journey and filling in forms for permission to study what's bin our own all along! And' – again he glared at Jack – 'never you try telling me I'm the only one to have read such things in the papers, John Huffam.'

The young man shuffled his feet, gazed at the box and then clicked his fingers. 'The local paper! We've the exact date on the lid, and these days everything's on microfilm, or computer. Anyone with the knowledge could read up on the subject and see if a detailed list o' the contents was given at the time. If it was...'

He waited for Barney to reach the obvious (to him) conclusion.

Mr Christmas hadn't made his millions by being slow on the uptake. He had also, in the course of a long lifetime, learned when caution must be his watchword. 'Anyone with the knowledge, you say? What *I* say is: no, not *anyone*. The ezackly right person needs asking, else...' With the stick carried mostly for show he rapped the side of the School Opening memorial. 'One heedless word to them that's *qualified*' – he favoured the history buff with a warning look – 'and it's goodbye, box. In the ordinary way I'd put such a request to Susan Jones, but so close to the wedding, no. The same with her daughter – but there's Jasper Merton, now.' He rapped the box again. 'That lad's another who knows his way around a keyboard! We'll lay the problem before young Jasper – and I'll need help in so doing, being unable to carry this gurt coffer by myself, using a stick as I do.'

'I could drive you in the truck, Mr Christmas.' Jack had taken the warning and was keen to make amends; or perhaps the history buff was keen to be on hand for the next stage of the proceedings. 'That all right by you, Sam? Mr Jinkins?'

'Straight there and back,' said Sam before Jinkins could argue. 'You'm paid to put this building to rights, not to be a taxi – even for the boss,' he added as Barney tried to smother a chuckle at Jack's look of dismay, even as Jinkins nodded his agreement.

There was an awkward pause.

'Circumstances alter cases,' said Barney at last, 'and I'd judge this occasion to be one such. Pick up the box, lad, and we'll be on our way.' He saw Jinkins frown. 'You can make up the time lost after we've talked with Jasper Merton.' He saw Sam blink. 'Or, just this once, and setting no precedent, maybe the case might be altered a second time?' He pointed to the box now in the arms of Mr Huffam, who didn't trust the rusted handle. 'Yes, maybe it could. I'll think it over!'

The blue-and-green van drew to a halt outside the cottage in Hempen Row. From the rear came scuffling sounds, accompanied by the shrill, rhythmic clink of metal. Mike Binns reached out a hand for the keys, then hesitated.

Gabriel, in the passenger seat, laughed. 'Want me to go ahead and break the news to Mickey?' he asked his brother-in-law.

Hesitation ended. Mike snatched the key-ring, stuffed it in his pocket, and squared his shoulders. 'No,' he said. 'For one reason why, he's currently from home – and for another, tidn none of his business. I ask you, whose house is this?'

'Not his, certainly,' said Gabriel. 'Leastways, not for much longer.'

'And even before then, mine.' Mike opened the door, climbed out, and slammed it shut. 'Son or no son, if I'd ever

180

wanted a dog – a dozen dogs – in my house I'd have took 'em, and not one word of permission sought – nor yet needed!'

'If you'd wanted a dog.' Gabriel had played his own small part in the rescue of shipwrecked Bran so long ago, but the young Binns had been the little black dog's saviour; and Gabriel didn't forget Mike's anguish when she had to be returned to her rightful home on the far shores of the Severn Sea. The handsome puppy sent from Wales as a substitute had failed to compensate; and after his death an oath was sworn that Mike Binns never broke.

Gabriel joined his brother-in-law at the van's rear doors. 'You'll be needing further help with that gurt old perch.' The two friends had struggled to transport Crusoe and his paraphernalia from the crowded Tuggs cottage to the little van that had been (Gabriel was thankful) entirely free of fish or any other human foodstuffs.

Joe bade his avian lodger a guilty farewell, but accepted his daughter's ruling that she was no longer prepared to house both the interlopers. Jolly black Turk, sensing sorrow, let his tail droop in a sympathetic curve and flicked his ears to and fro, but Charlotte couldn't hide her delight, and as a gleeful *congé* had even produced a new cloth for the parrot's cage. Crusoe at once began to chew an indignant hole, between beakfuls shrieking with laughter in the voice of the late Thomas 'Sandy' Joy until Lottie rammed a small dog biscuit through the bars and the bird was startled into silence.

'A cumbersome edifice,' said Gabriel as the wooden stand was borne, with great care, from the van up the short path to Mike's front door. Crusoe waited by the step with the cover off his cage, stretching his wings in the sun as songbirds sang in nearby trees, and gulls mewed overhead. 'Trust a master carpenter to get his money's worth o' wood.'

'But handsome, you can't deny. Fanciful. Unusual!' Mike, a little breathless from effort, unlocked the door and again picked up his end of the edifice. 'I've bin thinking. Once we've settled this where he'll feel happy' – they moved into the small front room – 'I'll concede how Lottie may have the right of it. Moving this contraption from once place to another idn a hurrying job, ladders and suchlike being of a breakable nature, and Lottie some years younger nor us' – some decades, in truth: but Mike would never say so – 'and, while we'm all across to Bideford these next few days, preoccupied with matters matrimonial, the poor bird's like to feel deprived of company, even stood right here before the window.'

Setting the stand in position, Gabriel had to agree. Hempen Row is a narrow cul-de-sac and sees little everyday traffic beyond local pedestrians. 'But, having found a willing victim, Lottie wadn agreeable to waiting, was she?' He chuckled. 'Afeared you might change your mind, no doubt. Mebbe, if they'd bin invited to the wedding—'

'Them and how many more? Susan and Mickey had it settled what was wanted from the start, remember. A small, select crowd to the register office' – Mr Binns savoured these words, happy to forget how very small the crowd first selected had been – 'and next day the blessing in church, with all invited. And everyone along to the party after.'

'Yo-ho-ho and a bottle of rum!' Crusoe knew about parties. 'Fifteen men on the dead man's chest!' Decanted from his cage he danced a wild jig on his perch, flapped his wings, looped the loop to land upside down on the topmost rung of a ladder, then climbed back up to grab the chain in his beak to ring the bell. Triumphantly, he rang it.

'Wedding bells!' Mike was delighted. 'Here comes the bride. Here comes the bride!'

'Man the guns! Abandon ship!' said Crusoe, and laughed.

'Here comes the bride!' persisted the bride's future father-in-law.

'He'll never learn it,' said Gabriel. 'Not in the time.'

'If we had a tape recorder...' Mike thought of the public address system he and Mickey had devised for Tollbridge occasions, and wondered how it might be adapted.

'Not in the time,' reiterated Gabriel. He knew how his friend's mind worked.

Mike sighed. He brightened. 'If Jan Ridd's agreeable, we could leave the bird with him while we'm away and ask everyone to say it to him. Help making him feel more at home.'

Gabriel looked pointedly at the elaborate trelliswork up and down which Crusoe was beaking, clawing and flapping his way. 'Move that thing again? No! Nor we haven't the time to make another, not even half the size. More-and-so, it could be upsetting for him to have too many disruptions all at once, missing Sandy as it seems he may—'

'Man the guns!' screamed Crusoe, in the voice of Sandy Joy. 'Man the guns!'

'Or maybe not.' Gabriel grinned. 'Well, if he'd be happy with just his cage, I reckon the Anchor could be the best place for him, after all. Not ezackly pining, is he!'

The parrot scrambled up to ring the bell again. Mike was suddenly thoughtful. Crusoe shrieked with laughter. He hung upside down on his perch, cackling.

'He seems happy enough,' said Mike slowly. 'Now Sandy Joy, rest his soul, wadn the only carpenter in these parts, for all he was one o' the best. You know, if either of us could find the time I'd rather like—'

'But we can't,' broke in Gabriel. 'If he hadn got old Barney breathing down his neck I'd suggest Cousin Sam Wilkins—'

'But he have,' said Mike, brightening, 'so you can't. But I know who might – and at a loose end while young Angela's away attending on her mother...'

'Handy Andy!' cried Gabriel.

'All hands on deck!' shrieked Crusoe. 'Man the guns! Pieces of eight! Abandon ship!' Once more at the top of the topmost ladder he rang a joyous bell.

When the builders' truck delivered Barney Christmas and the box to the far end of Hempen Row, Jack Huffam volunteered to find out who was at home, and to carry the box inside for his employer if anyone answered the door.

'Straight there and back, Sam Wilkins said,' Barney reminded the history buff.

'And circumstances alter cases, is what *you* said,' returned Jack, chancing his luck.

'Ah.' Barney hesitated. 'Precedence' – he began; but Jack was already out of the cab and hurrying up the short front path.

'Nobody home,' he announced after a few minutes. 'Should I now drive you down to your own place wi' the box for safekeeping?'

Barney shook his head. 'I know where there's a key.' Andy Marsh, after clearing the Mertons' chimney, had contrived under the name-plate on the gate a small cache, into which a spare key neatly fitted. 'You carry the box to their kitchen for me and we'll leave it with a note, then you can get back to your work.' A meaningful pause. 'But have no fear, I'll be sure to let 'ee know what's discovered. If anything is.'

'This Jasper: would it help to send him my photos?' Jack saw no reason why it should: there was no doubt as to the provenance of the box or the context of its discovery – but he wasn't going to say as much to Barney. He wanted to stay in the know.

'Ah.' Mr Christmas frowned. 'This would be the mobile phone, would it? You'm aware they don't work in Tollbridge, even so high up as here. More-and-so, I've no knowledge of such a number for either of 'em, neither Jasper nor young Jane.'

Observing Jack's woeful expression, he allowed himself to relent. 'But see here, it's worth a try. I'll write to explain what's wanted of him, and at the bottom you can leave your number. Doubtless he'll know what's best to do – out of working hours,' he finished sternly. Jack wasn't slow to take the hint.

The note having been accomplished, Barney waited at the Mertons' kitchen table for less than five minutes before starting to fidget. He locked the door, returned the key to its hideaway and stumped to the other end of Hempen Row, where he climbed the three steps of the old tin tabernacle, leaning heavily on the handrail and pleased to find it wobble-free. Handy Andy, indeed! Some of the older ones (he didn't include himself) would have to watch out! No lights under any nature of bushel for that enterprising young woman: she'd be worth every penny he chose to pay her, when the time came.

He tried the door of the Prue Budd Memorial Museum: locked. Nobody working there today? Well, Angela had a wedding to organise…

So much for the early start Barney Christmas had hoped to make, and the cup of tea he'd hoped someone else would make for him. He glanced back down the Row before deciding to give it up as a bad job: nobody there. Not a curtain twitched, not a door opened. The women were doubtless putting the final stitches to their wedding toggery, or shopping for last-minute frill-de-dills to outshine their friends. Every visit he'd made to the Anchor recently (and he didn't go every night) had been loud with husbands lamenting the efforts being made by wives to do Susan and Mickey proud – and lamenting the cost, likewise!

Barney chose to live up to his reputation by declaring that a clean handkerchief and a carnation buttonhole would smarten his funeral suit sufficient for any wedding: 'And as much as anyone reasonable should expect, more-and-so when tidn the full ceremony, for which it's only right an effort should be made. A blessing, however, is entirely otherwise and worth not nearly so much effort.'

'Or money,' someone commented out of sight, though not out of hearing.

Jasper Merton had opened his mouth to protest that only that week he'd driven Barney to a classy gents' outfitters in Taunton, but the old man skewered him with so ferocious a look that he shut up. Young Mr Merton, even now, didn't always remember to play Barney's game the way the old gentleman preferred it.

Still dithering between blue silk and soft white cambric for his top-pocket handkerchief (he'd bought both, but couldn't decide) Barney headed back down Stickle Street. He would call again at the old school to keep the builders on their toes – and because he was suddenly curious; he'd spotted no heavy equipment there earlier, yet the air had begun to throb, and the whole valley of the Chole echoed with a strange, high-pitched whine that sent the gulls screaming into the sky from Watchfield Point.

Barney looked up. He saw the Charybdis lifting off after the gulls, setting course for her base ship. He smiled.

Now he understood why the village had seemed otherwise engaged… preoccupied.

It was!

Chapter Nineteen

Two days later, Jasper handed Barney a printout of the 1875 newspaper article that covered the opening of Tollbridge School and described, in detail, the contents of the box.

'Pretty much what you'd expect,' he said. 'A set of postage stamps; ditto coins, with a half-sovereign from the actual year; a newspaper for that day; a list of pupils by name, ditto the teachers, the board of governors, the local worthies who gave financial assistance and – uh – the bloke who laid the foundation stone.' Something in his voice made Barney regard him sharply. Jasper grinned.

'Jerome Hockaday Christmas,' he said. 'Any connection?'

Barney squinted at the paper in his hands, then scowled. 'Very funny. I don't think.'

'There.' Jasper pointed. Barney peered more closely; started; then looked up and smiled. 'My apologies. 'Tis indeed one o' mine from afore the bad times come upon the family, when to be a Christmas still meant something in these parts.'

'Still does.' Jasper laughed. 'Don't try to out-misery Mike Binns! You'll never do it; he's got his act almost perfect and, especially at a time like this, why spoil his fun?'

Barney laughed with him. 'Jerome Hockaday Christmas,' he gloated. 'Laid the foundation stone! All the more reason for keeping that box where it belongs. So, you print me a paper that's easier to make out' – only strong emotion would allow Barney to admit he needed glasses – 'and I'll have copies found, or made, of all that's mentioned. There's old books and registers still about the village; there's folk that deal in old coins, and stamps, and newspapers – we'll set up a duplicate display, and never open the real box, not ever!'

'Angela and Susan could give us a few ideas,' said Jasper, 'but of course...'

'We wait for after the wedding,' decreed the scion of Jerome Hockaday Christmas.

On the third day, preparations for the imminent festivities were being finalised in many Tollbridge homes. Angela, in full organiser mode, crossed things one by one from numbered lists and stood over her mother as she packed and repacked her various accoutrements to her daughter's satisfaction. Angela did her best to chase Mickey Binns from Susan's door, with the warning that if he hadn't thought of whatever-it-was by this time, he'd left it so late now he might as well wait until tomorrow, when the small and select party embarked in the minibus for Bideford, and the register office.

'Tomorrow's too late.' Mickey held out a square gift-wrapped package. 'For Susan to wear to the wedding. If she likes it.' He took a deep breath. 'With... my love.'

Angela accepted the little package, and smiled. 'I'll give it to her, and I'll make sure she wears it – whatever it is.' She gave it a questing squeeze.

Mickey leaned forward. 'Bracelet,' he whispered, blushing; but, though she smiled again, his stepdaughter-to-be stood firm. He gave up trying to look past her shoulder in case his bride might be somewhere visible; sighed; and watched the door of Corner Glim Cottage close firmly in his face.

When, half an hour later, the fouled-anchor knocker rapped out another tattoo, Angela's eyes flashed. 'If Mickey's come back for more compliments he can go away again. You've already told him you like it, and that's enough!'

Susan had unwrapped Mickey's wedding bracelet – a confection of creamy-white seed pearls woven among sea-glass beads in shades of blue and green – and uttered a cry of pleasure before dissolving in tears. Angela passed her mother the paper hankies and beat a discreet retreat while she permitted one brief phone call to Mickey; she herself had to decide on which wrist the bracelet would better complement her mother's three outfits. The groom had made an excellent choice – as he'd been informed! Anything else was for tomorrow, not today! The timetable drawn up with such care was not to be overturned by unnecessary interruptions. Angela strode to the door, and opened it.

A completely unknown woman stood outside – or was there something familiar about her? Angela stared, and frowned.

The unknown's face had been widening in a smile that, as she saw Angela's frown, turned to a look of surprise. 'Oh,' said the unknown. 'I was looking for Susan Jones. They told me at the pub – I mean, isn't this her cottage?'

Angela sighed. 'It is, but didn't they also tell you she's busy at the moment? Very busy. Even more than usual – and for the next few days.'

'They did, but then she always is,' said the unknown knowledgeably. 'Workaholic isn't the word! I'm her editor,' she added. 'Belinda Bates.'

The name was familiar, though the two had never met. Could you recognise someone through an oblique business connection? 'I'm her daughter Angela,' said Angela. 'Helping her get ready to go away tomorrow – but not for work. That's not until next week.'

'Yes, she did tell me something about—'

'Belinda?' Susan appeared behind Angela to stare at the figure being barred from entry. 'What on earth are you doing here? If you were looking for me, you were lucky to find me. I thought I told you I was taking a few days off—'

'Even more incommunicado than usual.' Belinda nodded. 'Yes, I remember, and I had my suspicions – and it seems they were justified – but I'm in disgrace at home, so I thought, two birds with one stone: you know how nosy I am. Besides, if I can't get in touch with you here in the middle of nowhere, then *they* can't get in touch with me, even if they wanted to – which they probably won't, for a while – and it will give them time to simmer down.'

'You'd better come in.' Angela, relieved that it wasn't Mickey, ushered the editor inside and quickly closed the door, just in case. Not that she was superstitious (she told herself), and nobody seemed to bother so much about it these days anyway – but she didn't want to take the risk that anything might go wrong at the last minute by having the groom catch sight of the bride within twenty-four hours of the wedding.

'Have a cup of tea?' invited Susan. 'Coffee? Chocolate?'

'I had something at the pub when I checked in, thanks, which is where I heard all about the wedding. Susan, why didn't you tell me? I could have been your matron of honour!'

Susan winced elaborately. 'Angela refused to be a bridesmaid, and I would hardly want to risk being snubbed twice in a row—'

'Mother!' burst from Angela, who too late saw the twinkle in her mother's eye and the answering laugh in that of her editor. 'I wish you'd be serious about all this!'

'I am,' said Susan. 'Serious enough not to want to be mutton dressed as lamb, or to put anyone else through it. But what have you done that's so disgraceful, Belinda? Or was it just a convenient excuse to come snooping?'

Belinda sat down on the small couch that in emergency doubled as a bed. 'Fifty-fifty! I've known you a few years now, Susan, and something just felt different from your usual style about this incommunicado business. Call it instinct – I can't say more than that – but I *am* in disgrace with Alf and Freddie, so it seemed the perfect excuse to find out if my feeling was correct: which was confirmed all too quickly once I'd checked in at the Anchor and told them who it was I was here to visit.'

'Ah, feelings.' Susan turned to Angela. 'Belinda doesn't fuss about it, but under her other name she's a successful poet – Belinda Starling. Her *Enigma Versifications* stayed in the Sunday Times Bestseller List for several months, a couple of years ago.'

Angela, former librarian, was cross-referencing card index entries in her head and seeing jacket photographs on slim volumes of verse. 'Yes, of course! But I didn't realise you were an editor as well. Talk about versatile – your middle name, obviously.'

'At the moment,' said Belinda, 'my middle name's mud. Freddie broke up with his girlfriend, and you know how *intense* teenagers can be, and I'm afraid I said the wrong thing and Alf is almost as annoyed with me as Freddie, because I – I laughed so much.'

Angela blinked, but Susan looked startled. 'What *can* have been so funny?'

Belinda sighed. 'A short while back Freddie announced he wanted to turn vegan, and his father and I said, fine, just as long as you don't expect us to veganise too, and you take the appropriate multivitamins and supplements, and the first sermon you preach means you pay for them yourself – and he said okay, and he was as good as his word, bless the boy, and didn't nag once. We thought it was just another phase and didn't worry too much; we both expected it to wear off before long.'

'As they do.' Susan didn't go into details of Angela's teenage years. Angela grinned.

'But before it could,' Belinda continued, 'he tried to convert *her* and she wasn't having any of it. He had to admit that was fair enough – freedom of choice, and so on – but what seems to have upset him wasn't so much her saying she preferred a fully balanced diet, as having her laugh at him, as he thought.' She shook her head. 'I suppose that will have hurt him more than anything, and when I couldn't help laughing too...'

'Why should she laugh? What made *you* laugh?'

'She apparently told him that virtue-signalling was all very well, but he could never hope to get to heaven if he wasn't – wasn't willing to eat *p-pâté de foie gras...*'

'Oh, dear.' Susan choked. 'Oh, dear!'

Angela sighed. 'Did she mention trumpets?'

'That was the first thing I asked, of course, and he flared up and said yes, she did, and he took it for sarcasm because we all know very well she plays the flute. The poor lamb was so upset! He said he had every right to have his views treated with respect, not sneered at, and he – he didn't see what was so funny...'

'Not everyone these days knows that Sydney Smith quotation,' said Susan at last.

'No, but you do, and so do I – and Alf – and the girlfriend. It never occurred to me that Freddie didn't – or to her, poor girl. From what he said, she took his – his non-recognition as a joke, and laughed again, and one thing led to another – and when he came home and told us and I laughed too...' She sighed. 'It didn't help when I suggested he might try looking it up to give her the benefit of the doubt. He stood so much on his dignity, poor boy, and of course I don't blame Alf for standing with him, but there was a decided atmosphere – and you were being mysterious – so I packed a bag and drove down here and left a message with the office saying where I was, but not to tell the family unless there was an emergency.'

'There won't be,' said Angela with resolution. 'Fate wouldn't dare – and the village wouldn't allow it, either. Combe Tollbridge knows what it wants, which is for the next few days to go without a single hitch—'

'—you mean, with two singles getting safely hitched,' said her mother, laughing and blushing and pleased with her wordplay. Now that everything was ready it remained only to wait for tomorrow; she could leave details to family and friends, and just enjoy herself.

Belinda asked about wedding plans. Susan waved towards Angela.

'Sorted,' said the born organiser. 'Register office wedding, small and select, in Bideford; wedding breakfast in smart hotel; wedding night, anonymous ditto while the rest of the party drives home and the *Priscilla Ornedge* is dressed overall – flags, bunting, brasswork polished – the full pomp and circumstance, in fact.'

Susan giggled. 'Mike has looked forward to that quite as much as anything else. He'll be heartbroken if it rains.'

'It won't.' Angela was firm. 'The weather forecast is spot on and the barometer agrees it's Set Fair – and just as well,' she told Belinda, 'because next morning Mike and the others have an early start to catch the tide. Not me, this time; it's far too early, and there's the food to keep an eye on,' as if Tabitha Ridd hadn't successfully catered for many a Tollbridge celebration over the years. Angela was determined that nothing should go wrong.

'And if you – they – miss the tide?'

'They won't.' Susan, too, was firm. 'They're experts, every one – and you ignore the experts at your peril. Don't go thinking I had any real choice in naming the day, because I didn't. The moment I accepted Mickey, Mike and Gabriel took over: the old rascals had been planning various options for years, in secret. Not many brides can say they've had the date and time of their wedding chosen for them by the tide, but' – she bowed – 'meet me!'

'Unusual,' murmured Belinda, her eyes beginning to gleam at the publicity potential.

Angela shot her a suspicious look, and frowned her down. 'They'll take the *Priscilla* round to Bideford to collect the happy couple and bring them home in state for the blessing, and the party afterwards. They'll enter harbour with all flags flying and everyone waiting to escort them to the church – and I do mean everyone. There will be empty houses from one end of Stickle Street to the other, so don't plan any sightseeing trips for that day unless you're back in good time! Nobody will be able to get in or out of town because the road will be completely blocked, in case of burglars.'

Susan shot her daughter a quick glance, remembering Prue Budd's funeral and Rodney Longstone's solitary patrol of an empty village. Much had happened since then. For this latest Tollbridge occasion, the empty village had needed another security policy.

The London-based editor regarded her author with respect. 'I didn't realise you had the local police in your pocket.'

'The police? Goodness, no!' Susan was laughing again. 'They know nothing about it officially, though I believe a quiet word of warning did filter through to the right quarters from Jan Ridd at the Anchor, just in case. Jan used to be a copper, and he still keeps an eye on what goes on. He knows how far the village can push its luck—'

'—and pushes with them, more often than not,' finished Angela, proud of her part-time employer. 'Jan's Tollbridge born and bred,' she explained, as Belinda looked startled. 'He understands how things work – yes, it does take a bit of getting used to, but life's a lot easier once you do!' She exchanged a wink with her mother, who was laughing again. 'The road-block might even have been Jan's idea in the first place,' she went on. Susan was tactfully silent. 'One of the upalong farmers will bring a bulldozer tractor down from Combe Ploverton and skew it across the road just by the old school, so that you can only get in or out of Tollbridge on foot—'

'Or on a motorbike.' Susan thought of Andromeda Marsh.

'Or a bicycle,' said Angela, 'if anyone had the strength for it…'

Mother and daughter exchanged glances, hesitated, and collapsed in giggles. Belinda stared. 'But suppose there's an emergency?'

Angela grinned. 'No reason there should be, but if you're really worried Jan Safe – that's the farmer – will fix a notice telling anyone who needs to know to phone the Anchor, where someone will take a message.'

'But Susan's always told me mobiles don't work in Combe Tollbridge!' Belinda's family might currently be at odds with her, but this didn't mean they wouldn't want to contact her if anything went wrong.

'They don't,' agreed Susan. 'Which means whoever is sufficiently worried either walks down to the Anchor or goes back up to Ploverton to phone from the Pig—'

'And Tom Tucker, that's the landlord, can use his judgement quite as well as Jan Ridd if it's a genuine emergency or something that can wait another day,' finished Angela.

'Or the day after that,' said Susan, giggling again.

'This village,' declared Belinda, poet and publisher, 'seems to be a law unto itself.' She hadn't realised how far her best-seller had gone rogue in the years since she'd left London. Was she growing mad, bad, and dangerous to know? Might this be the reason Milicent Dalrymple was tempted towards a life of crime?

Would she get a sensible answer if she asked a sensible question?

'When will you be able to start work again? Have you found a pseudonym yet?'

'Next week, probably,' said Susan. 'And I have – and also, I think "Vesta Investigates" makes a better series title than "Vesta the Investigator" because the more research I do, the more I realise she wouldn't have been so much hands-on as supervising from a discreet distance. Vesta Tilley never wore male costume off-stage, not even at fancy dress parties, so she's going to have a sidekick, Paula, who'll be taught all the tricks just as Vesta taught them to Irene Adler. Paula's the one to do all the running around and dressing up and infiltrating suspicious households in pursuit of blackmailers and jewel thieves – as Paul, a boot-boy or a page or a scullery maid's visiting cousin. Paula will make regular reports to Vesta and Vesta will take appropriate action – but indirect, rather than physical.'

She frowned. 'I can work my notes up into an outline for you in a week or so – signed with my new name, which is inspired by one of the best. Dorothy L. Sayers had a music hall star, Cremorna Garden, really Rosanna Wrayburn. I prefer Roseanna with an "e", but Wrayburn spelled any way is a non-starter because it's so far down the alphabet. I want to keep the stage connection, though, so I think perhaps "Hall" for after. What do you think?'

'Roseanna Hall.' Belinda pondered. 'It'll do,' she said at last. 'Next week, then?'

'Or thereby, as they say in Scotland,' returned Susan cheerfully. Angela chuckled.

Belinda gave up. 'Is that where you're going for your honeymoon?'

'Gretna Green?' Susan laughed. 'That's a fairish journey when all we want is to be out from under for a couple of days while everyone plays Musical Furniture.'

'Musical Beds, perhaps.' A librarian should be accurate. Angela retrieved her notes from a pocket, waving the list in Belinda's direction. 'At least, beds is where it starts. We need to swap mother's small double for zip-up twins because a full-size double won't go up the stairs – but first the wardrobe needs shifting or the doors won't open – ditto the chest of drawers – and, being wider, the new bed will need the reading lamp moved, plus one for Mickey, which means the electrics want sorting – that's Andy's job – after which—' She saw Belinda's eyes widen, and laughed.

'You get the picture! It's all been measured and checked a dozen times; Mickey did a splendid plan on graph paper; and it's another reason I'm not joining the *Priscilla* when they go to bring the happy couple home. It's not that I don't trust Andy, but...' She hesitated, suddenly recalling her friend's enjoyment of the prawn trick. Logic, however, reminded her that Andy could have no possible grudge against anyone in Tollbridge, where she had been made very welcome.

Angela shook herself. 'Andy's one of my closest friends, but she doesn't really know this village too well.' At her side, Susan nodded as Belinda raised a quizzical eyebrow. 'If Mother left the keys with Andy, she might all too easily fall for, say, old Mike's excuses and let him in here to plant confetti bombs and booby traps all over the show. The locals tell an amazingly plausible tale: you just give 'em half a chance in the pub tomorrow!'

'Why not—?' began Belinda, but Susan forestalled her. 'Not tonight, because – well, at my age I'm not calling it a hen party, even if my friend Miriam does – Miriam keeps hens, so she's biased – but I'm having a modest pre-wedding all girls get-together here this evening, and of course you must come too. It'll be something of a squeeze, but the Anchor might be rather too lively tonight for someone who's in the middle of a – a domestic crisis.'

Belinda blinked, then remembered. 'Hardly a crisis,' she said. 'Partly an excuse to snoop, as I explained.'

'Definitely not a crisis,' said Angela. 'Nor even an emergency. Nothing's going to go wrong! Oh, a few – a very few – people might have acted worried about the ghost ship, but not seriously. Anyway, everyone decided that having the Charybdis appear like that out of the blue, a real-life landing with a guided tour and photos and hard facts rather than just a mirage floating in the air to fade away to nothing, should be seen as a kind of… counterpoint to any bad luck the fata morgana might have brought – if it did. Which it didn't.'

'It might have.' Susan was grave, but her eyes danced. 'However, as you say, lose on the spooky swings, win on the helicopter roundabouts—'

'The whirlybird roundabouts,' amended her daughter.

'Whirlpools?' suggested Susan; and the two collapsed in mild hysterics.

Chapter Twenty

Next morning Tollbridge turned out *en masse* to cheer the Bideford party on its way. The minibus, a glory of rich crimson paint and polished chrome, was garlanded with white satin bows and ribbons in nuptial celebration; the passengers wore cream rosebud *boutonnières*. Susan's nosegay of pale, sweet-scented flowers enhanced by wisps of fern was wrapped in a cloud of lace horseshoes (courtesy of Louise) and lace bells (Olive) stitched (by Amelia Martin) to a delicate gauze foundation. Mickey's bracelet was on Susan's wrist. In her hair she wore the fascinator created by Amelia from the lace butterflies and blossoms also woven by the two old ladies; Miriam Evans had dyed everything a soft cream, toning with both today's wedding outfit and tomorrow's blessing costume, which was of three-quarter length and a most elegant cut.

'You look pretty good, Susan,' was all Mickey said to his bride that anyone heard, but with the accompanying hug it was enough. Mike Binns was ready to burst with excitement, waving as people took photos and wishing he had ignored his son's preference for understatement and insisted on top hats for all. Climbing last into the minibus he caught the eye of Andy Marsh, who did a quick thumbs-up; Mike waved again before vanishing inside. The door closed. The engine started. The bus set off for Bideford.

Miriam, Andy and helpers then undertook the first phase of single-to-double occupancy at Corner Glim Cottage. Using Mickey's diagram Andy adjusted electric sockets as others shifted furniture, either across to the study or down the stairs, according to its ultimate destination. Her most urgent tasks complete, Andy hurried off to further carpentry; she'd been helping Mike with a special job, and had promised him she would finish it before tomorrow. She was observed in Farley's General Stores, buying a tin of grey paint.

In the afternoon, returning to Corner Glim, Andy kept quiet about what she'd been doing and joined the others in mopping, brushing and tidying. At last, the door was locked.

Miriam kept the keys until evening, when Angela would return in good time to authorise tomorrow's delivery men to deliver what was required for Phase Two.

Miriam invited all those in need of refreshment to tea and cake in Harbour Glim Cottage. 'Angela made the cakes,' was the bribe. 'And how she found the time I'll never know.'

'She wanted – wants – everything just right for her mother,' said Jane Merton. 'Oh, I do hope it all went well in Bideford.'

'We'll know for sure once the minibus gets back.' Miriam laughed. 'But we can guess it did, for if it didn and anything had gone amiss we'd surely know by now. Just you wait! They'll be out of that bus chattering and showing photos, with so much fidget and commotion telling ezackly how it all happened that nobody will hear one word anybody says – not until Mike wants us organised to help dressing the *Priscilla*. And then you'll be able to hear every dratted word!'

'Hence the bribery.' Andy winked at Belinda. 'Old Ange makes a wicked cake, so you've no need to worry, but even if she didn't it's all in a good cause.'

'The very best,' said Miriam; with which, nobody could argue.

The minibus returned. Miriam proved a true prophet. Amid the hubbub of voices only the loudest could be heard saying things had gone well, Susan had looked lovely, Mickey looked proud, and tomorrow's blessing would go even better than today's quiet ceremony with *all* their friends and family, not just a handful, celebrating the newlywed couple.

Mike and Gabriel pressganged cronies into draping M.V. *Priscilla Ornedge* with flags, promising drinks in the Anchor afterwards; Andy drew Mike aside for a quick, low-voiced consultation and went back to help Angela double-check her lists against those of helpful friends – the church flowers; the Anchor skittle alley decorations; the sweet and savoury, cooked and fresh contents of various fridges, freezers and old-fashioned larders. Tabitha Ridd had a list of her own, and everything was successfully ticked off. Angela thanked Miriam for her care of the keys and said she would be setting her alarm clock early for the morrow. She asked Andy to do the same.

'On my list,' said the handywoman smugly. 'But Mike's special job isn't quite finished yet, so I'm off to sort it now and I'm not sure how long I'll be. Expect me when you see me – or maybe not, if you're asleep. It all depends.' She was gone.

That night there was an inevitable outburst of partying in the Anchor, into which Belinda was inevitably swept as the target for Mike and Gabriel's best anecdotes. Jan Ridd entered into the spirit of the occasion by showing her the 'Lorna Doone' cannon-bullet in its display case, and selling her some of the tourist leaflets updated by Susan Jones-now-Binns writing as Lorinda Doone, Lorna's creative collateral. Belinda had known nothing of Lorinda – was curious about copyright – but over a second mug of cider muzzily decided that if it was anybody's problem it was one for Susan's agent, not her editor, to resolve.

Belinda heard the story of little Bran the Shipwrecked Dog, and promised to look out tomorrow for the grave of the Two Drowned Welshmen 'after all this time since the war, never forgot.' She heard about the Lost Silver Mine and added that leaflet to her collection; she made Jane Merton jealous by being permitted to know the true reason the squire's son was run out of town 'when they wouldn't tell me for years and years, because they've known me since I was a child and they think I still am.'

Landlord Jan had unearthed a tall, ladder-backed chair for Crusoe's personal use. The parrot's cage stood on a corner of the bar, the chair set within easy reach for him to scramble up and down the makeshift climbing frame as he pleased. He showed his pleasure by issuing frequent orders to man the guns or to abandon ship; but he showed no inclination whatever to welcome the absent bride, no matter how many times the welcome was repeated by any number of drinkers trying any number of voices.

Andy Marsh came in late, a smatter of paint adding grey to the pink streaks in her green hair. As she joined her friends she and Mike Binns exchanged meaningful looks, but gave nobody time to wonder why.

'Don't risk a third mug,' she warned Belinda. 'If you do, you might start to believe what these old devils tell you!'

'But they tell it so very well,' said Belinda. Mike and Gabriel preened themselves on this professional opinion and together told her why there was a gilded weathercock on the spire of Ploverton church, disagreeing only over which mediaeval pope had decreed it as penance for the squire's having murdered the parish priest in a quarrel over tithes.

'In short, midear,' Gabriel said, 'the Ankatells weren't suitable to squiring over the two villages, and good riddance to the whole boiling when they finally went—'

'—when the name of this place,' said landlord Jan, 'was changed from the Ankatell Arms to the Anchor, and the sign straightway chopped to kindling for the bonfire to roast an upalong pig – you'll likely have time to visit the Slandered Pig tomorrow, before the *Priscilla* gets back – which was another great village celebration.'

'Even greater to come, once my son and his wife are home!' Mike Binns drained his two-handled mug, pushed back his chair, and stood up. 'Regarding which, I'm off now for a timely start tomorrow. There's Bideford Bar needs crossing, remember, and an hour to be added each way for safety.' The old fisherman shook a stern finger at Belinda. 'Never take the sea for granted, midear. Tide tables may say three hours, but they can be no more than a guide, printed as they are so far ahead. How can paper and ink have knowledge beforehand of a storm come surging in from the west, or a cloudburst flooding down from the hills into the Severn? There'll be no risks took with my son and my daughter-law.'

'Nor with any on board,' said Gabriel.

'Who must *be on board* by the appointed hour.' Mike's gaze swept the crowded room. 'We'll have no delay, not even five minutes. And when we come back...'

Once more he exchanged a speaking look with Andy Marsh, nodded, smiled and bade the company, including Crusoe, a cheerful goodnight although the parrot still refused to bless the bride.

Next day's crowd of well-wishers was smaller than that of the previous morning, the send-off less hearty as M.V. *Priscilla Ornedge* left harbour. Not everyone drinking the health of the new Mr and Mrs Binns had been as strong-minded as the elder Binns about an early night. When Mike's triumphant farewell blast on the ship's whistle echoed round the valley, more than one pale face emitted an anguished groan.

Angela stopped waving, consulted her watch and turned to Andy Marsh. 'Did you finish Mike's mystery job in time? Will you be able to help with the delivery men?'

'I did, thanks – so yes, of course.' Andy's eyes danced. 'There's me, and Rodney Longstone, and any number of others you've only got to ask, but' – as she consulted her own watch – 'there should be time enough before they bring the beds for *you* to help Rodney and me. Come on.'

Angela wasn't sure how to take the unexpected coupling of these names. Andy was a good friend, but her sense of mischief – Angela thought of the prawns – could almost rival that of Mike Binns, with whom she had been going into whispering huddles for several days past. Angela was concerned for Rodney Longstone, being dragged in all innocence (she hoped) into the business, whatever it was.

Still, whatever it was, it seemed she was about to be let into the secret. 'Okay,' she said, and started in the direction of Baker's Cottage, in the shadow of Meazel Wood; but Andy had turned in the other direction and was striding purposefully towards Stickle Street.

'He's meeting me – us – in Hempen Row,' was the only explanation she offered. 'It was all arranged last night, before I joined you in the pub.'

Not another word would she say until, turning into Hempen Row, they saw the Mini Cooper outside the Binns cottage, its rear double doors ajar and Rodney gazing out to sea. Andy put finger and thumb to her lips, and whistled; Angela heard keys jingle in her friend's free hand.

The captain turned from his seaward trance to wave. When he saw Angela, he smiled a warm greeting. 'Don't you get a splendid view from here? Far better than Meazel Cleeve! I've been watching the *Priscilla*. Dressing her overall must have taken hours, but my word, it was worth it. A wonderful way for old Mike to pay tribute to the Ornedges, who did so very much for him in his youth.' He shook his head, gently. 'I know you've said more than once, Angela, that there's a lot in favour of elopement, and I do understand why, but in this particular instance I'm sorry. I think you're wrong.'

'No need to apologise! I think you're right,' she said. 'This once,' she added hastily.

Andy hid a smile. 'You're both wasting time.' Again she jingled the keys. 'Come on.'

For one dreadful moment, as Mike's door swung open, Angela thought of booby traps and held her breath. Then she looked; gasped; inhaled fresh paint – and sneezed. In the middle of the kitchen floor, surrounded by newspaper, squatted two large gunmetal grey bricks, each about four feet long. Each carried a heavy half-wheel to either side; each had a sturdy hollow tube protruding horizontally from one end, while at the other a length of narrow pipe rose at an angle from… the breech.

'Cannon!' cried Angela, wiping her eyes for a second look. 'Sort of,' she added, noting the purely ornamental nature of the side-wheels.

Andy laughed. 'Once a librarian, always a stickler! Cross-reference your mental index to rocket-launchers, and you've got it. Mike, bless him, suddenly set his heart on a twenty-one gun salute for when the *Priscilla* comes back. He says Crusoe first gave him the idea, but of course he didn't have time, by himself.' She wrinkled her nose. 'The paint's barely dry, even now: but between us we got the job just about done – though I admit the champagne was a big help.'

Angela stared. 'Champagne?'

As Rodney hid a smile, Andy smacked her lips. 'Mike Binns for president! He said in his young days they fired their rockets from milk bottles, but his son's wedding deserved the very best, and when I told him modern fireworks come with their own safety-tubes he said he'd paid full whack for the bubbly and it would be' – she giggled – 'a cruel shame to waste it: so we didn't. Don't look too closely, or you'll spot the mistakes. He gave me the final nod this morning that he'd pressganged poor Rodney into driving this lot up to the headland and taking charge…' Angela looked an astonished query, and the captain nodded.

'He swore me to secrecy,' he explained. 'We submariners, remember, are famously the Silent Service! He also said the only others he could trust to keep quiet were Andy, and your good self – for obvious reasons – and Sam Farley, for reasons equally obvious.'

'Sam lives there,' said Andy, forestalling Angela's next query, 'but never mind him now: we've work to do, down here and up on the Watchfield. Once we've helped load the car and driven round to unload outside the Printery, we two can go and arrange furniture or food or anything else that might crop up, and leave the rest to Rodney until zero hour.' She grinned. 'Perhaps we should synchronise watches!'

Captain Longstone tipped an invisible cap. 'Perhaps we should.' He looked at Angela. 'I do hope you'll be able to help us then, too. The fireworks remain in their box, in my car, until first sight of the *Priscilla* – Sam to keep watch – while I double-check the fuses and prepare the salute. Then we'll have you and Andy working one gun each while I do the countdown. With safety fuses and so on it's not strictly necessary, but I'll teach you the Navy way: more interesting than *one-thousand-two-thousand* for thunder after lightning.'

'You can count me in,' said Angela, 'if it's for Mother and Mickey. And Mike,' she added, her eyes beginning to dance. 'The old rascal.'

'Sorted, then.' Andy was brisk. 'Let's get on. Rodney, you remembered the dust sheets for your car?'

Again the captain smiled, and nodded. 'Naval training,' he said. The conversation became technical, practical and busy.

All was ready. People in their smartest clothes were leaving their homes as Sam Farley, high on Watchfield Point, flashed his mirror signal to those waiting below. A general cheer rang out. The newlyweds and their escort were now in sight – had rounded the point – were passing the harbour entrance.

Angela and Andy stood each to her individual gun, awaiting orders.

'If I wasn't a gunner I wouldn't be here,' chanted Rodney Longstone. 'Fire, *one!*'

Angela lit the fuse of the firework waiting in its tube, and retreated smartly. Rodney went on counting.

'Two thousand, three thousand, four thousand, five thousand, six thousand, seven thousand—'

With a whoosh and a bang, the first of twenty-one rockets soared into the air to explode in a glittering cascade of blue, gold and silver spangles.

'If I wasn't a gunner I wouldn't be here – fire, *two!*'

It was Andy's turn to light a fuse and retreat.

As Rodney went on counting, Angela set the third rocket safely in place.

'Two thousand, three thousand, four thousand, five thousand…'

More gold, blue and silver glittered from the second rocket down to the waters through which the little fishing boat was steaming.

'If I wasn't a gunner I wouldn't be here – fire, *three!* Two thousand, three thousand…'

Keeping careful time, Angela and Andy fired their rockets one after the other from the wooden cannon designed by Mike Binns. A proud, joyous fanfare sounded on the *Priscilla's* whistle: Mike was at the wheel. The rest of the party crowded the rails, waving and smiling at the welcoming crowd.

Mike slowed the engines as M.V. *Priscilla Ornedge* approached her regular berth.

Here was Susan in the second of her three Bristol outfits, wearing the same fascinator as on the previous day, carrying the same flowers. Miriam Evans had removed the outer lace wrapping and fashioned it into a shoulder corsage, designed by Amelia Martin. The hapless weaver had been forced by her stern apprentice to practise with a sample piece until she could have achieved the design in her sleep; Angela remembered the sticky tape, and would run no risks on her mother's special day.

As the spangles of the final rocket hissed into the harbour waves Captain Longstone produced binoculars, and passed them to Angela. 'They both look extremely happy,' he said, 'but I think you'd prefer to see for yourself.'

Her eyes were moist as, with a smile, she returned the binoculars and fumbled for a handkerchief. 'Yes, they do.' She blew her nose.

'Andy and Sam have stolen a march on us,' observed the captain gently. 'If we want to join the general welcome, we'd better follow their example!' He escorted Angela in her dash down Coastguard Steps and along Boatshed Row to the footbridge, and the harbour.

'Never known Mike more pleased with hisself,' Sam said to Andy. 'Talk about blowing your own trumpet!' The old gentleman, having leaped from the *Priscilla*'s deck, was rushing through the crowd announcing to all his brains, his brilliance and his skilled handiwork.

'Mine, too,' said Andy, as he paused near her to gloat yet again over the success of his twenty-one gun salute. 'You're not the only woodworker in town, Mike Binns!'

Mike looked at her, and grinned. 'Yours too, Miss Imperence. We make a good team. Coming with me?' He offered his arm, and with a quick wink for Sam she took it. 'Get me to the church on time!' cried Mike, leading her almost to the front of the procession that had been slowly assembling, making way for Mickey and Susan to head it. Slowly, the chattering throng moved off, and as slowly climbed Stickle Street for the blessing.

The older and more frail among the villagers had gone straight to the church and were waiting inside. The Reverend Theodore Hollington waited outside to congratulate the happy couple and guide them to the altar. Susan walked proudly with

208

her husband up the aisle, and didn't mind that her new shoes hadn't been completely broken in.

The ceremony of blessing complete, Tollbridge threw itself into photography, confetti, laughter and the lych-gate tradition. No fears now that Mickey Binns might put his back out, or drop his bride: his father whispered that he should look in a particular corner, where his collaborator had promised to hide a small set of wooden steps. Andy Marsh had kept her word. Mickey found the steps – adorned, like the gates, with a white satin bow – and carried them to the gate; he climbed up and swung himself over, and down. A smiling Susan began to follow, but paused halfway before jumping into his arms.

Everyone cheered her on. 'You'd best have worn trousers!' someone called as, with the bouquet in her hands, she hesitated. Her gaze swept a sea of friendly faces; she must make up her mind before she jumped. She touched the corsage at her shoulder, her eyes seeking out the lace-makers; she found Louise and Olive clustered with the twins and Amelia Martin and old Hilda Beacon and her sister Daisy – who had never in her life, that Susan knew, come first at anything.

'Daisy!' cried Susan, taking careful aim.

Hilda's delight that Daisy caught the flowers seemed so genuine that her younger sister pulled a single bloom from the bunch and gave it to her. Hilda, even more delighted, tucked it proudly in her new fascinator. Further cheers. The lych-gate bonds were loosed, Hilda appropriating the ribbon for a triumphal streamer – and Combe Tollbridge escorted Mr and Mrs Michael Ornedge Binns down to the Anchor, and their second wedding breakfast.

Belinda Bates won Mickey's heart by her admiration of his handsome beard. 'But don't tell your father I said so,' she whispered, loud enough for Mike to overhear. Mike only laughed, and thanked her for humouring his son on this special day of days.

Wanting to reassure her own family they weren't forgotten Belinda thought of sending a few explanatory photographs, but was reminded by Susan that she couldn't: 'Not unless it's from the Watchfield, which means climbing Coastguard Steps. You haven't eaten or drunk enough yet to justify losing the calories.'

At first sight of the magnificent cake Susan had again been touched to tears. Baked by Evan Evans, it had been iced and decorated by her daughter. On the upper tier Angela had constructed a pyramid of Turkish delight in pink and white cubes, lightly dusted with icing sugar: it seemed the diet she had imposed upon the bride could now be abandoned.

The bottom tier carried an open book with, on one page, an appearance of print that in close-up proved to be the names of the happy couple on repeat; the opposite folio showed a fishing boat in full sail, on calm seas, under a clear, sunny sky.

'A good omen for the voyage ahead,' approved Captain Longstone, who'd been consulted on maritime details because Angela's new family would be sure to laugh if she got anything wrong. 'Not that they need it! They look all set for fair winds.'

Did he (wondered Angela) remember his own wedding, and its sorry aftermath in that scandalous divorce? 'They do,' she said quickly, 'but I have to wonder how much is due to the Turkish delight! Which reminds me. I tried various recipes before I hit on the right one, and I'd be interested in your opinion of this.' She led him to another elegant pyramid of cubes, pale green and dusted with icing sugar. 'It doesn't always have to be rosewater or lemon, does it? Do try one!'

'I will,' said Rodney. He paused. 'If you will, too.'

After a moment, she smiled at him. 'Maybe I will,' she said slowly.

Spearing sticky cubes with forks they laughed together as they tried to keep sugar from drifting on their clothes. 'Very different from old Prue's peppermints,' was Rodney's verdict, 'but every bit as toothsome.'

Angela hesitated, then: 'I wondered if you might have preferred a Cornish pasty.' Nobody ever asked the captain a personal question. Was she pushing her luck too far?

'I'd rather have a tiddy-oggie than my favourite flavour? Why would you think that?'

She took a deep breath. 'Your, um, heritage. After your friend called you Restronguet the other day, I – I looked it up. Isn't it a river in Cornwall?'

He stared, then smiled, pleased by her tact. 'I'd rather hoped nobody had noticed, but Jonny isn't what you'd call subtle and I should have known that if anyone were to catch a slip like that, it would be your mother's daughter! But Mrs Binns' – he gestured with his glass in Susan's direction – 'isn't the only one to play about with words, though I'm a little surprised you, being a book person, didn't go further. Yes, it's Cornish, but Captain Restronguet is the anti-hero in one of those ripping yarns from last century: *The Rival Submarines* by Percy F. Westerman. I found it in my grandfather's house – a school prize, complete with name-plate – and I suspect it's what first inspired me to go into the Navy.'

'It's as good a reason as Mother's Milicent pseudonym.' Angela raised her own glass, and explained the gingerbread cakes of Susan's youth.

The captain nodded. 'Formative influences indeed! For myself, "Captain Restronguet" is the handle I use in' – he paused, and put a warning finger to his lips – 'in my secret life as a computer games developer: video games, if you prefer. I know people think I've been writing my memoirs since I came to live in Tollbridge, but' – again he paused – 'revisiting the past is the last thing I want to do.' He gave her a long, enquiring look.

Sympathy in her eyes, she nodded. 'I can imagine,' she said. Having his wife begin an affair with his father's young half-brother was surely bad enough, but on the way to the airport for a wild weekend the guilty twosome's car had sideswiped a lorry, loaded with confectionery, on the motorway slip road. Cut unconscious from the wreckage they'd been admitted to the hospital as a married couple because their passport surnames were the same...

For a member of the Silent Service, returning from a long tour of duty abroad, to be met by such newspaper headlines as 'Oh, crumbs! Caught out by a sticky situation' or 'A sweet pair of right jammy dodgers' must have been torture. For the quiet captain to have mentioned the episode, even obliquely, left Angela a little breathless.

'Forget the past,' she said firmly. 'Tell me about being a games developer. I thought you didn't like computers because you'd had enough of them in your service career.'

'In a way, yes; but from sheer self-defence I asked questions – and understood the answers, which not everyone did – and grew interested. A game-playing lieutenant introduced me to his online community, and things went from there. With the right sort of mind, and time to work at my own speed, it's possible to earn a modest living. The great attraction, for me, of Combe Tollbridge is that the broadband is so slow. I don't need to be distracted by too many outside influences – and it's easy enough to copy everything to a stick once it's complete, and send it by post if my publishers aren't in a rush, or by courier if they are.'

Angela knew that Farley's was a courier hub, but she'd never heard anyone mention the captain either sending or collecting. She had a lightbulb moment. 'Taunton twice a month,' she guessed. Rodney laughed, and once more raised his glass.

'Guilty as charged! As I have to go there anyway, it makes sense. You won't tell anyone else.' He didn't ask: he knew.

'Not a word,' promised Angela.

They smiled, clinked glasses, and drank to seal a bargain they both realised might well, in time, lead to promises of a very different kind.

Belinda, slightly flushed, materialised at Angela's side. 'I did an E.T. and phoned home from that quaint red box outside – it was wonderful! We forget how much simpler and more straightforward things were in the good old days. It belongs in a museum, but it still works!'

'Of course it does! Didn't we explain? It's original, and genuine – and necessary!'

'This whole place is original,' enthused the poet. 'Amazing! A step into the past with all mod cons – or at least, with the basics.' Was that a hint of slurring in her sibilants? 'Oh, I do see why Susan chose to live here. Talk about inspiration! Some of those old boys—'

Angela stopped her. 'Remember, don't believe more than half of what they say.'

'That's all very well – but which half? And which old boys in particular?'

Rodney watched Angela struggle between family loyalty and the truth. 'Barney Christmas,' he suggested. 'The stories of how he made his millions are never told the same way twice, even if on most other topics I'd say he's pretty sound.'

Belinda stared. 'But he's the one who told me Susan's going to live in a boathouse!'

'In Boatshed Row,' said Angela. 'Barney's having the whole lot converted into self-contained units as part of his hotel scheme, but he decided to give Mother and Mickey first refusal on the end one where he now lives, plus next door for Mother when she's working. They'll do a swap. Barney will buy Corner Glim Cottage, which is slightly more central and he's not getting any younger, while Mother and Mickey move the other side of the bridge just a bit farther away from Mike and the rest;

and Mother can be left in peace when she needs it.' She fixed the publisher with a look. 'The ideal solution, yes?'

'Ye-es,' agreed Belinda, slightly stunned but willing. 'I suppose it is – apart from keeping in touch with the outside world – but one day you'll have decent broadband...'

She saw Captain Longstone's grimace. She stopped.

She brightened. 'Talk about inspiration!' she said again. 'Why not go with the flow – make a virtue of necessity? You want to encourage visitors.

'Well, then, why not market Combe Tollbridge as absolutely *the* place to come for a total digital detox?'

Also available

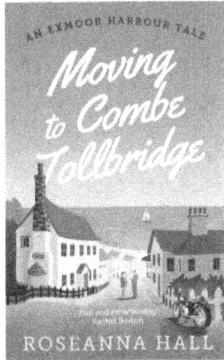

**Moving to Combe Tollbridge
(An Exmoor Harbour Tale, Book 1)**

When a cosy country cottage goes up for sale in
Combe Tollbridge, a small fishing village tucked away on
a quiet corner of the Exmoor coast, young couple Jane and
Jasper decide to make the move.

But while Jane is returning to the place of happy childhood
memories by the sea, another recent newcomer to the village,
Angela, has sadder reasons for her move.

Receiving a warm welcome from the colourful residents who call
the village home, all three soon become embroiled in rural life,
and find it not as sedate as they might have once imagined…

OUT NOW

Also available

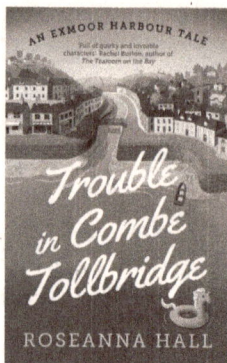

**Trouble in Combe Tollbridge
(An Exmoor Harbour Tale, Book 2)**

Combe Tollbridge, on the Exmoor coast, is a quiet fishing village always happy to welcome visitors for the sake of the local economy, but when an irritating journalist looks like staying overtime, a dine-and-dash couple plays tricks in the neighbourhood, and a family with more than one secret to hide features in the national news, the mixed blessing that is tourism becomes all too clear.

Meanwhile Professor Tolliday visits the coastal village for the first time in fifty years with his family. The once irresponsible student has come back to make belated amends, but it is his mischievous little granddaughter whose holiday fun causes the most trouble for the village.

OUT NOW

About the Author

Roseanna Hall is the pseudonym chosen by Sarah J. Mason for her Combe Tollbridge trilogy to distinguish these books from the seventeen 'Miss Seeton' mysteries she has written as Hamilton Crane, and the eight further mysteries under her own name.

The first Roseanna Hall was Sarah's grandfather's grandmother. Roseanna married John George and, in 1843, gave birth to grandfather's mother, Elizabeth.

Elizabeth George would be a grand name for an author, but someone else used it first.

Note from the Publisher

To receive updates on further releases in the Exmoor Harbour Tales series – plus special offers and news of other humorous fiction series to make you smile – sign up now to the Farrago mailing list at farragobooks.com/sign-up